Farther
Than I
Meant
to Go,
Longer
Than I
Meant
to Stay

Tiffany L. Warren

GRAND CENTRAL
PUBLISHING

NEW YORK   BOSTON

Copyright © 2006 by Tiffany Warren
Reading Group Guide copyright © 2006 by Hachette Book Group
Excerpt from *In the Midst of It All* copyright © 2010 by Tiffany Warren

Cover design by Melody Cassen
Cover photo by Ralf Nau/Getty Images

Grand Central Publishing
Hachette Book Group
237 Park Avenue
New York, NY 10017
Visit our website at www.HachetteBookGroup.com

Grand Central Publishing is a division of Hachette Book Group, Inc.
The Grand Central Publishing name and logo is a trademark of Hachette Book Group, Inc.

Printed in the United States of America

Originally published in trade paperback by Hachette Book Group
First mass market edition, November 2009

10 9 8 7 6 5 4 3 2 1

"YOU KNOW GOD IS LEADING YOU
AWAY FROM THIS MAN."

"Why are you ignoring the voice of the Lord?" Ebony asked slowly.

"At this point, I don't know what I know, except that I'm tired of being alone," I said.

"Do you think that God doesn't know that? Don't you know He will supply your every need?"

I furrowed my eyebrows. "Don't you ever feel lonely, Ebony? I thought you'd understand."

"I have dedicated my life to God, and I will remain single as long as He requires it. However, I do know that celibacy is a gift of the Holy Spirit."

"I don't want to be celibate. I want a husband," I whined.

"Even to the detriment of your own spirituality?" Ebony asked as she stood to leave.

I was afraid to answer that question, even in my own mind . . .

"This is Tiffany Warren at her best! . . . A wonderfully written story that captures your attention from the very first page."
—ReShonda Tate Billingsley, *Essence* bestselling author on *The Bishop's Daughter*

"This book made me open my eyes . . . Every woman should read this."
—Jackee Tolbert, Sister-to-Sister Book Club, on
What a Sista Should Do

Books by Tiffany L. Warren

The Bishop's Daughter

*Farther Than I Meant to Go, Longer Than
I Meant to Stay*

What a Sista Should Do

Coming Soon From Tiffany L. Warren

In the Midst of It All

Available February 2010

To Brent: my husband, rock, and best friend

ACKNOWLEDGMENTS

What a wonderful journey this has been! Of course, I can do nothing without Christ. Thank you, Jesus! Brent, thank you for supporting my dreams. No, *our* dreams. To my little chickadees (Briana, Brittany, Brynn, Brent II, and Brooke): Mommy loves you!

So many people have supported me that this page will not hold all of their names. To my mom, Libby: Go ahead and brag! Ain't nobody mad but the devil. To my mother-in-law Linda: Thank you for your constant promotion. Afrika, you are a fierce navigator and great driver! How many cities will we visit this time? Shawana, thank you for attending all of those book club meetings with me! You know I'm shy girl (yeah, right)! To my ATL connection, Tiffany: Do your thang, girl! I'm so proud of you.

Denise, you are a gem. Stay on the wall and keep allowing God to use you. Peggy and the entire staff at Tri-Com: I can't thank you all enough for your tireless efforts!

Bishop and First Lady Brantley and Lady Linda, thank you for your support, guidance, and prayers. Much love also goes to my entire church family at Zion Pentecostal

Church! INYTS. (So what if I stole it from Shellie!) Please keep the prayers coming!

Lastly, but absolutely not least, thanks to every book club that read my first book! I wish I could've come to all of your meetings. I love the feedback and the refreshments!

Thank you all! I pray that you enjoy reading this book as much as I enjoyed writing it.

Farther
Than I
Meant
to Go,
Longer
Than I
Meant
to Stay

Sin will always take you farther than you mean to go and keep you longer than you mean to stay.

—A wise Bible teacher

CHAPTER

One

❦

Past

I gazed blankly at the television screen.

After losing my career to Travis's criminal activities, I had no idea what to do with myself all day. I had no desire to start searching for another job; the whole idea was depressing. I chose, instead, to stay home and watch television ministers all day long. And between TV church broadcasts, I cooked.

I had been doing so much dieting that I'd forgotten how comforting food was. I totally rediscovered the joy of food. Yes, I'd lost fifteen pounds, but that didn't even matter. Being skinny was no longer a priority, not when my heart was broken and my life was in ruins.

During Joyce Meyer's broadcast, I heard a car pull up in my driveway. I peeked out of the window and saw Lynette's little red car. I didn't want to see her, or anybody else for that matter. Maybe she didn't catch the hint when I didn't answer the phone when she called, or respond to any of her voice mail messages. I just wanted to be left alone. I heard her banging on the door like a bill collector, but I didn't answer. She knocked for a good ten minutes before she left.

I inhaled the scent of the chocolate cake that I was baking. It was intoxicating. I'd made it especially sweet. So sweet that it was going to make my teeth hurt. It would be good with milk, but I was out of milk. It was going to have to be coffee.

I opened the refrigerator and realized that I needed a lot more than milk. It seemed like I'd just been to the store. But it had been two whole weeks. I was going to have to venture out again, but I'd wait until it was night. I would go to the twenty-four-hour Save and Go. Grocery stores were so peaceful at two o'clock in the morning. And best of all, I wouldn't run into anybody I knew.

Since Travis got me fired from my job, I'd seen two members from my church. Of course they knew all about me being fired. One of the problems with having bishops and pastors as the board of directors at the bank is that they all had wives. And some of them had nothing better to do than gossip about someone else's bad fortune. Well, I realized that running into people wasn't going to be very easy when the two I did see started offering condolences like one of my loved ones had died. I almost expected them to hand me a pot of spaghetti and some cold chicken. People always brought the most unappetizing food to the houses of the grieving.

I wished the cake would hurry and bake. I needed my sugar fix. I sounded like an addict. Speaking of addicts,

I wondered if Travis was addicted to porn. I never would've taken him for that type. When I thought of men who indulged in pornography, I envisioned greasy, slimy-looking characters who went out in the shadows and hid their dirty secret in garages and under beds. Maybe I'd driven him to it. Maybe he was sick of looking at my fat rolls and wanted to see some folks who weren't twice his size. Guess I couldn't blame him for that. But why'd he have to put it on my laptop unless he was trying to get me fired on purpose? That didn't make any sense. But then a lot of things weren't making much sense to me.

The cake had another twenty minutes to go and then it had to cool off, but I didn't think I could wait that long. I poured myself a huge glass of Pepsi. I grabbed eight ice cubes out of the freezer and placed them in the glass. When I went to reach for it, though, I slipped and knocked it off the counter. The glass broke into a hundred little pieces and Pepsi splattered everywhere. Tears sprang to my eyes—it was my favorite glass.

Still, the sound that it made when it fell, I liked it. It was loud and kind of sharp. That sound made me feel good. Even better than a slice of chocolate cake. Even better than that glass of soda would've tasted. I ran my hand across my arm, and there were goose bumps.

Before I could stop myself I broke another glass, and then another. And it felt *good*! I even saw the blood on my bare feet from where I stepped on a piece, but I didn't feel any pain at all. I ran out of glasses, but I still wanted to break something. I didn't want the feeling to go away. So I started on the plates. I was disappointed. The heavy pottery just didn't have the same sound as the glasses.

For a moment, I was dejected. And I started to reach for the broom. If I couldn't enjoy myself anymore, I should probably clean up. But then I got another bright idea. I bet the window would make a sound like the glasses. Actually, it might be even better! I hit the kitchen window with the broom handle, but not hard enough. I gave it another whack and then it crashed into a million little shards. I felt a smile creep across my face.

But the kitchen window wasn't enough. So I ran upstairs and started breaking all the bedroom windows. Faintly, somewhere in the back of my head, I could hear my burglar alarm going off. There must've been something wrong with it because it didn't go off until I got upstairs. Or maybe I just didn't hear it downstairs.

There was glass everywhere. Upstairs and downstairs. But there was nothing left to break and I felt melancholy about that. I looked out of what used to be my picture window in the living room. My next-door neighbor Clara was standing right out front, and so I waved at her.

"Charmayne!" she called. "Are you all right?"

"Me? I'm fine! Actually I'm better than fine. I'm great!"

"Well, your windows are broken."

"I know!"

Well, looking out at Clara gave me another idea. My car had six sturdy windows. I was sure breaking them would prolong my euphoria for just a little longer. I opened the door and went outside. I wasn't wearing shoes so I was making bloody footprints on the walkway. They looked funny so I let out a little laugh. Clara was still standing outside, so I waved at her again before I started bashing in the car windows. I heard Clara scream, but when I looked up she wasn't standing there anymore.

Then I heard the sirens . . .

Present

"How did we get here?"

I had no idea how to answer this question from my therapist, Dr. Rayna King. I wasn't exactly sure what she was referring to when she said *here*. She could have meant how I, Charmayne Ellis, ended up in her office as a patient. Or she could have been asking how I'd arrived at this point in my life. I breathed deeply while I contemplated a response to what seemed to be a simple question.

Dr. King affectionately called her office a sanctuary. From the inside you would never have guessed that the colorful and spacious room resided in a nondescript medical building, surrounded by dental clinics and pediatric offices. The walls were painted an appealing shade of lilac, and the lights were purposely dimmed to provide a backdrop of tranquility.

I was sitting directly across from Dr. King in a cushioned chaise while she rested on the burgundy velvet love seat. Conspicuously missing from this therapist's office was the obligatory couch where the patient spilled his or her guts, and the desk where the doctor silently judged sanity or insanity while madly scribbling on a yellow tablet.

My pastor's wife, First Lady Jenkins, had referred me to Dr. King. When she wasn't running her private practice, Dr. King served as evangelist in one of our sister churches. Her techniques, including praying and reading

Bible verses with her patients, were unorthodox to most of her peers, but she received high marks from the church community.

"I don't know," I finally responded. "Honestly, I never expected to find myself in therapy."

Dr. King smiled. "First of all, Charmayne, I want you to stop thinking of our meetings in clinical terms. I'm only here to help you figure out God's purpose for your life."

"I like to think of this in clinical terms, Dr. King. I'm sick, and I need treatment. It's better for me if I don't try to make it sound like something other than what it is," I said flatly.

"I agree. You are sick, but I believe your spirit woman is what needs to be treated."

I looked down at my arms and hands. There were dozens of tiny scars—a constant reminder of my illness. I wished that they were products of a vivid imagination, but no; they were cold, hard evidence that something wasn't right. I shook my head slowly and deliberately.

I asked, "How do you know that I don't just need some medication? Can't you just give me a prescription so I can get back to my normal life?"

Dr. King responded patiently, "I don't think you need meds. They are a last resort anyway. You had an episode that I feel was stress-induced."

An episode. That was a dainty name for something so ugly that it had my arms looking like a briar patch. It would have been nice to go back to what I felt was normal. I would have loved to just take up where I'd left off—in my career and my church duties. But Travis had ruined everything for me.

"So if you won't give me medication, how do you expect me to handle this mess?"

"First, we need to determine the root of your depression."

I sucked my teeth in a ghetto-girl manner. "I know the root. Travis Moon."

"I believe that your relationship with Travis was a symptom of something deeper. Together we're going to try to find out what that is."

I was skeptical of Dr. King's spiritual approach. My life had been fine before I met Travis. I was at the top of my game—spiritually, intellectually, and financially. I had been a bank president, making six figures a year. For ten years I had carefully chosen investments and was able to boast an impressive stock portfolio. But none of that meant anything anymore. I didn't think that my relationship with Travis was a symptom of anything. It was a tragic mistake that I couldn't take back, no matter how badly I wanted to.

I looked at my watch. There were ten minutes left in my session with Dr. King. It was my third visit, and we'd barely gotten past introductions. The whole thing was moving way too slowly for me. I had a life to reclaim, and I wanted to do it sooner rather than later.

Dr. King continued, "Charmayne, I've got some homework for you."

"Homework?"

"Yes. I want you to go home and read the story of Rizpah. It's found in Second Samuel chapter twenty-one, verses eight through fourteen."

"Rizpah," I repeated. "The name doesn't ring a bell, and I used to teach Sunday school. I'm ashamed."

"Don't be. Rizpah is one of the unsung heroines of the Old Testament. I believe that God will speak to you through her story. We'll discuss it at your next visit."

"Okay . . . ," I acquiesced, but I would have rather agreed to discuss me and my issues, and not those of a biblical character.

Dr. King pulled a little bottle of oil from her pocket and rubbed some on her hands. Then she reached out for my hands. I'd seen those saints whom I liked to call "deep" putting oil on their hands and head before they prayed, and sometimes we did it as a church when we were about to begin a fasting period. It felt odd doing it in the context of psychiatric medicine.

As if she could read my mind, Dr. King said, "The oil is symbolic, Charmayne. It reminds us of God's anointing that is present when we come together in prayer. I want us to pray for your healing, and I want you to believe that prayer."

I nodded and bowed my head. Dr. King prayed in a soothing voice that calmed me. I heard her send up on my behalf words that I had been afraid to utter. She squeezed my hands—willing me to feel God's Spirit in the room. After saying "amen" I left Dr. King's office. I was still filled with doubt, but I felt uplifted. That had to be a step in the right direction.

I walked into my home after my session with Dr. King, and it was strangely quiet. I suppose that it had always been that way, especially before I met Travis, but it was the first time I'd truly noticed. Everything was in place, but still I felt uneasy. I went through every room turning on lamps, even though it wasn't yet dark outside. The light helped to quell the unexplained panic that I felt rising in my belly.

I went into the kitchen to prepare my dinner—a protein shake and a garden salad. It wasn't a meal that I could get excited about, but a picture of my plus-size self in a bathing suit was taped to the refrigerator as incentive. I lost my appetite every single last time I got a glimpse of the photo—which was, of course, the desired effect. I remembered taking the picture. The women's ministry at my church had gone on a cruise retreat. I'd reluctantly worn a swimsuit at the urgings of my thin friends Lynette and Ebony. We'd gone to the ship's deck, wearing our suits, to get a little bit of sun. When I heard a little boy say to his mother, "Look at the fat lady!" I changed back into my sundress and hadn't looked at a bathing suit since.

Aside from my weight issues, everyone was always telling me how pretty I was. I could look in the mirror and see my caramel-colored skin and hazel eyes, but I didn't see the beauty there. I couldn't get past how round my cheeks were or that fleshy layer beneath my chin. The one feature that I did take pride in was my hair. It was thick, long, and healthy. I never went more than two weeks without getting it styled, and I spared no expense doing so. My stylist, Unique, worked in a shop in the "hood" area of Cleveland. She was so good that I traveled forty-five minutes from my condo in the suburbs and waited all day in the salon to have her lay my perm just right.

I listlessly chewed what was left of my salad greens, and then quickly moved from my kitchen bar stool to the living room sofa. I picked up my Bible from the coffee table and made myself comfortable on the soft leather. If the Lord had a word for me from the story of Rizpah, I wanted it right away.

I read aloud from 2 Samuel 21.

> *But the king took the two sons of Rizpah the daughter of Aiah, whom she bare unto Saul, Armoni and Mephibosheth; and the five sons of Michal the daughter of Saul, whom she brought up for Adriel the son of Barzillai the Meholathite:*

> *And he delivered them into the hands of the Gibeonites, and they hanged them in the hill before the LORD: and they fell all seven together, and were put to death in the days of harvest, in the first days, in the beginning of barley harvest.*

> *And Rizpah the daughter of Aiah took sackcloth, and spread it for her upon the rock, from the beginning of harvest until water dropped upon them out of heaven, and suffered neither the birds of the air to rest on them by day, nor the beasts of the field by night.*

> *And it was told David what Rizpah the daughter of Aiah, the concubine of Saul, had done.*

> *And David went and took the bones of Saul and the bones of Jonathan his son from the men of Jabeshgilead, which had stolen them from the street of Bethshan, where the Philistines had hanged them, when the Philistines had slain Saul in Gilboa:*

> *And he brought up from thence the bones of Saul and the bones of Jonathan his son; and they gathered the bones of them that were hanged.*

And the bones of Saul and Jonathan his son buried they in the country of Benjamin in Zelah, in the sepulchre of Kish his father: and they performed all that the king commanded. And after that God was intreated for the land.

It was just seven verses, but immediately I felt saddened by Rizpah's grief. I placed myself in her shoes, sitting out in the elements, mourning, grieving and lamenting. To passersby she probably looked quite pitiful—something like how I'd seemed to all of my family and friends. Her tears, however, masked an inner strength. I wondered if I would discover fortitude on the inside of me.

I understood the loneliness Rizpah felt when her sons were stripped from her so soon after she'd lost her husband. For my entire life I'd been surrounded by people, but I was no stranger to feeling alone.

As a girl, I was blessed to have the stability of a mother and father under one roof. I cherished the evenings that my mother, Claudette, baked cookies with me and my sister, Dayna. Mama would let us stay up late on Fridays to meet Daddy when he came home from his second-shift job.

Daddy always came in the house and scooped me up in his arms as if I weighed a feather. I didn't realize I was a chubby child; I just knew that my Daddy loved me and thought I was beautiful.

When I started going to school, and the teasing began, I didn't know how to take it. I ran home crying every day because of the cruel jokes and embarrassing pranks. Even worse, my own sister Dayna, a year younger than me, had become ashamed of sitting near me on the school bus.

Mama's solution to my weight problems was to berate me and deprive me of sweets and desserts. Gone were the nights of cookie baking. I sat alone in my room with tears in my eyes, reading books, while the aroma of the fresh-baked goodies wafted into my nostrils. Unbeknownst to Mama, I would sneak Little Debbie snack cakes from the store and guiltily munch on them while waiting for Daddy to come home.

Rizpah, a woman who had been dead for centuries, sparked new tears from decades-old hurts. I just sat on my couch crying for Rizpah . . . or maybe I was crying for me. Her despair reminded me of my own, and her loneliness of what I was experiencing right before I met the man who would change my life.

CHAPTER
Two

❧

Past

It was a hot and stifling Sunday afternoon, and Pastor Jenkins was running *long*. I enjoyed a good message, but if Pastor was going to get up there preaching for an hour he needed to take a special offering to get some air-conditioning. I fanned myself constantly to keep from forming perspiration stains on my new dress.

One of my best friends and fellow armor bearer, Ebony, passed me a note. It read, *Someone is looking at you.* I smiled, shook my head, and crumpled up the little slip of paper.

Ebony was referring to Marvin Baker. He was the only prospect of a husband that I'd ever had. Things hadn't worked out at all, but Ebony insisted that he still wanted to change my last name. She always imagined that she caught him gazing at me with longing in his eyes.

I ignored Ebony grinning at me, her gray eyes sparkling with excitement. Although she was eager to marry me off, she never seemed to want the same for herself. She was a beautiful girl, petite and shapely, though no one would ever know the way she covered herself in her "holy" garments. She had hair that came to the middle of her back, but it was always twisted into a neat ball at the nape of her neck. She refused to put on any makeup, not even lip gloss. Personally, I thought it was a waste, but she felt she was called by God to be single.

Finally Pastor Jenkins was saying the benediction, and I was so glad. As soon as we said "Amen," First Lady Jenkins sent Ebony on some errand. I stood next to her as she greeted the church members.

After everyone had said their hellos, First Lady turned to me and asked, "How are you feeling this fine Sunday afternoon?"

That was, on the surface, a fairly innocuous question. However, did First Lady Jenkins want to know how I felt in the spirit? If that was the case, I would respond, *First Lady, I feel good down in my sanctified soul.* However, if she was referring to my natural, physical existence . . . well, that was a whole other story.

I'd tried something new with my wardrobe that morning. Instead of my normal blacks and earth tones, I had listened to the advice of a bubbly salesperson and donned an orange dress. She told me that bright colors were really becoming popular for plus-size women (that's what she called us . . . I prefer *big girls*). She said that the bright color would draw attention to the dress and away from my weight. I wasn't so sure about that. I had all my armor on (not spiritual armor, but my serious one-piece body shaper), and still I thought I looked like an autumn pumpkin. Not to mention that my feet felt like sausages, crammed into size nine shoes when I really should have gotten size nine and a half.

I responded, "First Lady, I feel good today."

"Well, all right. You're looking good, too, honey."

"Are you sure this orange looks all right?"

First Lady laughed. "What you doing, girl? Fishing for compliments?"

"No. I wasn't sure about it when I put it on this morning."

"Well, you look lovely. So are you excited about the wedding?" She'd clapped her hands together when she asked. Obviously, *she* was excited about it.

I hesitated before responding. "Um, y-yes. Yes I am."

The wedding. My best friend was to be married in a week, and I kept forgetting that I was supposed to be thrilled about the event. Lynette and I had been best friends for fifteen years, but I had to question the friendship of a woman who insisted that I (all 260 pounds of me) wear a strapless gown.

When Lynette told me a year ago that she was getting married, I vowed to lose at least fifty pounds. When I started on the Linda Turtle weight loss regimen, I was pumped. Ms. Linda Turtle's television commercials depicted big girls who had been transformed into svelte fat-free vixens. I knew I was going to be a success story.

About six weeks into the plan, I had lost a grand total of five pounds. I'd followed that diet to the letter (okay, maybe I'd slipped up once or twice or thrice), but my reward was a measly five pounds. That's what I call invisible weight loss. I couldn't tell where on my body those five pounds were lost from, and as a matter of fact I don't think they were lost at all. I think they were just playing hide-and-seek and were readying themselves to reappear at any moment in a new form, maybe underneath my chin or on the back of one of my arms.

Needless to say, I gave up without much of a fight. I didn't have enough time to lose the amount of weight to actually make a difference. At 260 pounds, even if I lost 50, I'd still be fat. A fat girl in a strapless bridesmaid's gown.

Now, although I wouldn't be shapely for the blessed occasion, I still planned to have a smile on my face, because I truly was happy for my friend. Her two sons needed some type of positive male influence in their lives, and Lynette's fiancé, Jonathan, was the answer to her prayers. From the moment he walked into their lives he was better to those boys than their daddy ever was, and ten times better to Lynette. No, make that a hundred times better. Her ex-husband Brian was a treacherous leech.

I started to ask First Lady Jenkins if she needed anything, but I noticed a smile spreading across her lips. I followed her gaze across the sanctuary to Brother Marvin Baker. First Lady and Ebony were in cahoots on hooking the two of us up. They didn't care how many times I told her that neither one of us was interested. First Lady waved at him, and he slowly walked over. I knew he didn't want to come anywhere near me, but I wasn't hurt. The feeling was mutual.

I spoke first. "Praise the Lord, Bro Marvin."

"Praise Him," he said dryly.

First Lady smiled as if she had accomplished something, but Marvin just stood there looking constipated.

He was like all of the other brothers I'd ever encountered. He probably thought that I still had a thing for him. I did not. The whole relationship with him was one of my most humiliating experiences.

First of all, let me say that Mr. Marvin was not the best-looking brother around—and that's being nice. He was overweight, and all his clothing was just a little bit too snug. He had a mundane career—he was a research analyst at a law firm—but at least he did have a job. To top it all off, it was only a matter of time until the brother sported a George Jefferson hairstyle. But with all that going against him, he thought he was too good for me. It never ceased to amaze me how even the most undesirable brothers in the church were searching for the sisters who looked just like Halle Berry.

First Lady had made Marvin and me a team to plan a group outing for the singles committee. I'd thought that we had a lot in common. We both loved the Lord, we both loved the church, and we were both single and looking. I also thought that we had connected, but I was wrong.

Before we were even officially dating, Marvin had the nerve to go around telling members of the singles committee that I was stalking him. He said I was calling him and e-mailing him every day, wanting to pray with him. Excuse me for actually caring about him. And to set the record straight he called me as much as I called him. He didn't start flipping on me until a new sister joined the church, one whom he thought he was going to hook up with. All I had to take is one look at her and I knew she was out of Marvin's league.

After the new sister completely dogged Marvin, he had the audacity to come back and try to mend fences with me. As badly as I wanted to be in a relationship, I was not about to be a doormat; nor was I taking sloppy seconds. I told Marvin that we could be friends, so he decided to stop speaking to me.

My story with Marvin was the story of my relationship life. In high school, as big as I was, I was virtually invisible to the opposite sex. It didn't help that my best friend, Lynette, was in the homecoming court every year and a cheerleader to boot. Lynette never seemed to notice that the boys didn't like me. She always acted like I had some elusive secret admirer who would soon show his face. When this prince never arrived, I lived vicariously through Lynette's puppy love ordeals and prayed that it would someday be my turn to experience the giggles and butterflies in my stomach. I ended up spending prom night alone and in tears.

My college years were supposed to be better. If there was a guy on campus who appreciated a woman with a little extra meat on her bones, he was going to find me and we were going to live happily ever after. I even worked on my personality. I didn't want any hindrances when my prince finally came along. I brushed up on current events, read interesting novels, and honed my conversation skills—only to find that the *one* brother in town who liked big girls was already happily involved.

By the time I hit my senior year, I was distraught and discouraged. Lynette tried to include me in social functions and convinced me that the only reason I didn't have a boyfriend was that I'd been making myself scarce. I joined the Black Student Union with Lynette thinking that I'd meet someone who wanted to make a change in the world.

At the first meeting I was introduced, by Lynette, to a debonair young man named Justin. He was quite active in his church and couldn't help but tell everyone that he was saved. Even though I was nonchurched—my family attended on Christmas and Easter—I was thoroughly impressed by Justin's zeal and dedication. He invited me and Lynette to his church, and we both accepted his invitation with stars in our eyes. We both found Jesus—and Lynette found a boyfriend. I didn't hold it against Lynette. She had no idea that I'd hoped Justin would be my first real boyfriend.

I flourished in my church environment. I was a single woman in a sea of many single women. On the surface, it was perfectly acceptable to be single, as long as I was living my life for Christ. Beneath the facade, however, were hordes of single women who craved love, husbands, and children.

It was hard to be a church member and not be married. I felt that married women were validated by the fact that they'd been chosen. I was always hearing about the "virtuous woman" as the epitome of femininity and womanhood. The virtuous woman did it all: ran a business, took care of her household, and of course was the main jewel in her husband's crown. Most of the women of faith in the Bible had husbands backing them up, and the single women of faith were mostly harlots! I wanted to be a faithful wife and not a faithful woman of ill repute.

Lynette was waving to me from across the church. She started walking over with two of her other bridesmaids in tow. They looked like three models prancing down the catwalk. Lynette was five foot nine, taller than the other women, and weighed probably 140 pounds—and that

was after she'd eaten a big meal, wearing her heaviest
jeans and a sweater. This morning she was wearing a fit-
ted red suit, the skirt just barely reaching her calves. It
was sharp. Now, Lynette . . . she looked good in bright
colors.

"Praise the Lord, First Lady. Praise the Lord, Char!"
said Lynette in her most cheery, upbeat tone.

"You betta praise Him," replied First Lady.

"Hey girl."

"That orange is pretty," she said after appraising my
outfit with a swift glance.

"You think so? I think maybe it's too much."

"Not at all. You know, not everybody can wear
orange."

First Lady smiled, but I narrowed my eyes and
frowned. Lynette had just affirmed that I looked horrible
in the orange getup. She thought she was slick, but I
knew her too well. Lynette was one of those people who
didn't feel comfortable talking to others without compli-
menting them on something. Usually, if there were no re-
deeming qualities to my outfit, she'd comment on my
hair. She had never actually said that she liked my dress.
She just said that she liked the color orange. Slick, but not
quite slick enough.

Alicia, one of the anemic-looking bridesmaids, said,
"Charmayne, the rehearsal dinner is at Shenanigans
Seafood House. It will start Friday evening at six thirty.
Please be on time."

"That's not a problem. I'll be there."

I bit my tongue, not once but twice, to avoid saying
something nasty to Alicia. The only reason she was even
in the wedding party was that she was Jonathan's sister,

but she came in and promptly took over in the planning department. Somehow she'd forgotten that I was the maid of honor. I knew she was getting on Lynette's nerves, too, because Lynette was flashing her fake grin—the one where she would be grinding her teeth underneath her lips.

Lynette said, "Of course she'll be there on time. Charmayne, you feel like some dessert? I sure could use some cheesecake."

I didn't feel like dessert, but coming from Lynette this was not just a trivial invitation. Whenever she was under stress, or really needed to talk about something important, Lynette had to hash things out with a mouthful of something sweet. She was apt to come over my house at two o'clock in the morning with ice cream and cookie dough, and usually tears in her eyes.

"Mmm-hmm, I'll go as soon as I'm off duty."

I ignored Lynette's very audible sigh, and immediately responded to First Lady's signal to leave. I quickly collected her Bible and handbag and rolled my eyes at Lynette in the process. My best friend hated it when I was on armor bearer duty. She tried to pretend that I was being abused by our pastor's wife, but Lynette just didn't like sharing my attention.

Once inside First Lady's office, she plopped down in her chair wearily. I neatly placed her hat in its hatbox and handed First Lady her comfortable shoes. Ebony walked into the office right behind us, her errand completed.

"You know," said First Lady, "Brother Marvin is just playing hard to get."

Ebony gave First Lady Jenkins a high five. I laughed at their joint attack.

"Am I supposed to chase him?" I asked.

Ebony replied, "Absolutely not! He's just going to end up missing out on a good thing."

"I don't think he's concerned about that."

"He should be." First Lady eased her tired feet out of her pretty high heels. She'd shouted up a storm during service and was definitely paying the price.

I imagined Lynette waiting impatiently outside First Lady's office. "Do you need anything else before I leave, First Lady?"

"No, Charmayne. I think I can make it from here."

"Where are you off to in such a hurry?" asked Ebony.

"Lynette is having a crisis."

"Oh, brother! She's always having a crisis."

"I know. But she really needs me this time."

I walked around First Lady's desk and gave her a hug and planted a kiss on her cheek. "I'll talk to you tomorrow. Ebony, I'll call you tonight."

"Right after you rescue Lynette?"

I laughed and nodded. Ebony didn't care much for Lynette. She felt that Lynette was shallow and bothersome. Ebony hated that I was always there to clean up Lynette's messes and rescue her from her dilemmas. Lynette, on the other hand, found Ebony to be uptight and too deep for her own good. Every time Lynette heard Ebony quote a scripture she would roll her eyes and say something under her breath. Usually I felt torn between the two of them, because I always had to choose one or the other. They never wanted all three of us to do anything together, and if I chose one, I wouldn't get a phone call from the other for a week or so.

I stepped outside the office door. True to her character,

Lynette was standing there with her arms folded and lips protruding.

I laughed at her antics. "Girl, what is wrong with you?"

"Are you *finally* finished?"

"Yes. Why do you always hate on my ministry?"

Lynette rolled her eyes. "Ministry? Girl, please. I'm sure the Lord has more in mind for you than carrying other folks' Bibles."

I shook my head in silent resignation and followed Lynette out of the church. We headed for Lynette's favorite dessert spot. It was a tiny little coffeehouse called Coffee and Cake. Their coffee wasn't very good, but they ordered their desserts from someone who had definitely seen the inside of a Down South kitchen. The peach cobbler was heavenly (or should I say hellish? It had to be about three thousand calories per bite), and the sweet potato pie tasted like it was especially prepared to cap off a Thanksgiving feast.

"Charmayne," lamented Lynette in between huge bites of German chocolate cake, "I just don't know what it is!"

"Lynette. We've talked about this before. It's cold feet. That's all it is."

"I don't know, Char. I think the Lord might be telling me that Jonathan is not the one."

It was my turn to sigh. We'd literally had this exact same conversation about fifty times. Lynette was constantly searching for a sign that she shouldn't marry Jonathan. If the man was five minutes late for a date, or forgot to call when he said he would, or ordered her the chicken sandwich with cheese when he knew she hated cheese . . . it was a sign from the Lord.

"Well, it is important to obey the voice of the Lord."

"Exactly!" exclaimed Lynette, slamming her fist down on the table for an added touch.

I continued, "I have always made it a point to seek God's face on a matter until I feel His perfect peace."

Lynette frowned. "Could you be any more self-righteous?"

"Me? You're the one talking about hearing from God! I'm trying to help you out."

"To be honest, I'm not sure if God is telling me not to marry Jonathan."

"Could you possibly be confusing your own doubts with hearing from God?"

Lynette leaned over the table anxiously and said, "I don't know. It's just that sometimes he'll do something to make me nervous. Like just the other day he bought me yellow roses."

"Okay . . ." I hoped I rolled my eyes hard enough, because Lynette was being absolutely ridiculous.

"Come on, Charmayne! *Yellow* roses?"

"What is wrong with yellow roses? They're pretty."

Lynette threw her hands into the air as if she were only stating the obvious. "You don't buy yellow roses for your fiancée. You buy red roses. Yellow roses mean friendship. Maybe the Lord is trying to speak to my spirit."

"From what I can tell, Jonathan is a good man. You need to go before the Lord and pray, girl. That's the only way you're going to know for sure."

"But what if God doesn't say anything?"

"You've got to go by that feeling of peace. Let your spirit lead."

Lynette contemplated my words over another bite of cake. "He is a good man, isn't he? And the boys love him."

"So do you, crazy lady."

"Yes, you're right. I suppose I do."

"You suppose?"

"Okay, I do, but I can't believe next Saturday is coming up so quickly. It seems like he just proposed to me last night."

"Time flies when you're having fun, right?"

"I guess. Speaking of fun, I've got someone I want you to meet."

I groaned. Why couldn't Lynette just leave me alone? At age thirty-six I had only ever had one boyfriend, and that was in high school. His name was William and it turned out that he was dating me because he'd lost a bet, so I couldn't even count him as a real boyfriend. He took me to a football game and I sat in the stands cheering with him, feeling like almost like a normal teenager. When we went to the local hangout after the game, I ignored all the giggles and whispers and held my head up, totally enjoying being on the arm of a somewhat handsome and popular boy.

But then Lynette overheard some of the cheerleaders laughing about William losing a bet to one of the football players. She had tears in her eyes when she'd told me about this. We cried for weeks over that boy. Not because I'd liked him so much, but because he'd made me a laughingstock.

I shook my head adamantly. "Lynette. I do not want to be set up. You know how I feel about that."

Lynette pleaded, "But, Charmayne, this guy is different. He's got money and he adores thick women."

"Girl, I passed thick about ten dress sizes ago."

Lynette rolled her eyes. "You are not that big! Plus

you're solid. It's not like you have rolls hanging from everywhere."

She called me *solid*. Was that supposed to be a compliment? The fact that I probably could've been a defensive tackle for a NFL team had to be an asset.

"I'm not even going there with you, Lynette. You say this guy has money? What does he do?"

Lynette's big eyes widened with hope. "Does that mean you're interested?"

"Not yet," I responded with deliberate indifference. "Just answer the question."

"Well, he owns a funeral parlor."

"Oh, God."

"What? He's an entrepreneur."

I wasn't trying to be funny, and I surely didn't have room to be too picky, but come on. He owned a funeral parlor *and* liked big women? There had to be something wrong with the man.

"Lynette, I prefer professional men. You know that."

"He is a professional!"

"You know what I mean, Lynette."

Lynette pursed her lips tightly and rolled her neck. "Oh, just because you're a bank president and all, that means you can't be bothered with a simple hardworking brother?"

"Of course I can be bothered, but we probably won't have anything to talk about," I answered honestly.

"So you'll see him then? Tomorrow night at seven thirty."

"Do I have a choice?"

"No."

*   *   *

I walked into the restaurant, and I immediately spotted Lynette and Jonathan. He looked dashing in his tan sport coat ensemble. Lynette, who had her arm linked in his, was wearing a cream-colored linen cocktail dress. Her ebony skin glowed as she stood next to the man she was obviously in love with. As usual, I felt underdressed. I was wearing a black blazer and skirt that I'd purchased from Saks. The outfit was expensive but sensible— something I'd wear to work. I didn't even own a cocktail dress. Most of the cocktail dresses I'd seen didn't cover enough flesh to make them practical, and it wasn't often that I got the opportunity to wear one.

"Hey, girl!" Lynette was extremely bubbly that evening. She was smiling broadly, making sure the entire restaurant got a good glimpse of the orthodontic work she'd spent thousands of dollars on.

I responded apprehensively, "Hello, Lynette. Hi, Jonathan."

I nervously scanned the room, hoping to get a look at my date before he saw me. Lynette was grinning so hard, her eyes were little slits. There was nothing that amusing going on in the restaurant.

"So are you excited?" Lynette gushed.

I couldn't help but sigh. No. I was not excited, and Lynette had been my friend long enough to know that. I had pretty low expectations when it came to men—make that doubly low when it was a blind date. I had a theory about blind dates. Anyone willing to accept one had to be operating on some level of desperation.

"I'm not even going to acknowledge that question."

Jonathan covered his mouth with his hand and let out a miniature chuckle. Lynette elbowed him in the ribs, seemingly more out of playful annoyance than anger. She let out a little squeal as my "date" approached, but all I could do was drop my jaw in shock. Lynette mistook my expression to be one of pleased awe.

She said, "I know! Isn't he great?"

I had just received more confirmation that my best friend ought to be committed. The man standing in front of me was at least fifty-five, and that's being generous. He was wearing a brown, tight-fitting, polyester suit that was completely out of style, not to mention too hot for the muggy summer evening. His hair was an alarming, unnatural shade of black, and if my eyes were seeing correctly, his hair color seemed to run right on over onto the backs of his ears and neck.

"Well, well, well, Nettie, you ain't tell me she was a redbone!" exclaimed my date while smacking his lips. I was thoroughly terrified that he was going to take a bite out of my arm.

That time, Jonathan didn't even attempt to hide his laughter. I was sure that in a few years, I, too, would look back on the date and laugh. At the time, however, I was horrified beyond words.

Lynette giggled. "Charmayne Ellis, meet Willie Brown."

I extended my hand for a polite handshake, but Mr. Willie Brown was what they call an old-school Casanova. He took my hand, and instead of shaking it, bent over and planted a juicy kiss on my palm before I got the chance to snatch it away. I wanted to gag!

"Girl, I am pleased to make your acquaints."

Yes. The man said *acquaints*. I supposed that he meant *acquaintance*. If Jonathan laughed any harder, he was going to have an accident. He wasn't the only one, though. His fiancée was going to "accidentally" come home with a speed knot on her head from where I planned on popping her. I wondered where she knew Willie from anyway. He was probably someone from her mama's church.

"No, Mr. Brown. The pleasure is all mine."

He smacked again and rubbed his hands together. "Aww, thicky. You ain't got to call me Mr. Brown. Just call me Big Willie."

Before I could reply, the restaurant hostess came forward. She motioned for us to follow her to a table. For some reason my feet weren't moving. I stood there, stuck in place, lamenting the depths to which my love life had sunk. I wasn't sure I could make it through the evening— or the rest of my life, for that matter. Not if I could only expect the likes of Willie Brown for companionship.

Lynette pulled me by the arm. "Come on, Charmayne."

"Girl, I've got to go and wash my hand!" I was holding my hand out far away from my body, as if it were infected with the Ebola virus.

"Quit tripping, Charmayne."

Lynette literally dragged me to the table, and all I could think of was getting Big Willie's saliva off my hand. When we got to the table, Willie pulled out a chair for me. I sat down and scooted myself up to the table, because I didn't want him to try to push my chair in. I didn't want the man to have even the slightest opportunity to touch me again.

Lynette said, "So, Willie, are you going to be at my wedding? You know it's next Saturday, up at the church."

Willie grinned, exposing his aged gold teeth. "You

know I'm gone be there, sweetie. 'Specially if your friend here is also attending."

"Charmayne is the maid of honor."

Willie rubbed his hands together again and winked. "Well, then I'm gone be sitting in the front row."

It was the second time that evening I had the desire to vomit. I kicked Lynette under the table. Naturally, she ignored me. I had to have a serious talk with my best friend. Her matchmaking days were over.

Jonathan came to my rescue. He asked, "Willie, what's it like being in business for yourself? I bet it feels good."

Willie patted his oversize belly. "Man, it feels better than good. I set my own hours. I get up and go when I want to. If I wanted to go to the Poconos one week with my lady, I could just go."

How come Willie looked at me when he said *the Poconos*? He couldn't even take me to the corner store, much less out of state.

Willie continued, "I'm one of those men who want to take care of a lady. I don't want no woman of mine working."

Lynette said, "There aren't too many men like you around, isn't that right, Charmayne?"

"I can honestly say that I've never met anyone like you . . . Big Willie," I added with a tight-lipped smile.

I sipped my water and looked around the restaurant. It was a Monday night, so the place was pretty empty. It was a good thing, too, because I didn't want to run into anyone I knew while I was on a date with Willie Brown.

Willie asked, "Charmayne, what do you do for a living?"

"I work at the bank."

Lynette said, "She doesn't just work at the bank. She is the president of Grace Savings and Loan."

I kicked Lynette again. I had no intentions of telling that man all my business. I planned never to see him again.

"A president, huh? So you making the big bucks. I guess you don't need a man to take care of you," said Willie, almost looking sad about it.

I responded curtly, "If you're asking if I need a sugar daddy, then the answer is no."

Lynette laughed. "Well, I sure don't want to work. That's why I'm lucky that I found Jonathan."

Jonathan said, "I'm the lucky one."

Any other time I would have been irritated by their showing of affection. But anything was a nice diversion from Willie Brown's drooling over me.

Willie said, "Well, I'm happy for y'all. It's so nice to see young folks in love. It's real nice. I just got one question for you, Jonathan. Can Nettie cook? She look too pretty to be in the kitchen frying chicken."

"I'll have you know that my Lynette is very skillful in the kitchen," announced Jonathan proudly.

I almost choked on a mouthful of water. That was the first funny thing I'd heard all evening. Lynette's most complex culinary offering was beans and franks. If it wasn't for me, her sons would have been raised on frozen dinners and bologna sandwiches. She was looking at me with a *don't-even-think-about-opening-your-mouth* expression. She didn't have to worry. Jonathan was going to find out soon enough.

Willie said, "That is a blessing, man. A woman has got to know how to cook a good Sunday meal. I bet Charmayne can put her foot in some collard greens."

"Why do you think that?" I asked angrily.

Willie ignored my apparent insult and replied, "Girl, you just look like you can cook."

If I had a nickel for every time I heard that mess, I could've been someone's sugar mama. I didn't get big eating home-cooked food. I got big eating burgers four times a week. The fact that I could cook had nothing to do with it. I happened to have a grandmother who ran a soul food restaurant. I'd been making biscuits and candied yams ever since I could reach a tabletop. So, yes, I could put my foot in some collard greens, but I still hated people assuming that I could cook.

"I'll have you know, Willie, that not every big woman knows how to fix collard greens."

"I don't know why Charmayne is being modest tonight," Lynette said. "She cooks better than my mama."

With perfect timing a perky waitress walked up to our table. The restaurant's menu consisted of expensive soul food dishes, but I couldn't muster up much of an appetite. Out of habit, I ordered the chicken and waffles. I rolled my eyes as Big Willie ordered the Cornish hen and jambalaya platter (pronounced *coanish* hen and *jam-bay-layee*).

When everyone had placed their order, Lynette resumed the inane chitchat. I no longer wanted to be a part of their conversation, so I let my mind drift. Monday had been a very stressful day for me, and the rest of the week wasn't looking any better. I had gone against all my good judgment and recommended a friend's daughter to supervise a group of night-shift proof operators. After working for a few months, she'd started abusing the attendance policy. The girl had a long weekend every week. She, or somebody in her household, was forever getting sick, and it always fell on either a Monday or a Friday.

I guess it was obvious that I didn't plan on engaging in much conversation, because Lynette started talking about her favorite subject of late—her wedding. I say *her wedding*, and not *their wedding*, because the only thing Jonathan had contributed to the big day was his checkbook. Jonathan adored Lynette, though, so he would have probably spent his last dime giving her everything she wanted. I suppose some people would think that was a beautiful thing, but truthfully Jonathan needed to set some boundaries for Lynette. She would spend them right into the poorhouse if he let her. I'd seen her buy an outfit when she knew she should've been paying a gas bill or buying some groceries. I couldn't count the number of times that I'd had to loan (and I use that term loosely) her money to keep her from getting evicted or to get her lights turned back on.

I was glad when our food finally got to the table. It was another useful diversion, and I thought that maybe Willie wouldn't be able to talk so much once he started chewing on his tough-looking Cornish hen.

Toward the end of the meal, I noticed that it had gotten really warm in the restaurant. It felt like the air-conditioning had been turned off all of a sudden. I didn't feel too uncomfortable, but I couldn't say the same thing for Big Willie. He had big beads of sweat forming on his forehead.

Willie said, "It shole is hot up in here."

"It is kind of toasty," Jonathan agreed.

Willie took off his polyester jacket, and I was not the least bit shocked that he had huge perspiration circles under his arms. He picked up his white cloth napkin from the table and wiped his face. When he laid the napkin down, it was streaked with a huge black stain. First I thought that it was dirt; then I realized that it was his hair dye.

Lynette looked at the napkin and said, "What the . . . ?"

Willie was mortified, and I really felt sorry for him. He had gone through a whole lot of changes just to impress me, but I was sitting up there dogging the poor man. He snatched the napkin from the table and put it in his lap.

The waitress came back to the table and asked if anyone wanted dessert. Willie said "no" like he was in a big hurry to leave. Well, for the first time that evening, we were on the same page. Willie took the check from the waitress and gave her his credit card. It was sweet of him to treat everybody. He was probably a real nice man.

When we left the restaurant, Willie walked me to my car. I told him that he didn't have to, but of course he'd insisted. I felt really guilty, because I had no idea how to gracefully brush a man off. I'd never had to do it before. I was usually the brushee and not the brusher. I just knew that I was going to hurt his feelings.

Willie said, "You've got a nice car, Ms. Charmayne."

"Thanks."

"I guess it's no need for me to ask for your phone number."

"Willie, I'm sure you're a good man, but I don't think I'm the one for you."

"Well, you haven't even given me a chance."

"At this point in my life, I really don't have much time to waste on dating. If and when God sends me a husband, I'll know it."

"Lady, I hope everything works out for you, 'cause a nice car and a nice house shole can't keep you warm at night."

Willie opened my car door and stood outside until I pulled off. He was right in some respects. Nice things didn't replace having a man. On the other hand, I was not about to settle for a polyester-wearing, hair-dyeing, tired wannabe sugar daddy. It didn't get *that* cold at night. And if it did, I'd buy an electric blanket.

CHAPTER
Three

Past

I used my key to let myself into my mother's tiny one-bedroom apartment. I knew that it would take her forever to get to the door if I knocked. She was only sixty years old, but her ankles were weakened by all the years of carrying around excess body weight. I could hear her shuffling out of her bedroom as I opened the door.

"Charmayne? Is that you?" she asked, sounding just like a sweet old lady.

"Yes, Mama," I replied.

When Mama discovered that it was me, she let the *real* Claudette come out. "Well, you could knock on the door, or at least let somebody know you're coming by."

I had been coming by every Tuesday since she'd been diagnosed with high blood pressure. I was eighteen when Daddy died and Mama decided that she was going to eat herself into an early grave. Her emotional eating turned into a weight problem that caused high blood pressure.

Sometimes I look at Mama and see my own future flash before my eyes. I wondered who would take care of me when I was sixty, overweight, and sick. At least Mama had her memories of Daddy.

I ignored Mama's miniature rant and walked into the small but efficient eat-in kitchen. My mother always had to find something to complain about. I knew that she was happy to see me, but she never said as much. If it had been her sweet younger daughter, Dayna, she would've rolled out the red carpet.

I glanced in the sink and didn't see any used dishes. I asked, "Mama, what have you eaten today?"

"Oh, well, I had me some leftover Kentucky Fried Chicken for breakfast. I ain't thought about fixing lunch yet."

"Well, it's after two o'clock. You sit down, and I'm going to make you a salad."

I heard Mama grumbling under her breath. She hated when I made her eat healthy foods. Her high blood pressure was completely out of control, but she did not let that stop her from eating whatever she wanted. The thought of her having a stroke terrified me, but it didn't seem to faze her one bit.

She turned on the television in her sitting room. I heard her favorite soap opera come on. I chuckled softly as I got the salad fixings out of the refrigerator. I wouldn't let Mama fuss at me, so she was in there yelling orders at the television. Her favorite characters were hardheaded, though, just like me. They never took her advice, either.

I finished the chef salad and topped it with French

dressing—the only kind Mama would eat. I brought it along with a glass of Diet Pepsi into the living room and set it on one of her television trays. She frowned when she saw the contents of her lunch.

"Here you go, Mama."

She replied grumpily, "A salad. Well, if you wanted to make me something, why can't it be something good like a peach cobbler. I got the stuff in there."

"I am not making you a peach cobbler. Your doctor said you need to lose some weight."

"Well, ain't that the pot calling the kettle black. Dayna would've made me a pie!"

"Seeing that Dayna can't cook worth a lick, it wouldn't have been a very good one," I retorted.

"It would have been better than this old nasty salad."

I ignored Mama's insult to my weight and the side comment about Dayna. She was right, though—on both counts. I did need to lose weight, and Dayna's silly behind would've baked her a peach cobbler even if it would kill her. Dayna and Mama were each other's favorite people and they enjoyed indulging each other, although since Mama had been sick, Dayna had been doing all the spoiling.

"So I heard you had yourself a date. I see you wasn't gone tell nobody."

I sighed out loud. Mama knew all my business. You would think we lived in a small farm town the way news traveled. Mama had a secret network of spies—half of them were members of my church, and the other half she met at the bingo hall.

"Where'd you hear that?"

"His mama plays bingo up at the lodge. That lucky

heifer won last week, too. So what did you think of Willie?"

I replied honestly. "He was a nice man."

"Are you seeing him again?" She truly looked hopeful.

"No, Mama."

Mama sucked her false teeth and shook her head angrily. I guess she thought that Willie Brown was a good catch, and I was sure that she was going to tell me about myself. We'd had the same conversation on so many other occasions.

She ranted, "You act like you don't want no husband. Willie Brown is a good decent man. He would've taken care of you and two or three grandbabies."

"He wasn't my type, Mama." I was so tired of justifying my choices and taste in men to her.

"And what *is* your type? I think your type is invisible, 'cause I ain't seen you on nobody's arm."

"Mama—"

She continued the barrage. "I mean, all you have to do is look at your sister and see how happy she is. It ain't natural to be thirty-six years old and ain't never had a man!"

I silently endured Mama's attack. If she wasn't harping on my weight, it was my marital status. Most days she harped on both. I knew that she just wanted me to be happy, but she never acknowledged any of my achievements, only my failures. It didn't matter how many degrees I had, or how well my career was going. To Mama, if I didn't have a house full of babies and a man to cook for, then I didn't have anything.

It didn't help that my sister was living what Mama

considered to be a perfect life. Dayna was a stay-at-home mother of three. Her husband, Ronald, was a mechanical engineer bringing home a decent paycheck. They had the traditional little family. They even had a dog.

Of course I wanted all that. Not a day went by that I wondered if I'd ever have any children of my own. But I wasn't going to rush into anything just to please my mama. I was going to wait until the time was right.

"I'm waiting on the Lord to send me a husband, Mama."

She rolled her eyes at me. "Well, I wish He'd hurry up."

I straightened Mama's kitchen and made sure she had something readily available for dinner. She continued her grumbling, but I didn't say another word to her. I knew I could never win the argument, so I decided to save my breath for another time.

I left Mama's house feeling dejected. I was on my way to pick up Ebony and Lynette for Lynette's "surprise" bridal shower. She'd found out the plans a week ago when she had overheard Jonathan on the phone with his sister, Alicia. Lynette promised me that she would still act surprised.

Ebony was running late, as usual. She hadn't wanted to attend the function, but she was doing it so that I wouldn't be alone. I appreciated her for that.

When she got in the car, she asked, "Do I need a gift?"

"Of course you need a gift! It's a bridal shower."

"Well, let me put my name on yours. It'll be from the both of us."

I laughed. "You are so tacky."

I only had to blow my horn once outside Lynette's apartment. That was most shocking, because she was usually late for everything. I was almost 100 percent sure that her wedding would not start on time. The invitations said one o'clock, but I didn't anticipate the event commencing until three.

Lynette practically bounced to the car. Fresh from the salon, she looked immaculate. Her brand-new hair weave was cut in layers and flipped. Lynette spent a near fortune on her hair. She'd hired the top weave expert in the city. It was Lynette's ultimate goal to fool everyone into thinking that her purchased tresses grew naturally from her head.

"Hey, girl!" Lynette announced cheerfully as she closed her car door.

"Hey," I replied.

Lynette pursed her lips and said lifelessly, "Ebony."

"Lynette," replied Ebony in an equally deadpan tone.

I would've probably been laughing at my two friends had I not been feeling fat and lonely after listening to Mama's tirade. I wanted to tell Lynette that maybe I shouldn't have been so hasty in writing off Willie Brown. And I wanted to break down crying because I should've been happy that my best friend was getting married, but all I was feeling was envy.

Lynette glanced into the backseat of my car and smiled when she saw my gift. She picked it up and shook it like a little girl trying to figure out what was hiding in a Christmas package under the tree.

I fussed, "Stop that before you break it!"

"So it's something I can break, huh? Is this something kinky?"

Ebony sighed out loud. She had no problem displaying her irritation with anything pertaining to Lynette.

"I wouldn't buy you something kinky. Any gift from me is going to be sanctified and holy."

Lynette laughed, "Of course, but the Bible says that the marriage bed is undefiled. So I say, bring on the thong panties!"

I just shook my head, pretending to be disgusted at Lynette's antics. I knew how much my friend was looking forward to *all* aspects of marriage. She missed the physical companionship of a man, and was constantly groaning about how difficult it was for her and Jonathan to maintain a chaste relationship.

We pulled up at the downtown Marriott, and I paid to have my car valet-parked. Lynette clapped her hands and let out a little shout of glee. "The Marriott ballroom? Alicia went all-out, didn't she?"

I didn't respond, because I couldn't give an answer that wasn't disparaging to Alicia. The fact of the matter was that Alicia hadn't gone all-out. I was the one who'd paid for everything. Ebony, however, was aware of this fact and sighed again.

We walked into the dimmed ballroom, and everyone jumped out and shouted, "Surprise!" In my opinion it was moronic to throw a surprise party for a grown woman, but I found myself yelling with the rest of them.

I had a big smile on my face when everyone started taking pictures of Lynette. They had to capture her counterfeit shock and engrave it forever into a million photo albums. I even kept smiling when Alicia ran up and hugged Lynette. She put her arm around Lynette's waist and started to pose for pictures.

Ebony and I decided to let Alicia bask in her own glory. We walked off from the picture-taking unnoticed and found seats next to the buffet. I didn't realize how hungry I was until I saw the Buffalo wings and cocktail shrimp.

After everyone was finished fussing over Lynette, one of the evangelists blessed the food, and the rush for the buffet began. When it was my turn, I picked up two plates for my food. Not because I was being greedy, but because there was a fruit tray at the end. I hated to have my fruit touch barbecue sauce and potato salad and whatever else was on my plate.

I heard Alicia and another one of the bridesmaids snicker when I picked up my plates. Alicia whispered something under her breath like, "That's a shame." I inhaled a sharp breath and ignored them. I'd been overweight for as long as I could remember, but the mean jokes never got any easier to digest. Besides, I wasn't the only plus-size woman in the room. Ebony also heard the joke and picked up an extra plate herself. I appreciated the gesture, even though Ebony was even thinner than Lynette.

Ebony and I went back to our table and devoured the little finger foods that I'd paid for. When we were done, we made another trip to the buffet. Ebony was what I called a big-girl sympathizer. Even though she was a size eight, she'd make as many trips to the buffet as I did. She was a true friend indeed.

We were cleaning out the last of the wings when we all heard the screech of a microphone. Lynette was standing in the front of the ballroom grinning from ear to ear. I had to admit that she'd never looked happier.

"I just want to thank everyone for coming out tonight," she said. "I can't believe that my wedding day is almost here. I want to thank Alicia for coordinating this evening, and all of my bridesmaids for putting up with me."

I felt my body tense with frustration as I watched Alicia smile, nod, and take the credit for what I'd done. The other bridesmaids were sitting at a table with Alicia, and they were all applauding her.

Lynette continued, "And to my maid of honor and best friend, Charmayne, I don't even know what to say. You have been with me through all of my ups and downs. I love you."

Lynette put the microphone down and came over to the table and hugged me. There were tears in both of our eyes. All my disdain for Alicia faded into the background. My best friend had not forgotten about me.

"You know, I know you paid for this," she whispered in my ear.

Alicia, not to be outdone, ran up to the front of the room and picked up the microphone.

"Okay, ladies!" she screeched. "Enough of the sentimentality. Let's open the gifts! Whoo!"

Lynette opened up several small packages from Alicia first. They were all flimsy, see-through lingerie. Everyone oohed and aahed as Lynette held up the tiny slivers of fabric. Even the church mothers in attendance were whooping and hollering.

After many more of the same type of gift, Lynette went to open up my package. After seeing what everyone else had brought, I wished I'd given Lynette my present at another time.

Lynette said, "This gift is from Charmayne and Ebony, y'all."

She ripped the paper off the oversize box. When she

held up my gift, a deluxe Crock-Pot, silence fell across the room. It was broken only by the cackle of Alicia's laugh.

"Great! She can cook beans in her lingerie," Alicia joked.

Ebony leaned over and whispered, "Remind me to never sign my name to one of your gifts."

The entire room, Lynette included, roared with laughter. I could've died of embarrassment. I just meant to buy her something practical. She couldn't spend *all* her time in the bedroom.

Lynette said, "That's okay, Charmayne. I need this. Y'all ain't never had my cooking, but Charmayne has."

One of Alicia's friends whispered audibly, "I'm sure she's never seen the inside of a Victoria's Secret."

I had had all that I could take that evening. After Lynette was done opening her gifts, Ebony and I made a quiet exit. I wanted a slice of the cassata cake, but I thought if another person made a joke about me I would explode.

I didn't even make it to my car before the tears started burning the corners of my eyes.

Noticing my tears, Ebony tried to console me. "It wasn't that bad."

"It was, and you know it was, but thank you for trying to make me feel better."

She continued. "Truthfully, I think you're making too much out of this. Who cares about what Alicia and her friends say? They're like some type of college sorority rejects! They all need to grow up."

"You're right."

Although I agreed with Ebony, it didn't make the tears

stop flowing. Since her words weren't bringing me any comfort, Ebony remained quiet for the rest of the ride, periodically handing me tissues.

"It's going to be all right, Charmayne," she said on her way into her apartment.

When I pulled away from Ebony's place, the tears really started to flow and were joined by loud sobs.

I cried out, "Jesus, please help me lose this weight! I hate being in this body, and I hate being alone. Lord, please take this food addiction away from me. You know I can't do it on my own. Please, Lord, send a companion who will love me for who I am, and not for what he can see."

My prayer was sincere. But it didn't keep me from stopping at the Dairy Serve on the way home and ordering up a banana split. I was determined to start my diet after the wedding.

CHAPTER
Four

Present

"So what did you think of Rizpah?" asked Dr. King as she handed me a cup of hot tea.

I sipped and responded, "Well, I felt sorry for her. She had already lost her husband, Saul, and then David took her sons and had them killed."

Dr. King nodded her head so fervently that her long, thick braids danced across her face. She brushed them back effortlessly and said, "Yes. She was definitely worthy of pity. What did you think of her reaction to her sons' deaths?"

"The passage says that she sat outside on a rock wearing sackcloth, chasing the predators away from the dead bodies. I thought that it was a tremendous showing of grief."

I remembered the passage that had moved me to tears.

Rizpah had found out about her sons' murders and desecrated bodies and she'd sat outside grieving them.

Dr. King tilted her head to the side. "You could look at it that way. She was indeed grieving. I also thought that she showed great strength."

"I got that feeling, too."

"The verse says that she sat on that rock from the beginning of the harvest until rain fell from the heavens. Most Bible commentators agree that this was a period of at least six months. She refused to allow her sons' bodies to be desecrated, and was quite determined in her efforts. When David heard of her courageous actions, it moved him with compassion. He went and collected Saul's and Jonathan's bones, and gave them along with their offspring a proper burial."

"So what is the point of us reading this story?" I asked, still not quite knowing what Rizpah's dilemmas had to do with me.

"Well, let's examine it closely. Do you see any parallels between you and Rizpah?"

"Let me see. Well . . . she lost everything. She was a wife of the king, and he was slain. She lost her status and her money. Then she lost her sons, who were obviously dear to her. I've definitely lost everything important to me."

"You've lost a lot, Charmayne, but I suspect that you have an inner strength to rival Rizpah's. We are going to tap into it."

I laughed. If there was any hidden strength dwelling on the inside of me, I wished it would come forth. "Maybe. But my question is this. What did all Rizpah's strength do for her? Her husband and sons weren't any less dead after she sat on a rock for six months."

"True enough. She didn't bring any of her dead loved ones back to life. But the Bible says that it wasn't until her strength moved David to action that the Lord was entreated for the land. Her courage helped to lift the famine from Israel."

"I'm sure that she wasn't thinking of Israel when she went through all that."

Dr. King replied, "She probably wasn't. Nevertheless, her resilience through adversity had an impact on others. Don't you think it will be a tremendous witness to the Lord when you make it through all your trials?"

"If I make it through . . . ," I said. I took one glance down at the scars on my arms, unsure what story I'd be able to tell.

"Charmayne. You have got to stop trying to convince yourself that you've experienced a death-dealing blow. You have your health, your sanity—"

"That's questionable," I interrupted.

"Honey, you are not insane. When you woke up this morning, you knew your name and what day it was. You knew how to get up out of your bed and use the bathroom. There are folks out here a lot worse off than you. It's time-out for your little pity party."

I hung my head and stared at my lap. She was right, of course. I'd been through adversity before. Losing my father was much more troubling than the Travis drama, and I'd come through in one piece. Even though I was only eighteen when it happened, I held my head up, went to college, and graduated with honors.

When Dayna had gotten married, I'd found myself extremely distraught: My baby sister seemed to be passing me by. And yet I'd survived. My faith and prayers had kept me before, and surely they would continue to keep me. I took a deep breath, exhaled slowly, and looked up at Dr. King with new resolve in my eyes.

She continued in a more subdued tone. "It's all right, Charmayne. Everybody feels sorry for themselves at one time or another. Let's just not stay there."

Dr. King was standing in front of me with one hand resting on my shoulder. Her touch was therapeutic and calming.

I said softly, "Okay . . . so now what?"

Dr. King sat down on her love seat. "Now we go back to the beginning of this whole mess."

We were finally talking about me. "What do you want to know, Dr. King?"

"What was going on in your life when you met Travis? What was making you feel vulnerable?"

I answered without hesitation, "Lynette was getting married . . ."

CHAPTER
Five

Past

"Michelle, do you know what it means to be a Christian in the workplace?"

She sat silently, waiting for me to answer my own question. When it was obvious that I was waiting for a reply, she nodded.

I continued, "Well, let me tell you what I think it means. At all times, you should exemplify what God has done in your life. That includes being responsible, honest, and trustworthy. You have to show people who don't know Christ that there is something different about you."

I felt myself getting irritated, because Michelle was only barely paying attention. I could tell that she was nervous, and that she just wanted my speech to be over.

I cut to the chase. "If your attendance doesn't improve, I'm going to have to terminate you."

That sure got her attention. Her eyes started welling up, and I handed her a box of tissues.

"You don't have to cry, Michelle. This is not the end of the world. Just do better."

"Yes, Ms. Ellis. I will."

It was always hard for me to come down on employees, especially when they were saved and members of my own church. I thought that when I'd accepted the position as president, I'd never have to handle human resource issues again. I was supposed to have people working for me to handle all that ugliness. But Grace Savings and Loan was one of those for-us-by-us operations. It was owned and operated by a coalition of churches, and the entire executive board consisted of pastors and bishops.

Michelle reiterated, "I promise I'll do better. Just please don't fire me. I've got bills to pay."

"Michelle, all you have to do to keep from being terminated is come to work. It's as simple as that. For the next ninety days, I don't care if your baby is sick. Ask your mama to watch him. Everyone knows how you abused the attendance policy. You have to show me that you value this opportunity, because there are a lot of people out here in need of a job. Do you understand?"

"Yes, Ms. Ellis," responded Michelle in a timid tone.

"I guess that's it, then. I know you will do better."

"I will," she said again.

Michelle got to her feet and grabbed two or three tissues for the road. I was hoping she'd hurry and take the waterworks back to her own desk. I hated to seem unsympathetic, but I had a whole list of things to do that did not include me soothing anyone's hurt feelings.

"Well, Sister Ellis, I'll see you at church on Sunday."

"All right, now."

Soon after Michelle left, there was a knock on my office door. I hesitated to answer. I hoped that it wasn't Michelle coming back, because I didn't have anything else to say to her. The knock came again, more insistently. If it was Michelle, I couldn't act like I wasn't in my office. She had just walked out the door.

"Yes?" I called, hoping and praying that it was anyone other than Michelle.

"Maintenance."

I breathed a sigh of relief. It was the janitor coming to fix my broken chair. "Come in, please."

The man who opened my office door was not a typical maintenance man. He had stepped right out of someone's dreams. He was at least six foot two, had skin the color of coffee with cream and piercing light brown eyes. His dark hair was styled in a neat tapered fade. I wanted to reach out and touch him to make sure he was real.

I exhaled slowly and deliberately as he moved toward me in that tacky green uniform. Armani'd had this man in mind when he designed his first suit. But here he was, standing in front of my desk looking fine as I don't know what, and asking me a question. I didn't even hear what he was saying, though I distinctly saw his full, sensuous lips moving.

"Ms. Ellis? The chair. Where is it?"

I snapped out of my semi-trance and replied, "Oh. The chair. Uh, it's over there in the corner."

He smiled, revealing his perfect white teeth. "Okay. I'll just get busy fixing it for you."

"All right."

The expensive and broken chair had been a treat to

myself. The office was already quite ornate without the addition of a six-hundred-dollar ergonomic chair. When I'd accepted the position of president, I'd had the office redecorated. I chose a subtle African theme that boasted some original, costly artwork and a mahogany-and-glass desk. Wooden blinds on the windows added the special touch that made the office my safe haven. The chair had been the pièce de résistance, but broke after two days of sitting in it. *Ergonomic* had definitely not meant *heavy-duty.*

I tried to get back to work while the man fixed the chair, but I was just a little bit distracted. Oh, who was I kidding? I was never going to get any work done with him in my office. It was on occasions like this that I really wished I looked like Lynette. She would have had no problem tossing her hair weave flirtatiously and asking the man out on a date.

He started humming while he broke the chair into what looked like a hundred pieces. His voice had a deep, rich, and soothing tone. It was frighteningly masculine. I supposed that he could probably sing like Luther or Barry.

"What are you humming?" I asked, trying to sound coquettish. It wasn't working.

"I'm so sorry. I do that without even thinking. I must be disturbing you."

"Not at all," I responded, "it's a lovely tune. I think I've heard it before."

"It's something my grandmother used to sing. A church hymn."

"It's nice."

I turned to my computer screen and pulled up my e-mail

before I said something completely out of character. As tenacious as I was in other areas of my life, I'd never been one of those women to pursue a man or even make the first move. I could single-handedly run a bank and graduate from college with honors, but when it came to talking to a man I went to pieces. I chalked it up to self-esteem issues, because I generally assumed the answer would be a flat-out, resounding *no*.

"Ms. Ellis, can I ask you a question?"

"Yes, you may." I answered, returning to my professional tone. The flirtatious femme was not working for me.

"How can a man like me get to know a woman like you?"

I laughed, because I didn't know how else to respond. I hoped that it wasn't his idea of a joke. Was I supposed to believe that this man, a perfect ten, wanted to get with me? He would've made the most beautiful woman in the office stop and stare.

"Ms. Ellis, what's so funny?" He sounded offended.

I cleared my throat in a desperate attempt to regain my composure. "N-nothing. An inside joke."

"I've seen you come into the office every morning, and I've wanted to talk to you. I didn't think that a bank executive would give a janitor the time of day. I guess I was right."

He couldn't have been more wrong. "That's not true. I mean, you could start by telling me your name."

"Travis. Travis Moon."

"Well, my name is Charmayne. So you can stop calling me Ms. Ellis."

"It is a pleasure to meet you, Charmayne Ellis. After I fix this chair, do you think I could take you out for lunch?"

I wanted to say yes. I'd never been noticed by a man as fine as Travis. But the president of the company out on a lunch date with a building maintenance man? My colleagues just wouldn't have gotten it. And as much as I wanted to say yes, I wasn't exactly bold enough to swim against the tide. But hadn't I just the night before asked the Lord to send me a husband? Could Travis have finally been my answer after so long? And were his eyes actually twinkling?

I offered the only rational reply: "I don't think that would be a good idea."

"Why not? Oh, is it because I'm just a janitor? A low profession even for the blue-collar brothers."

"My brother, you are jumping to conclusions. If you were the janitor at the McDonald's down the street, then it wouldn't be a problem. I don't want to appear to be unprofessional to my staff."

I watched a slow smile spread across his lips. "But you *are* attracted to me, right?"

I smiled back without responding to the question. I had learned from my beautiful friends to never put all my cards on the table. There would be no admissions on my part until Travis put himself out there. But who was I to even think about playing pretty-girl games? And why would I even *want* to play games if this man had been sent by the Lord?

Travis smiled, enjoying the game. "Okay, you don't have to answer that. But how about this. What if I take you to a really secluded spot for dinner? I can guarantee there won't be anyone there that you know, and you can meet me there."

I bit my lip and tried to gather my wits. I knew three

things about the man already. His name was Travis, he was fine, and he had a job. But I needed to know one more thing before I accepted a date.

"Travis, before I say yes I need to know if you are a Christian." My voice trembled with nervousness. What if the answer was no?

Travis exhaled as if relieved. "Whew. You had me worried for a second. Yes, I am, and I love the Lord."

I smiled, also relieved. "So what church do you go to?"

Travis stuck his chest out and responded proudly, "Jesus Our Redeemer, Church of God in Christ. It's on Eighty-ninth and Superior."

"I know it. It used to be a Catholic church, right?"

"Yes. That's the one. So, what about you, Charmayne? Where do you worship?"

"Oh, me? I attend Bread of Life Apostolic."

Travis's eyes lit up. He asked excitedly, "So are you in ministry or anything like that?"

"No, well, not really. I'm not a preacher or evangelist if that's what you're asking. I do serve as an armor bearer for the First Lady."

"That's a ministry," Travis stated matter-of-factly while his deft fingers moved fluidly over the chair components.

I had no idea how the man could concentrate. "Most people don't see it that way. What about you?"

"I am a minister in training."

"Well, all right." It was my turn to be impressed.

Travis cocked his head to one side and grinned coyly. "So now, if you're done interrogating me, will you go out with me?"

I laughed. "Wow. You're persistent."

Travis looked me up and down. "I like what I see. Is Saturday night okay?"

His stare sent a chill up my spine. "Yes, that's fine," I responded quickly. "Oh, no, wait. I'm in a wedding on Saturday."

"Do you have a date for the evening?"

I wasn't comfortable with what Travis was suggesting. "No . . . but . . ."

"But what? Is anyone from work going to be there?"

The nervousness had returned to my voice. "A few people."

Travis bit his lip thoughtfully. "Well, it's up to you, I suppose."

It only took me a split second to decide. A man like Travis didn't cross my path every day. Actually, a man like Travis had *never* crossed my path—not on purpose. Still, I almost couldn't believe that I was writing the church address down on a piece of paper. It was the most impetuous thing I'd ever done in my life. I felt betrayed by my own limbs. My fingers were scribbling, and my head was steadily screaming *No*. My heart, of course, was a wide-open chasm aching for the possibility of love. And if not love, how about some romance? But why were scriptures coming to my memory—warning me? "The heart is deceitful above all things, and desperately wicked: who can know it?"

I handed Travis the address. "The wedding starts at two."

"Thank you for the invitation."

"You're welcome," I replied, although I was almost sure that he'd invited himself.

"And by the way, your chair is fixed. Should be good as new."

I walked over to the chair and sat down. As promised, it was fixed. Well, Travis had at least one talent. He was good with his hands. I allowed myself to imagine how they'd feel holding me. I thought that perhaps he could fix me.

The wedding day had finally come, and I was as nervous as the bride. After I invited Travis to the wedding, I begged Lynette to let my dress be just a little different from the other bridesmaids'. There was no way I was going to let this man see me in a strapless gown. I would've been too self-conscious, and he probably would have decided that I wasn't so attractive after all. It took me two days to find a seamstress who'd make a jacket for my dress.

We were in the bathroom at the church, and Lynette was obsessing over everything. Her dress, her makeup, her shoes, and the imaginary pimple that she thought was emerging on the side of her nose. More importantly, she was having a critical case of last-minute wedding-day jitters.

"Lynette, you have to stop crying if you want this mascara to set," I said after applying the mascara for the third time. "You're going to be walking down the aisle looking like a raccoon."

"I can't do this, Charmayne. I'm not ready to get married."

I dabbed at the streaking mascara. "Look, heifer, we are not going to go through that today. You are about to get married and you are going to be happy. Period."

"Are you sure? I don't know anyone who's really happily married." She truly looked worried.

"Yes, you do. Pastor and First Lady are happy."

Lynette nodded as if suddenly relieved. "Okay, you're right. But they're the only ones I know who are truly happy."

Alicia was storming around the restroom, trying to make sure everyone was ready to start, because the ceremony was set to begin in fifteen minutes. Some of the bridesmaids were still walking around in their undergarments. "All right, everyone! Let's hustle. We've got a wedding to do in minus fourteen minutes. Charmayne, I need you to take off that thing you're wearing over your dress."

"It's a jacket, and it goes with the dress."

"You're wearing that? Nobody told me about that."

"Nobody had to tell you," Lynette said. "Last time I checked this was *my* wedding. I don't need your approval or permission for anything."

Insulted, Alicia stomped away. Lynette started applying lipstick and smiling at her reflection in the window. She was a beautiful bride.

After blotting her lips with a tissue, Lynette said, "So tell me about this guy."

"It can wait until after the wedding."

"Girl, I need to get my mind off this thing for a minute. Tell me about the guy. What did you say his name was? Tony?"

"It's Travis, and I don't know what to say. So far he's incredible, but we haven't been on a date yet. We haven't even had a real conversation."

"Really? Then what's so incredible about him?"

"Just wait until you see him."

"He's fine, huh?" she asked with a knowing glance.

I fanned my face as if the temperature in the room had risen ten degrees. "Girl, yes."

"So how did you meet him?"

"Uh . . . well, I met him at work."

For some reason, I was hesitant to tell Lynette that he was a maintenance man in my building. I was not embarrassed by his profession, but I thought that maybe she wouldn't understand. I couldn't even say that I understood.

"That's good, Char. I told you to start looking at some of those executive brothas up in there."

"Mmm-hmm . . . Oh, look," I said, getting off the subject. "There's Alicia lining everybody up. Must be time to get this show on the road."

Lynette took a deep breath and exhaled slowly. "This is it?"

"Yes, sweetie. This is it."

Lynette embraced me, and it felt like it was for dear life. For a moment I thought that she really might be making a mistake marrying Jonathan. She seemed so unsure. I planned to keep the two of them in my prayers.

The bridesmaids were walking out, and I held Lynette's trembling hand until it was my turn. I didn't realize that my hands were trembling, too, until I let Lynette's go. I'd pumped myself up so much that I didn't know what I was going to do if I walked out there and didn't see Travis.

A million things were going through my head as I walked down the church's long center aisle. I was trying to smile for the photographs and not look too anxious that

I didn't see Travis in the crowd. I wouldn't have been crushed if he wasn't here, because something inside told me that the whole thing was one huge practical joke.

I got to the front of the church and took my post, right next to where Lynette would be standing. I took a deep breath and looked out over the congregation. I wanted to sigh with relief when I saw Travis sitting in the third row. He smiled at me and winked. I smiled back, and then I felt a jab in my back.

"What are you doing?" Alicia hissed in my ear. "He's smiling at me."

I wanted to burst into giggles, but I maintained my composure. She would find out at the reception. I couldn't even explain how good it felt to capture a man's attention over someone who was thin, perfectly pretty, and available. It was like a victory for all big girls around the world.

I floated through the rest of the ceremony on a cloud. After the newlywed couple was introduced to the church, the entire wedding party was asked to stay in front of the church to receive the guests. I had no problem smiling and hugging and kissing the people in the line, even though some of them were virtual strangers.

Finally Travis approached. He patted the flower girls on the head, but bypassed all the other bridesmaids and came up to me. Alicia's mouth was hanging open like an unlatched trapdoor. Travis grabbed my hands and kissed the backs of both of them.

"Ms. Ellis, you look amazing. I'm so happy you invited me."

Lynette saw Travis. I could tell that she was shocked, but she nodded with approval. I was sure she wasn't expecting Travis to be as fine as he was. His eyes were dancing in the sunlight that poured in from the church windows. Travis's eyelashes were so long and dark that they almost looked feminine.

"Thank you for coming. I'd like you to meet the bride and my best friend, Lynette. Lynette, meet Travis Moon."

"Well, Mr. Moon, what do you want with my friend?" asked Lynette, and in a tone that was only half joking.

"Honestly, I want her to be my lady. Is that okay with you?"

Lynette smiled and said, "Only if you really mean that."

"Well, I mean it. Charmayne, I'll meet you later on at the reception. Did I tell you that you look amazing?"

Travis walked away from the line and Lynette elbowed me in my ribs. "Girl, you weren't lying when you said he was fine!"

"He looks even better today than the first time I saw him."

She squeezed my hand. "Well, it's about time, girl-friend."

Next in line was Marvin Baker. He shook hands with Jonathan and hugged Lynette. I waited patiently for him to pass me by without acknowledging me. He shocked me by standing in front of me with his arms outstretched. I warily gave him a polite church hug.

"How are you doing, Charmayne?"

"I'm blessed. Thank you for asking." I was extremely perplexed. It had only been a week since he had tried to avoid speaking to me.

"You look nice," he added as he quickly moved down the line, leaving me even more flabbergasted.

Ebony, who was next in line, giggled and asked, "What do you think that was all about?"

I shrugged. "Marvin? I don't know."

"You are prime real estate now, honey," Lynette put in. "Travis is way up the food chain from the likes of Marvin."

Ebony's eyes widened. "Wait a minute. That light-skinned brother you were talking to was Travis? Does he have any brothers?"

I laughed at the sad irony of it all. Why was I only validated in Marvin's eyes because of Travis's attention? Why couldn't I be judged on my own qualities? First Lady was right, though. Brother Marvin had missed out on something good.

I continued to greet Lynette's unending line of guests, but my mind was elsewhere. I just couldn't stop thinking of Travis. He was real and I wasn't dreaming! A smile spread across my face and parked itself there—I was on cloud nine. I couldn't wait to get to the reception, just to see him again.

The entire bridal party arrived at the reception hall early, because we had tons of photos to take. The reception venue was breathtakingly beautiful. There was a private garden in the rear of the building, complete with every flower imaginable. On the far side of the garden was an enclosed pond that was home to about ten white swans. The place couldn't be any more romantic.

Usually, I was not a picture person. I always started out with an upbeat attitude about the whole thing, thinking that maybe I wouldn't look fat when I finally saw the photos. But it never failed. And I wasn't talking about the camera adding ten pounds. I was talking about coming to terms with the reality of how big I really was. When I looked in the mirror, I automatically imagined myself thinner. All it took was one really bad photo to bring a big girl back to reality.

The whole process was depressing. The night of the wedding, however, I became a virtual camera hog. Having a man like Travis on my arm was an ego boost. My newfound confidence had me posing with the likes of Alicia and hamming it up for the camera. I was probably setting myself up to have a heart attack when I saw the pictures, but for the moment I was living diva-style.

After the photography was done, the wedding party was announced as we walked into the reception. Of course, the first thing I did when I walked into the room was locate Travis. I guess I was still in utter disbelief that he was even there. He was sitting at a table full of beautiful sisters, but he didn't seem to notice any of them. He grinned at me from across the room, and I tried to smile demurely.

As soon as we were seated, the wait staff started dishing up the food for the bridal party. I saw that Lynette had spared none of her new husband's expenses on the catering. Who really needed lobster tail and filet mignon? She could have fed these greedy people baked chicken and meatballs, and they would've been satisfied.

As the bridal party enjoyed their meal, guests stood up to toast the happy newlyweds. After each toast Jonathan kissed Lynette as if to seal the words of encouragement. Travis shocked me when he rose to his feet, glass in hand. Since he'd only just met Lynette and Travis, I wondered what he could possibly have to say.

"Now, I just met this couple today, and immediately I

felt the Spirit of the Lord reveal to me that they were bound for a lifetime of happiness," Travis said. "I would like to toast Jonathan and Lynette that they should keep God first in their union. Through all of life's ups and downs, Jesus will keep you. For richer or poorer, He's a waymaker, and through sickness and health, He's still a healer! To Jonathan and Lynette!"

I felt a huge smile spread across my lips. I was touched by Travis's toast. It seemed as if he'd just preached a message, what with all of the "Amens" and "Hallelujahs" that were heard from the other guests. I felt blessed to have him interested in me.

That night was a night of firsts, because it was another one of my hard-and-fast rules to avoid the dance floor at all costs. It wasn't that I didn't enjoy dancing, but since I was seldom asked, I usually ended up dancing in a group of desperate-looking women or worse—doing line dances. I think a lonely woman invented the line dance. She probably got sick of going out to parties and night-clubs holding up the wall, and just started making up steps for every new song that hit the airwaves.

But the night of the wedding, everything was different. I had a date, and he belonged to me. I had a partner for every song. If I wanted to, I could get sore feet that night, and not just because my shoes were too tight.

The bride and groom had their first dance and then the bridal party danced. The best man didn't look too thrilled about having to slow-dance with me, so I did him a favor and extended my hand for an old-school 1970s-style hand dance. I probably should have been offended, but with Travis in the room I didn't even care that the brother thought dancing with a big girl would ruin his game.

When all the wedding formalities were over, Travis made his way over to the bridal party table. I could see that a dozen pairs of eyes followed him across the room.

Travis said, "Miss Ellis, may I please have this dance?"

I did my best to stifle the silly giggle that wanted to escape from my lips. "Yes, you may."

Travis was the perfect gentleman, his left hand resting high on my waist, but not high enough to graze my breast. His right hand was entwined with mine as he swept me across the floor effortlessly, as if I were weightless.

I couldn't believe that I was thirty-six years old and having my first real slow dance. It was so different from those obligatory gestures of a family member or friend to keep a girl from feeling left out. It was a real slow dance, from a man who found me attractive and was interested in me.

I closed my eyes and inhaled deeply, allowing all my senses to enjoy Mr. Travis Moon. He smelled incredible, almost intoxicating. I thought he was wearing Nautica or Burberry cologne, but I wasn't sure. I wasn't what you would call a connoisseur of men's fragrances. His breath even smelled good. It reminded me of the peppermint tea that my grandmother used to drink when I was a child.

I tried to make myself think straight. I couldn't let myself get too caught up too quickly. I knew absolutely nothing about Travis. If I kept letting my senses have their way, I'd be sprung on the man before I even knew his middle name. When did I get that shallow? I opened my eyes and tried to bring myself back down to earth.

"So, Travis, are you enjoying the reception?" I asked, hoping that conversation would cool the heat I felt rising within me.

"Yes, I am. I thought I'd never get to dance with you, though. The dinner was so long and drawn out."

"It was long, wasn't it? That's just like Lynette. She's the only sister I know who wants a five-course meal for her wedding reception."

Travis laughed. "You're right about that. Most of us just end up having that soul food buffet thing."

"Mmm-hmm. Spaghetti, chicken, meatballs . . ."

"Dressing and yams."

"Knowing those foods don't even go together!"

"That's all right, though! Everybody always leaves full and with a to-go plate!"

I put my hand on my chest to try to contain my laughter. "Travis, you are funny. Too funny."

"Well, I like hearing you laugh. It sounds like music."

That caught me off guard. Where in the world was Travis getting these compliments? If nothing else, he was an original. "I like your laugh, too, Travis."

I needed to pinch myself to make sure that it was all real. I knew that this had to be of the Lord. Travis had every single last qualification on my husband must-have list. In order for me to even think about getting serious with a man, he needed a job, he had to have some level of intelligence, and he had to be saved. Travis didn't just have the must-haves, he even had the icing. A part of me was concerned, though. It was that irritating little part of me that contains a trait called common sense.

I knew that I was playing devil's advocate with my next question, but I just had to know. "Travis, why are you here with me?"

"What kind of question is that? Are you serious?"

"Yes, I am. You could have any woman in this room,

and I'm sure you've got sisters chasing you down at your own church. So why are you with me?"

"I know you might not believe this, but some men happen to be attracted to beautiful, successful women. I'm one of them."

"Come on, Travis. You know what I'm getting at."

"I also am one of those men who adore big women. I admit it. There's a certain comforting quality to a plus-size black woman."

I squinted my eyes and pursed my lips. "Oh, so I remind you of Big Mama, huh?"

Travis laughed. "Actually, I didn't have a Big Mama. My grandmother was about ninety pounds soaking wet. I think it goes back to eating pancakes."

"What?"

Travis responded with a straight face. "Well, we always had Aunt Jemima's syrup on the table. She was nice and round, and I just felt right after a stack of pancakes."

I'd heard a lot of tales in my day, but that one took the cake. I guessed it shouldn't have mattered how he got to love big women.

Travis burst into laughter. "Charmayne! You look like you're about to choke on a chicken bone! I'm joking, girl."

"Oh. I'm glad."

"Honestly, I don't know why I like big women. It's just a preference, I guess."

"Okay. I accept that. But I have another question."

"All right. Go ahead and interrogate me."

"You didn't even know that I was saved when you asked me out. So . . . why did you?" I almost didn't even want to know the answer to this one.

"That's easy. God told me to, clear as day. As a matter of fact, I've never heard the voice of the Lord that distinctly."

I was speechless. I'd accepted so many negative things in the past with reference to men and myself that I was totally willing to embrace something positive. And Travis loving big women "just because" was better than positive—it was miraculous.

After we finished dancing, Travis and I decided to take a walk around the courtyard. I appreciated the fact that he didn't presumptuously try to hold my hand. It was only our first date. Besides, I could not have handled him touching me—I was still giddy from the dancing.

"It's beautiful out here," Travis remarked.

I nodded, not feeling the need to respond out loud. The silence was not uncomfortable, though. Travis seemed content to reflect on the beauty of his surroundings while I pondered on *his* beauty.

Inaudibly, I sent up a prayer of thanksgiving. *Thank you, thank you, thank you, Jesus. You said that you would give me the desires of my heart, Lord. You have done over and above that with this man. Teach me how to be the woman he needs . . .*

CHAPTER
Six

❧

Past

It was two weeks after the wedding, and I was starting a diet. Even if Travis did love big women, I was still uncomfortable when I was out with him. I felt like I had to prove to everybody why Travis wanted me. Maybe I really just had to prove it to myself. At any rate, I had confined myself to a diet and was sitting with Lynette watching her scarf down chicken and pasta Alfredo like there was no tomorrow while I picked at a mixed-greens salad.

"So, how was your honeymoon?" I asked.

"It was great. I mean it was Aruba."

"Must be nice."

Lynette laughed. "What do you mean, *must be nice*? Girl, you've got plenty of money. You can go to Aruba anytime you want."

"It helps if you have some company."

Lynette leaned forward in her seat and squinted suspiciously. "Mmm-hmm. Speaking of company, that's why I asked you out to lunch today. What's up with this Travis guy? What's his story?"

"His story?"

"Yes, you know. What's wrong with him? He seemed like a real Prince Charming at my wedding, but there's got to be some glaring flaw."

I replied with much attitude. "I really don't know what you mean. He's great."

"Nobody's perfect, Charmayne."

I knew exactly what she was getting at. She wanted to know why Travis wanted me. There just had to be something wrong with him if he wanted me, right? She almost sounded jealous—as if she wished she'd seen him first.

"Well, I haven't seen any problems yet."

"Okay, so where did you meet him? Give me all the details. You say he works with you. Did you meet him at a meeting, in the elevator, what?"

Again I hesitated when given the opportunity to disclose Travis's profession.

"He came to my office on business," I replied evasively.

"Mmm-hmm. What kind of business?"

"What's with the third degree?"

Lynette rolled her eyes. "Don't I always ask for details?"

"You just seem to be relentless today. Why?"

Lynette dropped her head and said in a very low voice, "I don't know. It just seems like he's out of your league."

"What's that supposed to mean?" My voice had gone

up an octave, and I was speaking much too loudly for the quiet restaurant.

Of course I knew what it meant, but how dare she? Did she think that I could never pull a man like Travis? Even if I didn't believe I could, she had no right feeling that way.

I continued, "And what man is in my league, Willie Brown?"

"Well . . ."

Tears formed in my eyes. "I can't believe you, Lynette! You're supposed to be happy for me."

"Of course I want you to be happy, but—"

I continued angrily, "But what? You don't think a woman like me can get a guy like Travis. Well, Travis is into me, girl. We've been enjoying these two weeks, and I have having the time of my life."

Lynette reached across the table and took both of my hands into her own. "It's not about you! You can pull any man you want. There's just something about him . . . Girl, don't get me wrong. More than anything, I want Travis to be the one."

My chest heaved up and down from my angry breathing. "I'm a grown-up, Lynette. You don't have to worry about me."

Travis teased, "Would you like a chocolate-covered strawberry?"

"Travis, no. I can't. I'm *supposed* to be on a diet!"

"Girl, you don't need a diet. Open up your mouth."

I dutifully obeyed, allowing Travis to place the richly sweet strawberry into my mouth. It was our two-week anniversary, and he'd brought me to the park for an anniversary picnic. I felt like my drab, boring life had been replaced with the contents of a steamy romance novel. Only I wasn't your typical romance-novel heroine. My character was usually the wise and homely friend who keeps the heroine out of harm's way.

"Travis, you are spoiling me. I'm going to get used to this."

"I want you to. You deserve it."

I didn't feel like I deserved Travis or the special treatment. All I could hear in my mind were the cheerleaders laughing at chubby Charmayne who'd never get a date. It almost felt like they were standing in the shadows watching me and Travis, waiting for their cue to laugh.

I was afraid to even pretend that my romance with Travis was going to last. What if it didn't? Then what would I do once I'd gotten used to the good life? It would be like going back to being blind after being granted sight.

"Charmayne, I want to show you something."

Travis reached into the basket and pulled out a thin portfolio. It looked old and worn, and the pages had yellowed somewhat. He handed it to me; it said BUSINESS PLAN on the outside.

"You want to start your own business?" I asked, genuinely interested.

"I always have wanted that, and, girl, you inspire me. I see you sitting in that big office, pulling in the long dough, and I know that anything is possible."

I quickly scanned the pages to see if there was any meat to them. I was surprised to find that it was actually a viable plan. Travis wanted to start a handyman service for the shut-in and elderly.

Travis asked, "Well, what do you think?"

"I think it's good. Once you save up enough money for your beginning expenses, you should be on the right track."

"Well, I have been saving. I've got ten thousand dollars, which should be enough to start and pay my bills for a few months until I get some clientele. I gave my two-week notice at work today."

I shifted uncomfortably. "You did? Wow, you're really serious about this, huh?"

He'd quit his job with just ten thousand dollars to his name? In the recesses of my mind, a faint alarm was going off. A man without a steady paycheck scared me. I guess no matter how much money I made, I wanted to know that my husband could provide for me. But then again, Travis was not my husband. I didn't even know if he was mine at all.

"You don't look too happy. You don't think I should've quit my job. Am I right?"

"I don't know . . ."

"You said it was a good plan, right?"

"Yes, but it always takes a new business awhile before it turns a profit. You might be in the red for two years or more."

Travis responded passionately. "I can handle that. I'd rather do that than sit around and wait for some fat tycoon to fire me whenever he gets ready. I think the Lord wants me to do this, so that I can leave a legacy for our children."

"Our children?" I asked with a nervous chuckle.

"Yes, Charmayne." Travis's voice was steady and sure. "God told me that you are my wife."

My eyes widened. "Your wife?"

I was stunned. It had only been two weeks, and honestly, I hadn't thought much beyond that. Dating a fine man and marrying him were two completely different things, especially when he was talking about quitting his job.

"Charmayne, I'm sorry. I shouldn't have laid that on you like that. But I'm intent on obeying the voice of the Lord."

"But we've only known each other a short time. How can you know so soon?" I wanted to hear more about his revelation from the Lord.

"I don't know. God knows. From the very first time I saw you in the elevator, God spoke to me. Remember I told you how clear it was? He said, *This is your wife.* It was like He was giving you to me. Right then and there. Like He gave Eve to Adam."

I gazed at Travis and pushed all of the trepidation and uneasiness out of my mind. All I could see in his eyes was sincerity and kindness. Who was I to be skeptical of God's plan?

Travis tried to lighten the mood. "Charmayne, you can stop looking terrified. I'm not talking about tomorrow, next week, or even next month. I'm just letting you know that after we have courted for a sufficient amount of time, I will ask for your hand in marriage."

I could feel my eyes blinking rapidly. I was trying to take it all in, but the deluge of emotions was overwhelming. Instinctively, I felt alarm, but I consciously replaced that feeling with joyful resignation. I refused to submit to a spirit of fear. Then Travis reached across the blanket and kissed me. Not a friendly, Christian date peck. He planted a *You-may-now-kiss-the-bride* whopper on my unsuspecting lips. As suddenly as he came at me, I thought it would be rough and demanding, but it was the softest thing I'd ever felt in my life. The girl who'd never had a real boyfriend turned into the thirty-six-year-old woman who had never been kissed by a man.

I forced myself to pull away. "T-Travis . . . don't . . . it's too soon for this!"

"Don't worry, Charmayne. That's just a promise of things to come," he replied in a soothing tone.

Of things to come? Well, if there was to be more than that, I didn't know how I would even survive the wedding night. My insides felt like liquid gelatin, straining to hold their shape but struggling against an intense heat. I knew that it was not love. It couldn't be—I barely knew Travis. So it must've been lust, plain and simple. I used to wonder how women could just throw all caution to the wind and end up pregnant and alone. I understood after that day. They felt the feeling I had when Travis kissed me that first time. It was frightening yet exhilarating at the same time.

He asked nervously, "Charmayne, are you all right?"

I was all right. I smiled at Travis and it was like I was seeing him again for the first time. I would go before the Lord, and I was sure I'd get confirmation. If it was finally my time to fall in love, I didn't want anything to be a hindrance—not fear, low self-esteem, or lack of faith.

CHAPTER
Seven

❧

Past

"He wants to marry me."

Ebony looked up at me from my thick Bible concordance. She had been invited to speak at a Women's Day breakout session and was searching for a profound topic.

"Who wants to marry you?" she asked incredulously.

"Travis." I inhaled sharply, waiting for Ebony to explode.

She didn't. "How do you feel about his proposal?"

"It wasn't exactly a proposal. He just said that God told him I was his wife."

Ebony nodded pensively. If she had any objections, I couldn't tell from her expression. She was good about not judging hastily. It was why I valued her opinion.

I asked, "Do you think it's a little bit premature?"

"That depends on whether or not God really told him you were his wife."

"How do I know? I want to believe it so badly."

Ebony put one hand up in a *stop* motion. "I learned a long time ago not to get involved with anyone's decisions of the heart."

I shook my head. "So that's it? That's all you've got? What good are you?"

Ebony smiled and patted me on my back. "I will advise you to stay prayerful. If there is any reason why you shouldn't marry Travis, the Lord will reveal it to you."

My doorbell rang, and Ebony got a pained expression over her face.

"Is that Lynette?"

I nodded. Ebony started packing her things up.

"Why don't you stay?" I asked. "We're giving each other pedicures."

"Not this time. I'm trying to hear from God for this seminar and she is sure to make my flesh rise up."

I laughed as I went to open the door. Lynette was all smiles and hugs. She looked great, as usual. Her hair was in a bouncy roller set, and she still had her honeymoon tan.

Lynette frowned when she saw Ebony.

"Are you staying?" she asked.

Ebony shook her head. "Not at all."

Lynette observed Ebony's worn-out jogging suit and run-over tennis shoes. She replied, "You should. Lord knows you could use a little glamour."

Ebony exhaled, looked at me, and said, "Down flesh! Down!"

I giggled as I walked Ebony to the door. The constant

sparring between Ebony and Lynette sometimes provided my life with much-needed comic relief.

Lynette plopped down on my couch prepared for her pedicure. I gave a pedicure to rival any day spa. Lynette and I had discovered my talent for it in college. I always felt cheated when it was my turn to receive the pampering, because Lynette was nowhere near as good as I was. It was one of the endless list of inequities dividing me from my best friend.

Ever since college, Lynette and I had dedicated one Friday a month to making ourselves beautiful. We never scheduled anything on these days. No dates were accepted for the evening, no matter how fine the guy was. (Lynette broke that rule more than once.) Lynette had promised that once she and Jonathan walked down the aisle, she wouldn't forget about our ritual and the girl talk that came with it. She didn't want me to ever be able to say that our friendship had changed when she'd gotten married.

Things did become different for us, though, when she and Jonathan started dating. It seemed like every outing turned into a couples affair, and they would either try to set me up with my complete opposite (like the Willie Brown fiasco) or just not invite me. All of our conversations focused on how wonderful Jonathan was. Lynette sounded like a broken record, but my complaints fell upon deaf ears.

"What is this?" asked Lynette suspiciously as she held up a *Bride Today* magazine that was sitting on my coffee table.

I'd bought it, on a whim, at the grocery store. It was as if the thick book, full of beautiful, expensive wedding gowns, was just calling to me. I didn't think that Travis and I would be exchanging vows anytime soon, but I had started to let myself get hopeful.

"It is a *Bride Today* magazine," I replied flatly, trying not to give away any clues with my demeanor.

Lynette placed one hand on her hip and rolled her eyes. "Heifer, I see what it is, I mean what is it doing on your table?"

"I bought it at the store. There are some interesting articles in there."

"Charmayne, stop tripping. Nobody buys a bridal magazine for the articles. Have you got marriage on your mind already?"

"I don't know. It would be nice if it did happen that way. Travis is a great guy."

"Is he giving you that vibe?"

"I don't know what you mean."

"Has he mentioned anything about his future plans in life? A man will share his plans with you if he plans on making it permanent."

I wondered if this was confirmation from above. "Yes, he's shared his business plan with me. He also said something about raising children."

Lynette moved from where she was sitting to be closer to me on the couch. "Oh, my God! He talked about children?"

"Well . . . he says that God told him I am his wife." Again I held my breath, waiting this time on an outburst from Lynette.

"What?"

"He said that when he first saw me, God spoke to him and said I was to be his wife," I repeated, hoping that it would sink in without incident.

Lynette lifted her eyes toward heaven. "Thank you, Jesus!"

"Do you think that maybe it's too soon?" I asked cautiously.

"It does not take a man long to know he wants a woman. As soon as Adam laid eyes on Eve, he knew he had to have her. You know what I'm saying?"

"Now, see, I know this is confirmation. He talked about Adam and Eve, too! I guess I'm just feeling a little uneasy."

"You just aren't used to being in love. You better hold on tight to that man. I know plenty of vultures that would swoop right down out the sky and gobble him up."

"Was it this way for you and Jonathan? Did you know right away?"

I remembered trying to tell Lynette that they were moving too quickly. She hadn't listened to me and she was happily married. Why couldn't I just put those nagging doubts out of my mind?

"Charmayne, I'm going to be brutally honest," Lynette continued. "A saved man is hard to come by, especially one as fine as Travis. And you're over thirty. Girl, you better quit playing and marry that man."

"The truth is," I replied, "I haven't made up my mind on Travis one way or the other. He seems wonderful so far, but I'm not one hundred percent sure."

"Follow your heart, girl. You'll make the right decision."

After Lynette went home to her husband and children, I sat on my bed, staring at my Bible. I was supposed to be reading, but I kept thinking of Travis and his roundabout proposal. I just couldn't ignore the uneasy feeling I had in my spirit.

I had never been a person who needed signs from God for me to know His will for my life. I'd always read the Bible and let the words jump off the page and speak to me. I trusted Jesus to confirm everything I needed to know with His word. The Bible says that He "knows the plans he has" for me. After reading and praying I then allowed the peace in my spirit to gauge my success in decision making.

But the thing with Travis was unlike anything I'd ever had to decide. Maybe the uneasy feeling was just the butterflies people felt when they fell in love. Or did the butterflies only happen in love songs and romance novels? It was my *real* life, but I didn't know what to do or think. Lynette was right about one thing for sure—I was not used to being in love.

I closed my Bible and knelt on the floor next to my bed. I wanted to pray about my situation, but I didn't even know what to pray for. I meditated quietly for a few moments, running Bible verses through my mind. Then, since I couldn't think of my own words, I started to pray His word.

"Cause me to hear your loving-kindness in the morning; for in you do I trust: cause me to know the way wherein I should walk; for I lift up my soul unto you. Your word says that many are the plans in a man's heart, but that it is your purpose that will prevail. Lord, show me your plans for my life. In you, O Lord, do I put my trust; let me never be ashamed. I am casting my burden on you, Lord, because your word says you will sustain me."

When I was finished with my prayer, I laid my head on the pillow, knowing that everything was going to work out fine. I knew that if I trusted in the Lord, He would move all obstacles and show me the way to go. As I drifted into a wonderfully restful sleep, I felt the peace in my spirit return.

CHAPTER
Eight

~∞~

Past

My previous night's prayer had helped to calm all the fear I'd allowed myself to experience. I was out on a date with Travis and enjoying every minute of it. Travis, on the other hand, seemed to have something weighing on his mind.

Travis held the door open as we walked into a casual-dining restaurant. The place was crowded and noisy, and we were told that we had at least a forty-five-minute wait. That minor irritation did nothing but put him more on edge.

"Do you want to stay or go?" Travis asked. He was about to explode with nervous energy.

"We can go if you want. To tell you the truth, I'm really not that hungry," I replied honestly.

"I had something I needed to talk to you about, and I need to do it tonight."

Suddenly I felt alarmed. "Okay, but this is not the place to do it. I can't even hear myself think in here. Let's go to Handel's." I really wasn't in the mood for ice cream, either, but Handel's was quiet and we wouldn't have to scream at each other in order to hold a conversation.

We drove to the tiny ice cream parlor in silence. I kept wringing my hands, because I didn't know what to do with them, and I kept looking out the window, because I didn't want to look at Travis. The fact that he was so troubled had me truly concerned. What bomb was Travis going to drop on me? I prepared myself for the worst. Had he heard God wrong when it came to marrying me?

We got to Handel's and sat down at one of their outside tables. It was a warm evening, but not the typical muggy and humid of a July night in Cleveland. The only other people in the parlor were a couple sharing a milk shake. That was a good thing, because Travis had the most somber of expressions on his face.

I couldn't wait any longer. "Travis. What is it?"

He sighed wearily. "I don't even know where to start, but I need to tell you everything about me, before we get in too deep. Actually, I hope that what I tell you will bring us closer together. I have to know that you can accept me, even though I have some things in my past."

"What kinds of things?" I tried to make my voice sound steady, but I could feel it trembling, and my knee was shaking under the table.

He took a deep breath. "I served five years in the state penitentiary for drug trafficking. In all, I have four felonies on my record."

This was not what I'd expected. I'd thought he wanted to break up with me or tell me that he wasn't ready for marriage. Now all my doubt changed to paralyzing fear.

I felt that I was receiving the answer to my prayer. The Lord must've been telling me no, even if I wanted it to be yes.

Finally I replied, "Travis, this is a lot to lay on me at once. I need to let it sink in before I give you an answer."

Travis, sounding irritated, said, "I understand that. I expected you to react badly."

"I don't think I'm reacting badly. I just need time to react, period."

I thought of all the negatives that could've come from his prison life. Besides the fact that I thought he'd never have what I considered a real job, he could've had communicable diseases. I was furious that he'd kissed me and swapped bodily fluids without warning me first.

"How long have you been out?" I asked, desperately trying to ignore the answer that I was receiving from God.

"Going on a year."

I pieced together a response in my mind. I hoped it sounded compassionate and understanding.

"Travis," I started warily, "I do not have anything against a man who has paid his debt to society and turned his life around—"

"But?" he asked.

I guess my tone implied the fact that there was going to be a *but*. It really didn't matter how I tried to sugarcoat it; the *but* was going to negate it all. The *but* was always something unkind and hurtful. This time was no different.

"But, I don't think that after waiting all these years for a husband, the Lord would send me someone who can't attain the kind of success in life that I hope to have."

"You think I'll never have what you have?"

It took all of the Holy Spirit on the inside of me to keep from screaming! How could Travis not understand my concerns? He had made choices that had landed him in prison and I hadn't. It was as if he wanted me to feel sorry for being a success.

My voice was steady and sure as I explained my stand even further. "It's not about possessions. It's just that I want to be able to respect my husband and submit to his leadership. I don't think that I could ever submit to you. Our marriage would be a disaster."

I'd said it, and once it was out it sounded callous and mean, and not entirely truthful. Travis dropped his head sadly. When he looked up again, there were tears in his eyes. I didn't want to know what they meant. I just wanted to run away and pretend I'd never even met him. But I was trapped, at an ice cream parlor, forced to witness the pain I'd inflicted.

Travis had not made a sound, so I asked in a whisper, "Do you want me to call a ride? You don't have to take me home if you don't want to."

Travis was obviously offended. "That's ridiculous. Of course I'll take you home. There is nothing that you could say or do to me that would change the man I am or the one I will become."

He stood from the table and quickly wiped his eyes. I felt sad and confused, and I regretted making things so final. Why was it so complicated? I was hurting, too. I was feeling a pain that I'd never known. What type of cruel test was this for me to receive? Why let me set my feet down in the Promised Land and then hurl me back into the wilderness?

CHAPTER
Nine

~∞~

Present

Dr. King told me that I was making progress. I couldn't say that I agreed completely. I was still angry enough to do bodily harm to Travis if I saw him, and I was still alone. I didn't *want* to be either of those things, but I was, so I wasn't sure where or how I was progressing.

"So you broke up with Travis when you found out he was a convicted felon?" asked Dr. King.

"Yes," I responded defensively. "I could just feel that the Lord was telling me no."

"But something made you take him back."

I narrowed my eyes and replied, "Stupidity. That's what made me take him back."

"It was more than stupidity, and probably not even stupidity at all."

"Desperation, then," I said matter-of-factly.

Dr. King responded, "Go deeper than that, Charmayne. Something made you think that for some reason, you didn't deserve to have the man God had planned for you. Something made you think you had to lower your standards."

I nodded, in total agreement. In the beginning, no one could've told me that I made a wrong decision backing away from Travis. As attractive as he was, I was going to wait on the Lord. But a whole chain of events and a host of feelings got me to thinking I was going to lose the best thing I'd ever had.

"Tell me, Charmayne, how did it make you feel when you were out with Travis? The other women would be looking at you on the arm of this fine man. What did that feel like?"

I grinned. "It felt good, Dr. King. I actually felt equal to any skinny model type out there."

"So Travis was what you could call a trophy piece."

I agreed. "Yes. Having Travis built my self-esteem."

Dr. King shook her head as she sipped her tea. "No, Charmayne. It didn't build your self-esteem. Having a good-looking man—or any man, for that matter—doesn't change the way you feel about yourself."

I didn't answer, but I let what Dr. King was saying sink in. I thought about how self-conscious I was with Travis. I knew that everyone was looking at us, and I was glad the thin, pretty women were jealous. But I still wanted to be them. I still wanted to be a size eight.

Dr. King interrupted my thoughts. "Do you have your Bible with you today?"

"Yes," I replied, pulling my miniature King James Bible out of my purse.

"Good. Open up to Genesis and go to chapter twenty-nine."

As I flipped to the scripture, Dr. King scanned the page. She continued, "Read verse seventeen aloud."

I read, "Leah was tender eyed; but Rachel was beautiful and well favoured."

Dr. King commented, "In describing Leah, the word says that she was 'tender eyed.' *Tender* in this passage could mean soft, delicate, weak of heart, timid, or soft of words. I believe that this was describing not her looks, but her personality. Why do you think she's described this way?"

I smiled to myself. I thought of Lynette and her constant matchmaking attempts. If the brother didn't have anything going on in the looks department, she always started off talking about his personality. I thought that Leah must not have been much to look at.

"Maybe because her compassion was the most memorable thing about her."

Dr. King nodded. "I think that she was probably someone who was loved after people took time to know her. Rachel, on the other hand, was probably first noticed for her beauty. Perhaps more people took time to build a relationship with her because they were drawn by her beauty."

"That kind of reminds me of me and my sister, Dayna."

"Who would you say is the Rachel between you two?" Dr. King asked with interest.

I laughed aloud. "Guess!"

Dayna was so beautiful, and everyone always said that we'd look like twins if I were one hundred pounds lighter. When we were girls, she had all the male admirers in school and at church. That turned into her having all of the beaus and gentlemen callers when we got older.

I remembered crying into my pillow on the nights of all of the school dances. Homecomings, winter balls, junior proms were all sad occasions for me. During those times, Daddy had always tried to make me forget my troubles. We'd watch movies and make Jiffy Pop popcorn. Daddy's efforts softened the blow just a little bit. Later, Dayna would come home and recount the night's events to Mama; they would stay up late into the night giggling like best friends. Mama never seemed hopeful that she'd share those times with me. She resigned herself to the fact that she only had one beautiful daughter.

"So you can relate to Leah?"

I replied emphatically, "Yes. I know what it's like to be outshined by a beautiful, younger sister."

"Were you jealous of her?"

"Actually, I wasn't. I was just as enamored with her as everyone else," I answered. "Generally, I tried to protect her. Her looks never seemed to keep her from making bad decisions."

Dr. King said, "That sounds similar to your relationship with Lynette."

"It does, doesn't it?" The fact that Lynette was a lot like my baby sister had never even occurred to me."

"We're going to skip some of this. Start reading again at verse thirty and go down to thirty-five."

I continued to read.

And he went in also unto Rachel, and he loved also Rachel more than Leah, and served with him yet seven other years.

And when the LORD saw that Leah was hated, he opened her womb: but Rachel was barren.

And Leah conceived, and bare a son, and she called his name Reuben: for she said, Surely the LORD hath looked upon my affliction; now therefore my husband will love me.

And she conceived again, and bare a son; and said, Because the LORD hath heard I was hated, he hath therefore given me this son also: and she called his name Simeon.

And she conceived again, and bare a son; and said, Now this time will my husband be joined unto me, because I have born him three sons: therefore was his name called Levi.

And she conceived again, and bare a son: and she said, Now will I praise the LORD: therefore she called his name Judah; and left bearing.

Dr. King took a huge breath before she started. "Whew! This passage is so rich, and saying so much. What is your first reaction to reading this?"

"Immediately, I feel sorry for Leah. She knew her husband loved Rachel, and with the birth of every son she hoped to earn his love."

"Yes, yes. I don't even think that she wanted to take all of his love away from Rachel. I believe that like you, Leah didn't harbor any jealous feelings toward her beautiful sister. She just wanted her fair share of affection. Read chapter thirty, verses fourteen through sixteen. These verses really made my heart ache for Leah."

I read,

> *And Reuben went in the days of wheat harvest, and found mandrakes in the field, and brought them unto his mother Leah. Then Rachel said to Leah, Give me, I pray thee, of thy son's mandrakes.*

> *And she said unto her, Is it a small matter that thou hast taken my husband? and wouldest thou take away my son's mandrakes also? And Rachel said, Therefore he shall lie with thee to night for thy son's mandrakes.*

> *And Jacob came out of the field in the evening, and Leah went out to meet him, and said, Thou must come in unto me; for surely I have hired thee with my son's mandrakes. And he lay with her that night.*

Dr. King asked, "Tell me, Charmayne, do you think that Leah had high self-esteem?"

"No, not if she felt she had to buy her husband's affections with some fruit," I replied, still feeling sorry for Leah. I hadn't ever read that Bible story to focus on Leah's hurt; only on Rachel's disappointment at not bearing children.

"I believe that Leah had very low self-esteem," said Dr. King, "although she had much to be proud of in her life. She had sons, wealth, and a husband who cared for all of her needs. Do you see where I'm going with this?"

I thought that I did. Of course, I was supposed to be looking for the application of Leah's story in my situation. I had been proud of my career, education, and financial status, but I hadn't thought enough of myself to do better than Travis. I'd ignored danger signs that I would have easily picked up if it had been Lynette or Dayna romancing him.

I nodded slowly. "Dr. King, I never thought that I had a self-esteem issue. I've even mentored young women with low self-esteem."

"You know, I believe low self-esteem is birthed when we start to view ourselves through the eyes of others."

There were plenty of eyes on me—critical eyes. It seemed that Mama had nothing but complaints about my life, and she had no problem voicing them. Lynette, and just about everyone else I knew, thought that I should be married. In their eyes, validation came with marriage; validation of my beauty, validation of my womanhood, and validation of God's favor. I had completely ignored the fact that I had all of these things without a husband.

Dr. King continued. "I've got some more homework for you, Charmayne. I want you to start changing the way you think, and we're going to do that with something called affirmations."

"I've heard of affirmations, but I don't see how they'll help me."

"Every time you have a negative thought about yourself or your situation, you will cancel that thought with a positive affirmation. If you can include scripture in that affirmation, it's even better. Let's try one. The thought pops into your head that you need a slice of cheesecake. You feel guilty and think to yourself, *I'll never lose this weight.* Now give me your affirmation."

"Okay, let me see. I can say to myself, *Yes, I can do it, with Jesus' help. The Bible says that nothing is impossible with God.*"

Dr. King replied, "That's exactly what I want you to

do. You'll find that the more you use scripture to back up your affirmations, your faith will increase."

I bit my lip pensively. The whole affirmation plan sounded like a good idea, but practicing it would be quite another thing. I knew plenty of verses that applied to my situation, but I'd never used them before.

As if she were reading my mind, Dr. King said, "Charmayne, I know that this exercise might seem a little elementary. The idea of it is to get in the habit of being a positive thinker. Let's try it for a week and see what happens."

"Okay," I replied. I was still skeptical, but willing.

That evening, after my session with Dr. King, was the first test of my new "affirmation" plan. I'd been doing well on my diet, and the pounds were slowly but surely melting away. That was a good thing, but I was tired of protein shakes and salads. I wanted some smothered fried chicken and mashed potatoes.

It didn't help that I hadn't seen Travis in four months, and I had no reason to believe I'd ever see him again. But every time the phone rang, my heart would start racing. I was hoping that it was Travis on the line, but also dreading the possibility. Just thinking about him made me want to raid the refrigerator on a junk-food binge.

I tried to take my mind off breaking my diet by listening to my voice mail messages. I had three new ones. One of them was from Lynette. She called just about every day—to make sure I was still alive. The second was from Mama. She didn't have enough money for her prescription and wanted me to bring her fifty dollars. The third message was from my first choice on the employer list.

They were calling to tell me that they had filled the position with someone more qualified than me.

As I walked back into the kitchen, I felt the tears stinging my eyes. Why did it have to be so hard to bounce back? Was my one bad choice going to destroy the rest of my life? I grabbed the flour out of the cupboard and started adding seasoning for my fried chicken batter.

Then I realized what I was doing. I was slipping into a pity party. It had happened so quickly that I hadn't even had the chance to stop myself. I put the flour down and closed my eyes, silently praying to the Lord for an affirmation.

I whispered, "I am a skilled and educated young woman. I was qualified for that job, and I am qualified to do many other things. I will succeed, in the name of Jesus."

My telephone rang and I answered on the third ring. "Hello."

"Hey, girl. How you doing?" It was Ebony. Her cheery tone made me smile.

"I believe I'll make it," I replied, actually believing the sentiment.

"All right now! I'm calling to invite you to a speaking engagement of mine. I'm speaking at a women's shelter on Saturday at three. I need an armor bearer."

I laughed. "I haven't been anyone's armor bearer in a while."

"You're the one I want," Ebony said. "I know that you're a prayer warrior, and some of those women need a mighty deliverance."

"Mmm-hmm. You just want somebody to carry your Bible," I joked.

Ebony chuckled at our ongoing joke. People always made light of our commission as armor bearers. We knew that we were called to do much more than carry Bibles and deliver messages.

Then Ebony's tone became all business. "Seriously, girl, I need you."

"I'll be there. Thanks for asking."

"Don't thank me. I'm just doing what God said to do. See you Saturday."

"All right."

I hung up feeling much better. Ebony's call had been confirmation of my affirmation. I was qualified by God no matter what any human resource department thought. I paused for a moment, and then wiped the flour from my hands. I felt myself walking over to the cupboard and putting the flour back in its place. I then went to the refrigerator and took out a fresh lemon. That evening, the devil was defeated. Instead of fat and calorie-laden smothered chicken, I dined on grilled chicken flavored with lemon and herbs.

CHAPTER
Ten

~⧸⧹~

Past

My breakup with Travis was more devastating than it should have been. I hadn't been dating him long, so it should've been short and sweet, but it was not. I found myself walking around in a melancholy funk, wanting to cry all the time but willing the tears not to come. It was certainly not the peace that I was used to after obeying the voice of God. Perhaps God hadn't said no. Maybe He'd just wanted me to wait.

I tried to counter my feelings by putting on my corporate hat. I had an important meeting with the board of directors about my plan for community reinvestment. When I had accepted the position at Grace Savings and Loan, I was hoping that I'd be able to make a difference in the church community. I knew all kinds of saved folks who were completely bound when it came to finances. I believed that it was greatly due to a lack of education about money. It was my dream to implement a plan to transition convicted felons into career positions, including nontraditional small-business loans. I'd finally garnered enough support to get the board to consider a proposal.

I pressed my intercom button and said, "Donna, did you order the deli trays for my meeting?"

"Yes, Ms. Ellis!" she responded cheerfully.

"Thank you," I said, wishing that I could borrow her positive attitude and take it with me into my meeting.

I walked over to the conference room and steeled myself for what would probably be a dead-end meeting. It was nice to be part of a church-run organization, but some of the members of the board had no sense of what it took to run a financial institution.

"Does everyone have a copy of the agenda?"

I waited a few moments for the rustling of the papers to die down. I wanted to make sure that they all heard about my plans, because I needed them to give me a unanimous vote. It was not an easy thing to get a roomful of ten clergymen to agree.

When everyone was settled, I cleared my throat and began. "What I have proposed, as you can see, is a way for people to improve their standard of living, not just a handout. By training individuals who have had run-ins with the judicial system, we will empower them instead of making the church a crutch. The investment that Grace Savings will make is relatively small, especially when compared with the benefits. To put it simply: The more gainfully employed saints we have, the stronger, more financially secure our congregations will be. And this is how we can become the pillars that our African American communities need."

I took a deep breath and waited for the objections. I hoped that my presentation, along with my research and statistics, was convincing, but inevitably at least one person was not going to agree. Bishop Donaldson cleared his throat.

I knew that he would be the one to object. Bishop Donaldson had never wanted to hire me for this position—he had someone in mind from his own congregation. He was old-fashioned, and would have rather had a black man at the helm of the bank. He was against women in leadership positions, period. Not one female minister or evangelist would ever grace his pulpit.

"And how do you propose we choose these worthy individuals?" Bishop Donaldson asked. "You're talking about giving loans to ex-felons here. How do we know whom to trust?"

"I leave that up to the heads of the respective congregations," I said, my negotiating skills kicking in. "Typically, we are looking for individuals who have been outstanding examples in the church and have completely turned their lives around. I'm speaking of someone who is working steadily, even if it's menial labor, and who consistently makes financial offerings to the church."

"Are there any types of ex-felons we'll exclude? What about those with fraud charges or thieves?" asked Bishop Gordon. "No matter how much we want to serve the church, we are still a financial institution."

I replied calmly, "I'm glad you asked that, Bishop. We will look at each individual on a case-by-case basis. There will be a list of criteria, with the type of crime being only part of it. Remember, we want to assist those who normally wouldn't be given a second chance by society. It is my dream that an individual can come into the church and start over."

Bishop Donaldson chuckled. "That's a noble sentiment, Sister Ellis. Very noble indeed. I don't know how practical it is, though. If we do this, we'll need to take it slowly. There are wolves out here that would take advantage of the church—"

"But there are also sheep," Pastor Jenkins interjected. "And these are the ones Charmayne is seeking. We shouldn't discard an idea just because it may attract wolves."

"I agree," said Pastor Strong. "There is a poverty stranglehold over our congregations, and I think that this is a move in the right direction. If we are successful, maybe more Christian business owners will follow suit and employ members of the body of Christ."

Pastor Frank, who was usually quiet in the meetings, added, "I move that we implement this program, at least in its preliminary stages. I trust that Sister Ellis will provide us with the details, and some general guidelines for applicants."

"Of course. The documentation on this project is already prepared."

Pastor Jenkins said, "I second that motion."

"All in favor?" asked Bishop Gordon.

When all of the other board members had agreed to the plan, Bishop Donaldson reluctantly added his approval. I could've squealed with delight, but I didn't. I almost never gave way to displays of emotion at work.

After the vote, Bishop Donaldson said, "I want to see

the paperwork on this, first thing in the morning. I still have some reservations."

I eased back into my chair. Now that I'd gotten the approval of the board, the real challenge was making the program work. I finally had my chance to create a success story, and in the process maybe win over my critics.

I was on cloud nine as I walked back to my office. Even the thoughts of Travis that lingered in the back of my mind couldn't dampen my mood. Donna handed me a message as I entered my office.

"It's from your sister," she said. "She's going to be half an hour late for your lunch date."

I was glad that she'd called, because I had forgotten all about the lunch. We were planning a surprise party for Mama's sixtieth birthday. I should say that Dayna was planning it, but she wanted to make it seem as if I was involved.

"Donna, I need you to print out the documentation of the Teach a Man to Fish program. Fax a copy over to Bishop Donaldson immediately. The rest can go in the regular mail."

"Will do."

I returned a few telephone calls and then headed out to the Italian bistro that Dayna picked for our lunch meeting. That was one thing we had in common—our love of Italian food. The difference was that the thick pastas and creamy sauces seemed to have no detrimental effects on Dayna's figure. She was built like our father. He was five foot four, and couldn't have weighed more than 130 pounds.

Even though Dayna had said she was running late, she actually beat me to the restaurant. She had an irritated look on her face, and she was looking at her watch.

"Hey, baby sis!" I called across the patio, trying to

sound as upbeat as possible. Dayna looked up and her expression immediately changed. She grinned and shook her head.

"I see some of us are still operating on CP time," Dayna joked.

Of course, I knew that she meant "colored people." I'd heard Dayna say that line thousands of times. I'd seen her break off promising relationships if the brother had a problem picking her up on time for a date.

Since it was a sunny afternoon, we decided to be seated on the patio. Usually we didn't indulge in outdoor dining, because the humidity would cause our hair to swell into thick Afros. That day, however, the air was not the least bit moist.

We ordered our food from an overly friendly waiter— I was having the antipasto salad and Dayna chose the sausage marinara. My stomach started to grumble just thinking about what my sister had ordered, but I was trying to eat healthy.

Dayna pulled a huge notebook out of her bag and placed it in the center of the table. "Everything is in here! It's going to be a perfect party, Charmayne."

I picked up the notebook and flipped through about twenty pages of caterers, locations, and a guest list that had over two hundred people. Who was Dayna kidding? Mama did not have that many friends.

I laughed. "I was thinking we were going to do something just a little bit more intimate."

"Intimate? This is Mama's sixtieth birthday. It should be a bash."

"And who is going to pay for all this?" I asked, already knowing the answer.

"Well, I'll chip in, but I thought you were going to handle most of it. You know Erin just started kindergarten at Sacred Heart. That tuition is kicking my butt."

I shook my head and frowned. Dayna and Ron always had big plans for everything, but never any money. The year before, they had wanted to get Mama a big-screen television for Christmas, but they wanted me to come up with one thousand of the fourteen hundred dollars. They didn't get me that time; Mama got a robe and slippers.

"Well, if I'm paying for it, then I get a say in how much we're going to spend. We need to scale this thing way back. You act like Mama's getting married."

"Not that you would know anything about that," Dayna said under her breath, barely loud enough for me to hear.

I folded my arms and squinted angrily. "I see you been talking to Mama."

"She just mentioned that you dogged out yet another perfectly eligible bachelor."

"You and Mama need to mind y'all own business."

"And what about that guy I saw you dancing with at Lynette's wedding reception?"

"Oh, he's history, too."

Dayna shook her head and asked, "Why, Charmayne? Don't you want to be happy?"

"Who said that I wasn't happy?" I responded, my voice going up an octave. "I don't need a man to make me happy."

Dayna rolled her eyes. "The only women who ever say that are the ones who *don't* have a man. I believe that God created us to want a husband. Saying that you don't need one is unnatural."

It was my turn to roll my eyes. I had heard this line of reasoning so many times that I could repeat it verbatim. In fact, I'd heard it so much, I was starting to believe it. As much as I hated to admit it, I did feel that there was something missing in my life without a family.

"Are you going to try to bring a date to Mama's party? She would be so happy if you did."

I thought about who I could bring. I wished Travis had waited to tell me about his felonies. It would've felt nice to have Mama doting on my boyfriend for a change.

"Don't worry about me. I'll have a date," I replied, not knowing at all if that was the truth.

CHAPTER
Eleven

~~~

Past

When it finally sank in that my first romance was over, I called Lynette to receive some compassion. Lord knows I'd cried with her through enough breakups. But instead of being kind and supportive, she tore into me like a lion into a freshly killed antelope.

"I cannot believe you," said Lynette in a bitterly scolding tone.

"Well, believe it," I replied with a conviction that I didn't truly feel. "I'm not just going to marry the first man who comes along. I've waited far too long for that."

"The first man! He's the *only* man you've been the least bit interested in since Marvin Baker. You act like you just have eligible bachelors lining up to be with you."

"I'm not about to argue with you on this one. The Lord said no, and that's that."

Lynette scoffed, "You kill me with *the Lord said this* and *the Lord said that*! Since when did you become such a deep wonder? You've been hanging around with Ebony too much, and she don't have a man, either!"

I purposely ignored her dig at Ebony. "I'm not trying to be deep. I just know that Travis is not the man for me."

"And you're sure about that? Did Travis do or say something to influence your decision?" asked Lynette.

I thought about the felonies. I wondered if God's hand was truly in the situation or if Travis's revelation had been the *only* reason for the breakup.

"Look, Travis told me that he's a convicted felon. Even if I didn't think God was directing me, I'd still say no."

"What brotha doesn't have felonies these days?"

I was taken aback. I'd expected Lynette to back me up, but she was nowhere near being in my corner. I started thinking that I'd called the wrong friend. I should've known better. Between the two of us, I was the one with common sense. Lynette's nonchalant attitude was what drew me to her in friendship. I'd always lived vicariously through her.

"You're talking crazy, Lynette! You know the kind of man I want to get with. And that man does not have prison time under his belt."

"I'm not the one who's crazy. Let me bring you back to reality. You are thirty-six years old. You're overweight to a fault. Yet one of the finest, saved men in Cleveland wants to be with you. But you, all of a sudden, are hearing from heaven that he's not the man the Lord sent."

Her words hit me like a boxer's blows. "I don't have to listen to this!"

"You need to listen to this! You are so caught up in your own deepology that you're going to miss out on a good man."

I responded angrily, "Well, maybe if you had been sensitive to the Spirit of the Lord in your life, it wouldn't have taken you so long to find Jonathan. I don't need the hard knocks, I can just look at yours."

I was not surprised when I heard the dial tone in my ear. Lynette was good for hanging up on people, especially in the heat of an argument. I hadn't meant to throw her past mess-ups in her face. I wished that I had more experience with men. It frightened me to think that Lynette's rant included so many elements of truth.

Ebony and I sat in First Lady Jenkins's office, licking stamps and putting them on invitations to our annual women's conference. I couldn't believe that it was already September and conference time again. It seemed as if we had just finished all the work from the previous year's event.

To top it all off, Mama's birthday party was a week away and I still had not found a suitable date. Of course, I hadn't actually asked anyone, but it wasn't like I had a little black book or anything. My choices were slim to none—closer to none. I was trying to get up the nerve to ask Brother Marvin, although he was my absolute last resort.

When I'd told Ebony about my breaking up with Travis, she was characteristically silent. She'd nodded and whispered *Jesus* under her breath—probably a prayer for my strength.

"The conference is going to be so anointed this year," she said, trying to lighten the mood. "I can't wait to hear what the Lord has to say to the women."

"I know! I'm looking forward to it, too," I replied, trying to catch some of Ebony's enthusiasm.

"I'm sure the Lord has a word for you, Charmayne. Be encouraged."

I nodded and continued my stamp licking. Sometimes Ebony's stoic manner got on my nerves. I needed her prayers, but sometimes I just wanted her to get real with me. That was the reason I needed a friend like Lynette. She would pray for me, too, but only after she'd gotten angry, tearful, and bitter right along with me.

First Lady breezed into her office looking as if she didn't have a care in the world. I knew that to be untrue— she had more cares than the average woman. I admired her ability to retain her joyfulness even in the midst of trials.

She said, "Ebony. Will you please go make one hundred copies of this memo to the auxiliary heads and ministry staff? I want to make sure no one says they didn't know about their special offering."

Ebony graciously took the memo from First Lady's hand. I was glad that she hadn't asked me, because the copier needed replacing and would only print ten copies at a time without jamming. Ebony's job would take at least an hour to complete.

When Ebony was safely out of earshot, First Lady asked, "Charmayne, how are you? You seem too quiet."

"I'm blessed, First Lady," I replied with an upbeat tone, trying to mask my true feelings.

I knew that First Lady wasn't going to accept my

response. She'd only asked me how I was doing because it was obvious something was wrong.

She asked, "Whatever happened with that young man you were dating? I haven't heard you talk about him since Lynette's wedding."

"I broke up with him, First Lady," I replied sadly. I swallowed hard to keep from crying.

"So soon? He seemed so nice."

I felt the tears welling up in my eyes. "He was! I don't know what's wrong with me!"

"Well, now, I'm sure you had a good reason," she responded in the caring tone she used when she counseled the women of our church.

"He has felony convictions and he spent time in prison."

First Lady nodded pensively. Lynette had made me self-conscious about my *deepology*, so I didn't say anything about how I felt in my spirit.

"Did you go to God in prayer before you made your decision?"

"Well, no, but the night before, I'd prayed about the whole situation because I was feeling uneasy. I believe that the Lord exposed Travis's past as a way of saying no."

"If you feel that the Lord is telling you no, you did the right thing. There's nothing wrong with you."

"But," I cried, "I don't feel any peace about anything. Shouldn't I feel peace when I follow the will of God?"

"You will feel peace—just don't let the devil take it away."

First Lady got up and walked to the other side of her desk. She perched on the edge directly in front of me.

"You know," she continued while handing me tissues

to dry my tears, "Prince Charming doesn't always have to come in a pretty package."

I supposed that she was referring to Travis's looks. She wasn't telling me anything I didn't already know. In fact, I'd always expected my Prince Charming to be more of a court jester. It wasn't until I'd met Travis that I even dared to dream about someone tall, dark, and handsome.

"I know, First Lady."

"Brother Marvin asked Pastor about you the other day."

My eyes widened with disbelief. "He did? What did he ask?"

"In a roundabout way he asked if you were dating anyone."

I didn't know whether to be indignant or joyous. Why, of all people, would Marvin ask our pastor who I was dating? If he wanted to know, then he could've asked me himself.

I said, "Well, I had thought of inviting him to a birthday party, but I didn't think he'd be interested."

First Lady responded excitedly, "So now that you know he's interested, what are you waiting for? Ask him! He's right outside Bishop's office. They'll be leaving for Toledo soon. Hurry and catch him."

First Lady's enthusiasm was infectious, because before I knew it I was rushing out into the hallway, looking for a brother who barely even said hello when he saw me. I nearly collided with him as he walked out of Bishop Jenkins's study. I greeted him with a big smile, but I thought I detected a hint of nervousness on his face.

"Praise the Lord, Brother Marvin!"

"Praise Him, Charmayne," he responded quietly.

"Um . . . how have you been lately? We haven't talked in a while."

The nervous look changed to irritation. I wasn't sure that First Lady Jenkins knew what she was talking about. Marvin didn't seem at all comfortable with talking to me.

"I've been good."

"Look, I was wondering if you'd like to go with me to my mother's birthday party," I blurted almost unintelligibly. I hoped that he didn't ask me to repeat myself, because I was sure that I couldn't.

"You mean as a date?" Marvin asked, clearly not thrilled with the idea.

I stumbled over my words. "I mean, not necessarily as a date. More like an escort."

Marvin's eyes shifted from left to right. I guessed that he was trying to find a way to refuse without seeming like a jerk.

I decided I'd make it easier for him. "You know what? Never mind. I don't know what I was thinking." I willed the tears to stay in their places. I would not give Marvin the pleasure or guilt of making me cry in front of him.

"It's not that I'd mind, really. I just think it might give people the wrong impression," he explained feebly.

I turned and walked away—quickly. I sped past First Lady's office, although she was standing outside her door looking hopeful. I couldn't blame her. I should've known better. Plus I'd forgotten about the new single sister who had joined our church. She looked like a mixture of Vanessa Williams and Angela Bassett. No doubt, Marvin had again set his sights on an unattainable prize. Oh, how I wished that I didn't care. I *did* care, and I let the devil and Marvin Baker steal any lingering vestiges of peace.

CHAPTER
Twelve

❧

Past

The whole episode with Marvin almost made me cancel the outing that I had planned with Lynette. There was an event going on at the local Christian bookstore, and one of my favorite praise-and-worship singers was going to be there. I decided to go anyway, because I needed something to lift my spirits.

It was Lynette's turn to drive. When I heard her honk the horn, I took my time. I was still a little bit angry with her because of our last conversation, even though she'd apologized profusely.

Finally I emerged from my condo and walked to the car. On the way I noticed that my usually manicured lawn was looking ragged. I'd been too preoccupied with men to call my landscaper.

I got into the car without a word. Lynette asked, "Are you going to be like this all night?"

"Like what?"

"Pouty and angry. I thought you accepted my apology. What more do you want, my firstborn?"

"Does he do yard work?" I said with a tiny smile gracing my lips.

"If the price is right," replied Lynette with a chuckle. She exhaled a release. The joke had eased the tension.

I didn't tell Lynette about what had happened with Marvin. Number one, I was too embarrassed that I'd allowed myself to get dismissed by the likes of him. And number two, the last time we'd talked I was crying about Travis. I didn't want my life to seem like a sob story. Besides, between me and Lynette, I was the strong one. I was the one to solve all the problems.

We got to the bookstore, and I wasn't surprised to find it packed with people. There weren't many activities in our city that saved folks could participate in, so the gatherings at Imani Christian Books were always well attended. Lynette waved to a few of her friends from a sister church. When she went over to talk to them, I tried to fade into the background.

I got a cup of cocoa from the free-refreshment table and found a nice cozy spot on the wall in the back of the store. There I could brood about my thoughts without anyone asking me what was wrong. I could've even cried if I'd wanted, because people would have just assumed I was lost in the spirit realm.

I closed my eyes and listened to the sweet soprano voice singing CeCe Winans's "Alabaster Box." The lyrics of that song always spoke to my heart. It was the story of the woman who lay before Jesus and anointed his feet with oil and washed them with her tears. I could imagine myself being that woman. No one knew her story, or why she had been saving the costly box of oil. Some of the Pharisees scoffed at her for being wasteful, but she didn't care. No one knew her pain or her struggles but Jesus. I felt like that sometimes.

My eyes were still closed when I felt someone brush against my arm. I thought nothing of it at first, because it was so crowded, and because I was enjoying the music. But then a very familiar voice gave me an unexpected jolt.

"Hey, Charmayne." It was Travis—the last person I wanted to run into.

"Hi."

I didn't want to start a conversation with him—I had no idea what to say. For some reason I felt like I should be apologizing to him. It felt rude to walk away, so I just stood there, pretending to be engrossed in the singing.

He tapped my shoulder. When I turned to look at him, he was smiling. "We don't have to act like we're strangers, you know."

"I know."

Travis continued, "So how have you been?"

"I've been good," I replied.

"I haven't. I've missed you, Charmayne."

I glanced around nervously, trying to spot Lynette in the crowd. I refused to make eye contact with Travis, although I could still feel his eyes as if they were burning a hole right through me. I spotted Lynette, but she was too far away to even notice that I was in need of rescuing.

I smiled nervously. "It hasn't been a long time, Travis. I just saw you a few weeks ago."

Travis took both of my hands in his. "It's been like forever. My heart jumped for joy when I saw you here tonight."

Why on earth did he have to say things like that? It sounded like something out of a romance novel, but good nonetheless. I could feel every last one of my defenses crumble. Travis was still holding my hands and massaging the center of my palms with his thumbs.

"I don't know what to say." It was hard to gather my thoughts with him gazing into my eyes.

"Say that you believe what I believe—that this is the Lord bringing us back together."

As if on cue, Lynette finally decided to show her face, saving me from responding to Travis and giving me a chance to get my head together. Lynette looked at Travis suspiciously, and then over to me with questions in her eyes. I hoped that she could read the desperation in my face.

She said, "Brother Travis. It's good seeing you again."

"Same here," Travis replied, taking his eyes off me for only a second.

Lynette chuckled. "If I didn't know any better, I'd think I was interrupting something."

I snatched my hands away from Travis. "No, girl. Not at all."

The disappointment in Travis's eyes was apparent, as was the relief in mine. Lynette linked arms with me and started swaying back and forth to the upbeat song that was being performed. She swung me around until my back was to Travis.

Lynette mouthed the words, *You okay?*

I nodded and mouthed back, *Thank you.*

I guessed that Travis had given up on getting a response out of me at that moment, and since Lynette and I kept dancing, he moved across the floor to the other side of the room. I felt myself relaxing and loosened my grip on Lynette's arm.

I tried not to notice what Travis was doing and who he was talking to, but I couldn't help but see him talking to a gorgeous young woman who seemed to be smitten with him. Immediately I felt an enormous amount of jealousy. I panicked. Before I could force my mind to entertain rational thoughts I pushed through the crowd until I was close enough to touch Travis.

I desperately grabbed his arm and said, "Travis. We need to talk."

Travis seemed to note the urgency and passion in my request and ended his conversation abruptly. The woman rolled her eyes at me as she strode away, but at that point I didn't care—as long as she was gone.

"Charmayne?"

"Look, I don't know how I feel, Travis, and I don't know if I believe what you believe, but . . ."

Travis's eyes lit up. "But you're willing to give us a chance?"

"I-I don't know."

"Well, tell me something . . ."

I thought quickly. "Do you want to come to my mother's birthday party with me? It's next Saturday."

Travis smiled. "Of course. But you know that's a big step, introducing me to your mother."

"It's just a birthday party."

Lynette walked up again, this time too late to stop me from doing any damage.

"Charmayne," she said, "Jonathan just text-paged me. He needs me at home."

"Oh, okay. I'm ready anyway."

"I can take you home if you want," Travis interjected.

Lynette said, "I'm a horrible night driver. I need Charmayne. She's the navigator."

Before I could object and remind Lynette that she was only a horrible night driver when she wasn't wearing her contacts, she was saying her good-byes to Travis and dragging me out of the bookstore. She glared at me all the way to the car. I knew she was angry when she slammed her car door. Lynette usually babied her used BMW like it was one of her own children.

Lynette started to question me as soon as we closed the car doors. "What was that all about?"

"What?"

"First you thank me for rescuing you, then you're up in his face like a lovesick teenager. I'm trying to back you up, but I don't even think you know what you want."

I sighed. "I don't know what happened, really. I saw him with that other woman and got insanely jealous."

Lynette shook her head in disbelief. "But I thought that you didn't want him. Do the words *The Lord is saying no* ring any bells?"

"I'm so confused, Lynette. What if that wasn't the voice of the Lord? What if it was just my own insecurities?"

"Girl, I believe Jesus gave you good sense. Stop trying to be so deep about all of this."

I slumped down in my seat, weary from the mental anguish. "I don't know what to do."

"Remember when I was having doubts about Jonathan?" Lynette asked. "You were the one to reassure me."

I nodded and remembered Lynette's wedding day. She was so uncertain, even though she knew that Jonathan was a good man. Maybe I was experiencing the same thing.

I listened to Lynette tell me all the reasons why I should get with and stay with Travis. I didn't need to be reminded of my limited options for male companionship and my obvious handicaps in that area.

I decided to be totally honest. "What if I told you that Travis wasn't a corporate executive, but was the maintenance man in my office?"

Lynette was stunned. After a noticeable silence she said pointedly, "I'm surprised you even gave him the time of day."

"Well, I did. So do you still think I should pursue him? Especially with his felony convictions?"

"Girl . . . I don't know. You need to pray on that."

I laughed at the irony of her words. I had been praying fervently and still had no idea which path to take. I couldn't depend on Lynette, Ebony, or First Lady to make this decision for me. I had only the voice of the Lord to rely upon, and I wasn't sure if I was hearing Him.

Honestly, when I saw Travis and that beautiful woman, I wasn't thinking about felonies, job descriptions, or even the voice of God. I was thinking that someone was trying to steal my man. I wanted Travis in my life regardless of the risks.

I asked, "If Jonathan had told you that he had a felony record and was making a modest blue-collar income, would you still have married him?"

"Of course not," Lynette responded without hesitation. "But I am not you."

"What does that mean?"

"You are paid, girl. I needed a man to come in and take care of me. You don't. You know full well you can afford to take care of that man."

"I'm not trying to take care of a man."

"Right. You're just trying to be an old maid."

I repeated. "I am *not* trying to take care of a grown man."

"So you compromise a little bit. That's what relationships are about anyway."

If I had any sense of inner tranquility about my decision to break up with Travis, it had been replaced by turmoil. I didn't even want to pray about it anymore. How could I have peace when I was going out of my mind with loneliness? What I wanted was a perfect life. I wanted a family and I wanted a man. I wanted Travis.

Why was I torturing myself anyway? I deserved to be happy. I deserved to have my dreams come true! I had a fine, saved brother who was obviously enamored of me and I was about to lose him just because of a few little flaws.

I was reminded of the fruit pies that my grandmother used to make when I was a little girl. Grandma would send me and Dayna to pick peaches from the trees in her backyard. We were so little that most of the time we just picked up the best-looking windfall from the ground around the trees. They were bruised and banged up, but we were proud of our harvest.

Grandma never said anything negative about our mutilated peaches. She took them from us, ever so carefully, and rinsed them gingerly in her big aluminum tub. As she peeled them she talked about how good the pie was going to be when she was done. She'd have me practically drooling thinking about the sweet, juicy pie that we were going to eat after dinner. And it never failed. Every single last time, Grandma turned those wrecked, beaten-up peaches into the best pie I'd ever eaten in my life.

CHAPTER
Thirteen

❧

Past

For the first time Ebony decided to voice her opinion on my problems with Travis. We were sitting in First Lady's office putting the final preparations on the women's conference. When I'd told her that we were back together, her face had immediately darkened into a frown.

"Why are you ignoring the voice of the Lord?" she asked slowly, deliberately enunciating each word to convey the desired emphasis. "You know that God is leading you away from this man."

"At this point, I don't know what I know, other than the fact that I'm tired of being alone."

"Do you think that God doesn't know that?" Ebony continued. "Don't you know that He will supply your need?"

I furrowed my eyebrows until they almost connected.

"Don't you ever feel lonely, Ebony? I thought you'd understand."

"I have dedicated my life to God, and I will remain single as long as He requires it. I do know that celibacy is a gift of the Holy Spirit. The Apostle Paul tells us in First Corinthians seven, verses seven through nine, that not everyone can walk this path."

"I don't want to be celibate. I want a husband," I whined.

"Even to the detriment of your own spirituality?" Ebony asked rhetorically as she stood to leave.

I was afraid to answer that question, even in my own mind.

It was the day of Mama's birthday party and I was apprehensive, though not about Travis. Over the course of the week we'd reconnected—over the phone. There was something youthful and elementary about staying up all night talking about nothing in particular, but not wanting to hang up. I found out things about Travis that pleasantly shocked me, like the fact that he read Tolstoy and enjoyed spa pedicures. Actually, aside from his felony record, Travis was beginning to look like the perfect man for me.

What worried me was Dayna and, of course, Mama. It was almost inevitable that at the birthday party, one or both of them would do something to humiliate me. My life had been their ongoing, secret inside joke for so long that I didn't think they could handle me in a situation not ripe for ridicule.

It calmed me a little bit to know that Lynette and Ebony were going to be there, too, even if neither one of them really agreed with me and Travis getting back together. Lynette would have my back regardless, and Ebony would be praying for me.

Travis had insisted on picking me up for the evening, even though the only transportation he had was his work van. I agreed only because I knew it was a pride thing. Besides, I'd rather be riding up to Mama's party in a clean, albeit a little rusty, van—with a man—than in my shiny Infiniti riding solo.

I couldn't help but beam when I watched Travis step out of his van from my window. He looked like he'd just stepped off a Parisian catwalk—and he was with me. I noticed two women who were waiting on the bus; they were staring at Travis. *Ha!* I thought, *he's mine!* Well, he was mine for the evening, at least. We hadn't discussed taking it any farther than that.

I was still all smiles when I opened my door. It was the first time Travis had been to my home, and he was obviously impressed. The majority of my home was decorated with an Asian theme. I'd spent thousands of dollars on furniture, because I felt that if I was going to be a homeowner, then I should go all-out. The living room was filled with blue-and-white ceramic pieces that gave it a delicate and feminine feel. The family room was also filled with Asian pieces—wooden carvings, bamboo baskets, and a burgundy-lacquer-and-glass coffee table. I watched Travis's eyes take it all in and I was glad that I'd had my cleaning lady come an extra day that week.

I had also taken a great deal of care in getting myself ready. My hair was freshly styled in an elegant updo that slimmed my facial features. I'd chosen a pretty and feminine black cocktail dress. The A-line bottom flattered my figure and hid any bulges left visible by my girdle. I'd topped the outfit off with a silver wrap and shoes. When I'd looked in the mirror at my reflection, I was more than pleased.

After scanning my home, Travis's eyes rested on me. "You look good, baby. Are you ready?"

I nodded, because I was too excited to say anything. His eyes told me that he found me beautiful and desirable. And then he called me *baby* and almost made me lose my mind. No man had ever, in my life, used a pet name for me. At work I was Ms. Ellis. To my church family I was Charmayne or Sister Ellis. Even my daddy, who'd loved me more than anyone, had called me by my full name—Charmayne Jean.

When we got in the car, I was finally able to speak. "You look good, too."

Travis laughed, probably at my delayed response. "Thank you."

Dayna and I had compromised on a much more scaled-down version of her original party plans. I agreed to go semi-formal and have it catered, but we rented out the local community center and had a sister from my church do all the cooking.

I was glad I'd let Dayna splurge just a little on the decorations, because she had transformed the plain gymnasium into an elegant ballroom. Mama was sitting at the head table looking nowhere near her sixty years. No one could look at her and tell the way her health had been failing. Her salt-and-pepper-colored hair was swept into an alluring updo. She'd even let Dayna give her curls that cascaded down the side of her face.

It was obviously Dayna's plan that she and Mama

look like twins for the party. They were both wearing silver gowns, and Dayna had twisted her hair into a similar style as Mama's. Dayna's little girls, Erin and Koree, were also wearing silver, and she'd forced Ronald Jr. to put on a miniature tuxedo with a silver cummerbund. Only Dayna's husband seemed to rebel. He was wearing a brown suit, with not even a hint of a silver accessory.

Instinctively I grabbed Travis's arm as we made our way over to Mama's table. There were little name cards to mark our seats. Dayna had made it a point to place me near the end of the table while her family unit surrounded Mama on either side. She also didn't have a place set for Travis, so she obviously assumed that I wasn't bringing a date. I made every effort to contain my fury, but my light skin color betrayed me. I could feel the redness creeping up my neck.

Travis squeezed my hand and asked, "Are you okay?"

"Yes. I'm fine." I smiled bravely. "Come on, so I can introduce you to Mama."

Mama squinted suspiciously as Travis and I approached. I prayed silently, *Lord, please don't let her embarrass me.* Dayna walked up behind Mama just as I was about to make my introduction.

"Charmayne," Dayna said. "I'm glad that you *finally* made it."

I could've slapped her. I didn't know why she always felt the need to show me up. She already had Mama's favor. Besides, we weren't that late.

I ignored her and said, "Happy birthday, Mama. I have someone here that I want you to meet."

Travis extended his hand to shake Mama's and smiled

that charming smile of his. Mama was enchanted, but Dayna snorted under her breath. I wondered what the joke was.

"Mama," I continued, "I'd like you to meet Travis Moon."

Mama smiled and then yanked my body down until my ear was next to her mouth. She whispered loudly, "Is he your man?"

Dayna, who had heard the question, snorted again. "I'm Dayna. Charmayne's sister. It's a pleasure to meet you, Mr. Moon."

"Likewise," replied Travis.

Mama looked up at Travis and said, "Sit down, right here, and tell me about yourself."

Dayna frowned. "Mama, that's Ronald's seat."

"Well, it's okay, Dayna. I already know Ronald. I'd like to get acquainted with Travis."

I smirked at Dayna, and she marched off to attend to some imaginary business. I breathed a sigh of relief. Mama seemed to approve of Travis so far.

He sat down beside Mama and asked, "What birthday is this? Your fortieth?"

Mama giggled and smacked at Travis's arm. "Honey, I ain't seen forty in a long time."

"Well, you don't look old enough to have a thirty-six-year-old daughter, that's for sure."

Mama blushed. "Yes, I do, but it is quite gentlemanly of you to say otherwise. Somebody raised you right."

I scanned the room for Lynette and Ebony, because it was obvious that neither Travis nor Mama needed any input from me. Neither of my friends had arrived yet, but I watched with amusement as Dayna tried to force

Ronald, who was at the appetizer table, to come over to Mama.

I listened to Travis as he charmed my mother off her feet. He talked about his work, and she seemed enthralled. How exciting could home maintenance be? I heard him tell Mama that he'd just landed an out-of-town client. That was news to me. Perhaps he'd forgotten to mention it. I made a mental note to ask him about it after the party.

I waved to Lynette and Jonathan when they came in. Lynette walked around the table and hugged Mama. Jonathan kissed me on my cheek.

"Lynette, have you met Charmayne's date?" Mama gushed.

"Yes, I have. He was at my wedding."

Mama frowned. "Charmayne, why didn't you introduce us at Lynette's wedding?"

"I'd only just met him myself," I replied truthfully.

"You see how she treats me?" Mama asked Travis. "She's so embarrassed of her dear mother that she won't even introduce me to her dates."

I shook my head and sighed. Nothing was ever going to change with Mama. Lynette squeezed my hand, silently offering her support.

While Mama and Travis continued to chat, Lynette looked at me with a sparkle in her eyes. She took my arm as she and Jonathan left to find a seat. I excused myself from Mama and Travis, who barely noticed that I was getting up from the table.

Lynette grinned from ear to ear. "Girl, your mama is drooling over Travis and he's eating it up. I bet she'd marry you off to him tomorrow."

I laughed. "Tonight, honey. She really likes him."

"What about Dayna?"

"Dayna is too busy trying to run the show to be concerned with Travis."

The next sounds we heard were Dayna's voice combined with a shrieking noise—feedback from the microphone that Dayna was holding. She was announcing that it was time for everyone to take their seats, and that dinner and presentations were about to begin. Lynette sat down at her table, and I took my seat next to Travis. Dayna had a chair added to the head table so that all of her family was represented properly.

Dayna announced, "This birthday celebration is in honor of my beautiful mother, Claudette Ellis. Words cannot express how much I love and cherish her. I'm going to try to sing a song tonight that depicts just a fraction of what I feel for my mother."

I growled under my breath. "I *knew* she was going to sing!"

Travis smiled at me and put his arm around me lovingly in an attempt to calm my nerves. I was still furious. Dayna knew that I couldn't sing a lick. It was a chance for her to outshine me—again.

Ebony walked into the party just as the music began. She waved as she sat down at a table with people she didn't know. Most of the guests were members from Mama's church, which she rarely attended.

Everyone listened in awe as Dayna sang "You Are So Beautiful to Me." In my opinion she added way too many runs and extra notes, and sang the same verse too many times, but everyone else seemed to enjoy it, especially Mama. There were tears in her eyes as her favorite daughter sang to her. It was just what Dayna needed to draw attention away from me and Travis and place it back where she wanted it—on herself.

The audience gave Dayna a standing ovation. I felt betrayed when my two friends stood clapping as loudly as everyone else. I couldn't be the only one in the room not giving Dayna accolades, so I stood with the others.

After Dayna sang her song, the dinner was served. It was adequate, to say the least. I hadn't agreed to Dayna's plans for a five-course meal. We stuck with a tossed salad, chicken, vegetables, and roasted potatoes. It was standard fare, but it was tasty and filling.

Next on Dayna's program came the presentations by her children. Erin and Koree did a little dance that wasn't even cute. I felt sorry for them little babies. Mama looked pleased, though.

Mama clapped her hands and bragged to Travis, "You see! Those are my granddaughters. They will be dancing with Alvin Ailey one day."

Travis nodded in agreement and clapped as fervently as Mama. Dayna had Ronald Jr. recite a poem by Langston Hughes. He stopped and started about five times, but finally made it through the entire piece.

"That's my baby!" shouted Dayna, sounding exactly like Mama. I shook my head and clapped. I hoped Dayna was done humiliating her family for the evening.

After the presentations, a jazz band played while everyone enjoyed chatting or dancing. I'd wanted to have a soloist from my church sing a song or two, but Dayna had stubbornly objected. She said that she didn't want to make Mama feel guilty for only going to church a few times a year.

Mama finally turned her attention back to me and Travis. She asked about his family, and again I found out information I'd never known. Travis was an only child, and he had been raised by his mother. I wondered to myself just what were me and Travis talking about on the phone that I had neglected to collect such pertinent information.

"Charmayne," Mama said as the night drew to a close, "you better hang on to this one. I know a good man when I see one."

I didn't know how to respond to that, because—other than Daddy—Mama absolutely did not know a good man when she saw one. And it wasn't like she was going to pray for me, either. Mama's approval of Travis was almost a warning. I watched as Travis continued to smile and chat with Mama. If he was trying to win her over, then his mission was accomplished.

On the way home I asked Travis casually, "When were you going to tell me about your client?"

"I just finalized the deal this afternoon. I was going to tell you tonight."

I nodded. "So how far out of town is your client located?"

"Just in Detroit. Four hours away at the most."

"Detroit? How are you going to swing that? Are you moving there?" There was a bit of alarm in my voice. I was not sure that I wanted this relationship at all, much less a long-distance one.

"My old friend Les and his wife live there. He said that I could crash with them for the four days out of the week that I need to be in town. I'm only going to have to give him two hundred bucks a month."

"Is that practical?"

"Well, before I pick up and move to another state, I want to make sure that this client is going to work out. It's a new senior center, and they want me to do all nonurgent maintenance requests for a flat rate every month. I don't know how much work they'll have me doing, or if I'll even like it."

I wanted to ask how he'd even found the client, but I didn't want to seem like I was prying. For some reason, I sounded to myself like a nagging wife, asking question after question.

Breaking the brief silence Travis asked, "So are you going to take your mother's advice?"

"What advice?"

"She told you to hold on to me."

I looked into Travis's eyes, and I couldn't see anything in them that would cause me any harm. All I could see was the intensity of his feelings for me. Travis just *had* to be a blessing from heaven. It was only my reckless emotions that were causing me to feel any doubt.

I answered seriously, "I'd like to, Travis. Just give me something to hold on to."

CHAPTER
Fourteen

~∞~

Present

When I first walked into the job interview, I truly felt confident. The job was supervisor of sorter operations at Union National Bank. It was the first bank job I'd applied for since I resigned from Grace Savings and Loan. I was more than qualified for the job, I was completely prepared for the interview, and I was looking *good.* I was down to a pleasingly thick 190 pounds, and for the first time since I could remember I actually shopped in a normal-size women's store for my interview suit.

The first sign of trouble was when the receptionist told me that it was going to be a panel interview. I hated those. The idea of having three or more people shooting questions at me seemed like cruel and unusual punishment.

Still, I held my head up and put on my game face as I sat down in front of the three interviewers. One of them was a very young woman whom I figured was the human resource representative. She looked like she'd only graduated from college the week before. There was a seasoned-looking African American woman and an older gray-haired gentleman. I chose to focus on the black woman, hoping she'd be an ally.

The first questions were standard fare. I was asked about my background, my strengths and weaknesses, my goals and ambitions. I'd asked similar questions so many times that I recited the proper responses with ease.

My supposed ally was the one who ventured into dark waters. "It says here on your résumé that you were the president of Grace Savings and Loan. This seems to be a backward career move for you. Do you care to elaborate on why you left there?"

No, I didn't want to elaborate at all, and I couldn't believe that she'd asked the question. Of course, she couldn't call up Grace and get a definite answer. It was against the law for them to discuss the terms of my resignation.

"It was a joint management decision," I replied dryly, hoping that would satisfy the hungry interviewer.

She frowned. "I see." She then started scribbling furiously on her little notepad. I wanted to get up and smack her.

It only went downhill from there. Another interviewer, this time the gentleman, asked, "After commanding an entire financial institution, do you think that this entry-level supervisor job will provide you with enough of a challenge?"

"Anytime I'm in a new environment with new people, there is enough to keep me interested in my work. I put my heart and soul into everything I do," I answered with a smile.

I was getting irritated with the whole interview. I hadn't gone through an entry-level interview in years, and I was starting to be sickened with the canned responses that were expected. What I really wanted to say was, *Look, this job is paying a quarter of what I was making at Grace. I can do it with my eyes closed, so let's cut the games. I can start immediately.* Of course, I had to sit there with my interview smile on and my eyes bright, glassy, and eager.

The wrap-up part of the interview couldn't come soon enough. I had expected a tour of the office, and to be introduced to the operations staff. That was not going to happen.

"Ms. Ellis," the black woman said. "You have an impressive list of qualifications here. Unfortunately, we don't have any positions available that match your skill set."

I wanted to scream. I'd gotten up early in the morning for that interview. I'd paid seventy dollars getting my hair done. Worse of all, they knew I could do the job—of that, I'm certain.

She continued, "We will put your résumé in the up-and-coming file and contact you when we have something on tap that would better utilize your education and experience."

I forced myself to smile through dry thank-yous and good-byes. I didn't go out of my way to leave an impression because I knew that I'd never hear from them. Their up-and-coming file was probably at the back of somebody's filing cabinet.

*   *   *

I'd thought I was beyond the habit of healing myself with food, but after that interview I needed a good hearty meal to lift my spirits. I decided to go to the grocery store and get the ingredients for my stuffed chicken Parmesan. But I would not go wild: I would only buy one chicken breast and get the whole wheat pasta. That would keep me from overdoing it and killing my diet.

I boldly marched past the in-store bakery to the meat department, but my nose was still accosted by the aromas of baking bread, cakes and cookies. I read in a diet book once that a dieter should stick to the outer aisles of a grocery store, because that's where the healthiest foods were stocked. Well, I guess my neighborhood store got smart and put the bakery right between produce and meats. I was tempted, but praise God, it was going to take more than a whiff of a doughnut to push me back over the two-hundred-pound mark.

I picked a juicy-looking chicken breast and headed for the pasta aisle. Halfway down, I stopped the cart abruptly, as if I were about to run over a small child. Standing in front of me was Travis.

I wanted to take my cart and run in the opposite direction, but my feet were frozen in place. First my hands started to tremble, and then my entire body followed. My heart was beating so quickly and so loudly, I was sure the man could hear it. I opened up my mouth to speak, but the only sound that came out was something of a croak. The sound got the man's attention, and he turned around. I was only partially relieved to see that it wasn't Travis after all.

"Ma'am, are you all right?" asked the stranger.

"Y-yes. I'm fine." I tried to smile then rushed away.

But I was not fine. If the man had truly been Travis, I didn't know what I would've done or said. After all the therapy I'd had, I still was unable to fathom the thought of coming face-to-face with Travis.

Maybe the whole thing was hopeless. Perhaps I was never going to recover from what that man had done to my life. It was bad enough that I couldn't get a job; I was also a broken-up shell of a woman. I stood there in the grocery aisle crying. All my comparisons to Rizpah and Leah were pointless. I was nothing like them. I prayed for strength to leave the grocery store, and after a few deep breaths I was able to walk again. I left my cart where it was and went home to nurse all my reopened wounds.

CHAPTER
Fifteen

❦

Past

Travis and I had decided to spend the day at the art museum. It was one of my favorite pastimes. I enjoyed examining the pieces and trying to figure out what was going through the artist's mind at the time of creation. My favorite exhibit was the Egyptian ruins.

We stood, in awe, looking at the mummified remains of an Egyptian princess. If the painting on her sarcophagus was any indication of her beauty, then she had been stunning.

I remarked, "I bet she never had to lift a finger to do anything."

"Is that what you want?" Travis asked. "To never lift a finger?"

I thought about the question for a moment. I had never

envisioned a time in my life that I wouldn't be working to achieve something.

I shook my head. "No. But I would like to find out the one thing I was put on this earth to do, and then do it."

"What makes you think it's only one thing?" asked Travis. "Maybe God has several things for you to do. Maybe being at home and never lifting a finger would free you to fulfill God's purpose."

I tilted my head to one side and smiled. "Are you saying that if we get married, you don't want me to work?"

"I'd only want you to work if it was necessary for our survival. I would want you to enjoy being a wife and let me worry about providing for our household."

"That's rather primitive, don't you think?" I quipped, eager for the discussion to continue. I wanted to know Travis's mind on the issue.

"I don't think so. God gave Adam everything that he needed for his bride. He had a home and a job."

"Well, we're a long way from Adam and Eve, and you're going to have to show me the money if you want me to leave Grace Savings and Loan."

Travis smiled. "Not yet, but I will."

"I'm sure you will," I beamed. "You can do anything you want, with God's help."

Travis led me to a bench outside the exhibit and motioned for me to sit down. I wondered what he wanted to say.

"Tell me about your dreams, Charmayne. You know all about mine."

I thought for a moment. "Well, I want to be able to retire comfortably in the next five years and raise at least two children."

"Is that all?" Travis seemed surprised.

"No," I continued. "I also want to open a women's relief center."

"What's that?"

"It will be a place where women who have been broken and abused can come and put their lives back together. They can live there or just attend the career readiness program." My face and hands became animated as I shared my vision.

"I'm impressed," responded Travis. "What gave you the idea?"

I looked into the distance, remembering what had birthed my dream. "My father died when I was eighteen, and my mother was totally destitute. She'd never worked and didn't know where to start. My sister and I both got jobs to help out, but she never really landed on her feet. I worked two jobs all the way through college."

"Two jobs?"

"Mmm-hmm. I worked on campus during the day and as a mail handler at night for the post office. All that while I attended classes full time."

Travis laughed. "Guess you didn't have too much time for partying."

"No, I didn't," I mused. "But it was a good thing. I did well in school, and now I take care of my mother."

Travis put his arms around me and squeezed me in a loving hug. "You are an amazing woman."

I hugged him back and felt a warm feeling on the inside. I could've stayed in his arms forever.

The Teach a Man to Fish program was having a better response than anyone had ever expected. Entrepreneurs from all over the city were presenting their business plans to Grace Savings and Loan for whatever amount of loan money they could receive. Of course, most of the business plans needed work, and some of the applicants had poor credit histories, but even these were not insurmountable obstacles. We started classes at Grace to instruct individuals on creating business plans and on how to repair their credit.

The stream of applications seemed endless. We hired two new loan officers to help with the load, and as the last phase of the approval process, the applications ended up on my desk. I didn't usually involve myself in such operational procedures, but the program was my baby, and I didn't want anything to go wrong.

Randy Haskins, my most productive loan officer, was standing in front of my desk waving a thick folder. I assumed that it was another loan to be approved.

"Charmayne, this applicant is named Travis Moon. I need you to look over his application."

My eyes widened. Travis and I had been having intimate discussions every night since my mother's party, and he had not even hinted that he had applied for a loan at Grace. I could've helped him dispense with some of the formalities if I thought his application looked good. Travis was someone who had surely turned his life around. He could've been the poster boy for the program. He should've told me.

I held out my hand for the application. "Let me take a look."

I first looked at the credit scores page. His credit was better than average, and he didn't have any collections listed. He didn't have any credit cards, but that wasn't necessarily a bad thing. I had already seen his business plan, but I flipped to the budget page. It was flawless. Travis was requesting a twenty-thousand-dollar loan to purchase much-needed equipment and supplies. Since he had already invested over ten thousand dollars, it was not an unreasonable request.

Randy asked impatiently, "So do you think he's a good risk?"

"So far, so good. Did you meet with him face-to-face?"

"Yes, ma'am."

"And what did you think?" I was asking because I wasn't sure I could be objective when it came to Travis.

"I thought that he seemed like an honest hardworking man. He's probably the best applicant I've interviewed since we started the program."

I responded, "Well, Randy, as long as you have all of your documentation and have all of your i's dotted and t's crossed, I think this loan is an acceptable risk."

"Thank you, Ms. Ellis."

Randy walked out of my office and I felt my stomach drop. I picked up the telephone and immediately dialed Travis's number.

"Hello, my love," said Travis, noticing my number in the caller ID.

My tone was all business. "Hello, Travis."

"Is there anything wrong?"

"I was just wondering why you would apply for a loan at my bank and not tell me about it."

"You found out?"

I was starting to get irritated. "Obviously. It was brought to me for an approval."

"Was it approved?" Travis asked excitedly.

"We'll get to that in a moment," I stated, trying to maintain my professional composure. "But first, I need to know why you kept something like this a secret."

There was a distinct pause before Travis replied. "You're not my wife yet, Charmayne."

I didn't know how I felt about Travis's words. Part of me knew that he was right—I wasn't his wife—but another part of me felt he was up to something deceitful.

"You're right, Travis. But in the future, I'd like a heads-up if you're going to transact any major business at Grace Savings and Loan. I may be able to help."

"Not a problem," said Travis. The smiling tone of his voice calmed my fears.

"By the way . . . your loan was approved."

"Hallelujah! Glory to God! You won't regret this," exclaimed Travis.

"All right, baby. Talk to you later." I hung up hoping I wouldn't regret my decision to help Travis.

Even though I felt some apprehension, approving the loan had been a sensible move. It seemed that my entire life had been a series of sensible moves. I'd watched from the sidelines as my sister and my friends fell in and out of love. I was there with the tissues when their hearts were broken, and I helped them avoid the men they'd wanted out of their lives. But that was never for me—I'd chosen to be safe.

Maybe that was the problem. Maybe I needed to follow the advice I'd given so many times. I was always telling someone to "step out on faith" or "let go and let God do it." It sounded so easy when I was telling it to someone else, but I didn't know if I even believed my own rhetoric.

At a little after five o'clock my receptionist, Donna, knocked on my office door. She was grinning from ear to ear, and I was sure that she was about to tell me why in the next ten seconds.

She whispered loudly, "Ms. Ellis, there is a man here for you."

"Thank you. I'll be out shortly," I replied blandly. I hid my excitement at Travis's surprise visit because I didn't want to feed Donna's curiosity.

"Is he a date?" asked Donna. I was almost offended by her nosiness. Did she forget that I was her boss?

I frowned and responded, "He's a friend."

Donna continued unashamed. "But didn't he used to be a janitor here?"

"Yes."

Donna stood at my desk for a moment, looking as if she wanted to say more. In my opinion, there was nothing left to say.

I asked, "Is there anything else, Donna?"

"No, I guess not," she replied, disappointment lacing her voice.

Donna turned and left my office. I knew that by the end of the next day, the entire company would know that the president of the bank was dating an ex-janitor. I had no idea how my peers would react to the news, and I didn't really care.

I smiled at Travis as I finally emerged from my office. He was dressed to impress in the same suit that he'd worn to my mother's birthday party. Even though I loved him in that suit, I would've liked some variety. We were going to have to make a shopping trip one day.

We drove separately to a little Chinese restaurant that

was one of my favorites. It was quiet, secluded, and rarely frequented by anyone I knew. Plus they served the best shrimp egg foo yung I'd ever eaten.

When we got to the restaurant, Travis's friends were waiting for us in the vestibule. I looked forward to conversing with someone from Travis's circle. Travis and his friend hugged and gave each other one of those intricate handshakes while we women watched with amusement.

Travis introduced us. "Charmayne, this is my oldest friend, Les, and his wife, Anna."

Les was just as fine as Travis, but unlike Travis with his raw masculinity, Les was what I called a pretty boy. His skin was light and creamy like butter, and he had the most captivating green eyes. His hands sparkled with several diamond rings. I wondered if fine men always ran in packs.

Compared with her husband, Anna was as plain as they come. She was petite and mousy. Her hair was dull and lifeless, but it was obvious that she'd attempted to style it. And while her husband was all flash, she wasn't wearing any jewelry except a plain gold wedding band.

When we got settled into the table, Travis announced, "I want you all to be the first to know that today my application for a twenty-thousand-dollar small-business loan was approved!"

"Well, all right, man! Congratulations!" exclaimed Les before I got the chance to say anything.

Travis continued, "I was afraid at first that they wouldn't even give me the loan, because of my background. I couldn't have done it without my lady here, and Jesus! He's able!"

I did my best imitation of a church organ and said, "You betta testify!"

We enjoyed a lively dinner, with Travis and Les talking mostly about their high school glory days. Apparently they had been quite the players. From the way they talked, it was amazing to me that anyone had been able to get Les to settle down, especially the demure and homely Anna.

At the end of dinner Travis and I parted ways with Les and Anna. They were going to visit with her family for a couple of days. We promised to get together again before they went back home to Detroit.

Travis walked me to my car. "Are you ready to go home?" he asked.

"Why? What do you have in mind?"

"Well, it's so nice out tonight, and you know winter will be here before you know it. I was thinking we could go down to the lake."

I smiled, thinking of the romantic possibilities. "I'd like that."

Travis insisted that we ride together in my car. He turned the radio dial to a rhythm-and-blues station. He hummed along to an old DeBarge classic.

"You're in a great mood," I remarked.

"Girl, you just don't know! It's like my life is finally coming together. I've never felt so sure of myself."

Once we got to the lake, Travis found a huge rock for us to sit on. I looked out over the water and could tell that an autumn storm was brewing. The waves were crashing across the pier and making the docked boats bob up and down like apples in a barrel. The storm was a way off, though, because the air was still warm and muggy. It was already October, but it felt like July.

I was so caught up in the wonderful view of the lake

that I jumped when Travis grabbed both my hands in his. The action was surprising yet tender. His eyes were sparkling with what I presumed was joy over his loan approval. I smiled up at him proudly and lovingly.

"God is good," he said.

"Yes, He is," I replied.

Travis let my hands go and lifted his arms toward heaven in a miniature praise. I nodded in agreement.

"Charmayne, do you realize that you have been the answer to my prayers? Since I've met you, only good things have happened in my life."

"It's not me, baby. It's your season."

"I wanted to do this all on my own. Like I landed my first real client on my own. I want you to know that I can be a provider for you—felony record and all. The Lord has just been granting my every request."

Next, Travis reached into his suit pocket and pulled out a small jewelry box. I felt my heart begin to race. The look that Travis was seeing on my face at that moment was true astonishment. Travis took my hands again—I was sure that he could feel them trembling.

"Charmayne . . . you are a wonderful woman. You're everything I've ever wanted and I'm sure everything Jesus ever wanted me to have."

Travis took an expensive-looking ring out of the little box and placed it on my finger.

"And now, I'm officially asking you to be my wife."

I stared down at the ring, my eyes blinking rapidly to try to slow the tears. The ring was clearly an heirloom, but it had an ageless beauty. In the center of the gold band there was a large princess-cut diamond surrounded by at least a dozen smaller diamonds.

"It's b-beautiful," I stammered.

Travis beamed with pride. "It was my grandmother's ring. I know she would be proud for you to wear it."

I was filled with joy and apprehension. I wanted to just say yes with total abandon, but something inside kept telling me that it was all too good to be real.

But it *was* real! I finally had the one thing I'd always dreamed of having—the love of a man. The ring on my finger was not a mirage, and the pleading in Travis's eyes was not my imagination.

"So will you be my bride?" he asked again.

"Y-yes."

Travis clapped his hands together gleefully. "Thank you, Jesus!" he shouted as if he wanted the angels in heaven to hear him.

And that settled it. I was marrying Travis—the man of my dreams. And what could be wrong with a man who thanked Jesus for having me?

CHAPTER
Sixteen

~∾~

Past

The first person I shared my news with was Lynette, and she was giddily happy for me. We screamed, yelled, and cried, and then we screamed some more. She almost seemed happier than I was, although I didn't know if that was possible. I was literally ecstatic.

Telling Mama was more of a challenge. Her only response was, "So you marrying that pretty boy, huh?" I couldn't tell if she was for or against my decision, but she seemed content not to try to talk me out of it. I guess she'd been trying to push me off on a man for so long that just about any man would do—even a pretty boy.

I didn't call my sister; she called me. I knew that Mama would tell her before I got the chance.

When I picked up the phone, Dayna said, "So what

color will the bridal party be wearing? I'm thinking a peach or rose."

I laughed. "Well, hello to you, too."

"You can dispense with all the pleasantries. We've got a wedding to plan. As the matron of honor, I think my dress should be stunning. I am the matron of honor, right?"

I actually was thinking of asking Lynette to be my matron of honor, but that was something I had plenty of time to decide.

"I don't know, Dayna. Do we have to talk about this right now?"

"What do you mean, you don't know?" Dayna spat indignantly. "I'm your only sister! What is there to decide?"

"Right now, I'm deciding to get off the phone. I'm having company later."

"Company? You think it's wise to have your man all up in your house before you get married? Fornication is still a sin."

I shook my head and laughed. "For your information, Lynette and Jonathan are coming over for dinner. They want to get to know my fiancé."

"And you didn't invite me and Ronald?"

"Maybe next time, Dayna. I'll call you later on, okay?"

Dayna did not reply. I knew she'd hung up because I heard the dial tone after a few moments of silence.

Travis was nervous about having dinner with my friends. He'd already met both Lynette and Jonathan, but he wanted them to accept his friendship. Travis knew how important Lynette was in my life, and for some reason he felt that he had something to prove to her.

I also wanted the evening to be a success, so I pulled out my entire arsenal of recipes. I prepared a salad with three different kinds of lettuce, carrot slivers, Parmesan cheese, tomatoes, olives, and my own secret sweet-and-tangy salad dressing. For the main course, we were to dine on stuffed chicken Parmesan with homemade marinara sauce and angel-hair pasta. And for dessert, a specially prepared tiramisu.

Lynette and Jonathan arrived just as I was putting the finishing touches on dinner. Travis answered the door to my home, looking fine as ever in a thick black turtleneck and dress slacks. I gave him a smile of encouragement, and he seemed to relax a little.

"Lynette and Jonathan! Come on in," said Travis.

"Hey, Travis!" exclaimed Lynette as if she'd known him for years.

Jonathan said, "It's good seeing you, man."

Lynette pushed past Travis and Jonathan and came directly into the kitchen. She snatched my hand viciously to take a close look at my ring. She squealed with pleasure.

"This is what? About one and a half carats?"

"Just about."

"Go 'head girl! How did he afford to pay for this?"

"It was his grandmother's ring."

Lynette followed me back out to the living room. Both men stood up, and Jonathan gave me a hug.

I said, "Don't stop chatting on account of us. Dinner is just about ready."

"Honey, we were just talking about romantic honeymoon spots. How does Saint Thomas sound?" asked Travis.

Lynette nudged me suggestively and said, "It sounds romantic."

I replied, "It sounds great, Travis. I love Saint Thomas. I went there on a cruise once. They have some of the world's most beautiful beaches."

"Well, Saint Thomas it is."

Jonathan said, "Man, that's going to cost a grip."

"That's all right," I beamed. "Travis landed his first huge client."

Jonathan asked, "What is it that you do?"

"Well, I started off doing air-conditioning and ventilation systems along with general maintenance for corporations. But while I was working during the day, all my mother's friends and the elderly saints in the church would ask me to take care of repairs in their homes. When my side income surpassed my paycheck, I knew that there was a market for my services."

"All the money these days is in the service industry," interjected Jonathan. "If you can fill a need, you can make a fortune."

"Exactly. A friend of mine in Detroit gave me the heads-up about a senior condominium community. They were looking to contract someone like myself to address the larger maintenance requests that their general staff couldn't handle. I accepted the contract on faith, not knowing if I would be able to procure all of my start-up expenses. But the Lord came through for me with a small-business loan."

Jonathan was clearly impressed. "It sounds like you've got a plan! I wish you all the success in the world."

I was so proud of how well Travis articulated his

plans. I was probably more impressed than Lynette and Jonathan. I wanted to kick myself for almost letting him get away. That was nothing but the devil trying to keep me from what God had for me.

I ushered everyone into the dining room to start our meal. I'd called my housekeeper to come in an extra day, but Travis had insisted on polishing my cherrywood dining room furniture so that it looked brand new.

Lynette asked between huge bites of food, "So have you two set a date? I know I'm in the bridal party, right?"

I replied, "Of course. You're the matron of honor. It'll probably be the first weekend in December."

Jonathan asked, "That's only two months away. I had no idea you two were that serious."

"Neither did I! What's the rush?" asked Lynette.

"Why wait?" asked Travis.

Lynette thought for a moment and said, "I can't think of any good reason to wait. I guess we have a wedding to plan."

"So, Jonathan, how's married life so far?" asked Travis with a smile. "Am I in for the shock of my life when I take Charmayne down the aisle?"

Jonathan responded, "Travis, man, finding Lynette was the best thing that ever happened to me. And I mean that."

Travis smiled at me, "I feel the same way about Charmayne. It's funny, though, 'cause I thought she'd never even want to talk to me."

Lynette was apparently intrigued, "Really? Why not?"

"Well, how often does the president of the bank give the time of day to the man who empties the trash cans? I guess our hooking up was something like a miracle."

"It was God!" said Lynette supportively. "Plus you're not the janitor anymore."

"You're right. I was the janitor. But now I'm an entrepreneur. God is good."

There were two people I was afraid of sharing my news with—First Lady Jenkins and Ebony. First Lady believed in long courtships and even longer engagements. Ebony had already expressed her displeasure at my decision. I wished that I hadn't shared with either one of them my earlier concerns about Travis.

I sat in First Lady's office putting the final touches on the travel plans for our conference guests. First Lady had glanced at my ring, but she hadn't yet made any comments.

"Come here, girl, and let me see that ring."

I dutifully obeyed. She pulled my hand in close for inspection and squinted.

"Have you set a date?" asked First Lady pointedly.

"First week of December."

"You aren't wasting any time, are you?"

"Why wait?"

First Lady sat down at her desk and exhaled slowly. "The passage of time can repair impetuous decisions."

"We're not acting impetuously, First Lady."

"I seem to recall a conversation we had about the Lord telling you—"

I interjected before she could finish. "I know. I was just afraid, and you know the Bible says that He has not given us a spirit of fear."

First Lady sighed and pressed her lips into an almost invisible line. This was her look of frustration. I'd seen

it many times in the past, but it was the first time she'd
ever used it for me.

"Are you at least having premarital counseling?"

"Yes. We've already made an appointment with
Pastor."

First Lady paced back and forth across her office as if
she was troubled. Her pacing was making me nervous, so
my leg started to shake.

"Charmayne, I hope that this move is not being made
out of a sense of desperation."

"Certainly not." I was starting to get offended, but I
tried not to let on by any of my facial expressions.

"I'll just say one more thing. If he loves you and wants
to marry you now, he'll love you and want to marry you
a year from now."

"Thank you for your advice, First Lady. I'll take it into
consideration."

I was glad that was her last comment, because I was tired
of hearing everyone's opinions on my life. Of course, it was
sage advice, perhaps for a young teenager trying to rush
into marriage. I was way past youthful indiscretion, and I
recognized a once-in-a-lifetime opportunity.

Ebony rushed into First Lady's office just as First
Lady was leaving. Ebony had completed some errands
and we were going to finish the travel arrangements together. Our relationship had been strained since Ebony
had expressed her feelings about my dating Travis. I still
valued her as a friend, though, and above all a sister in
Christ.

She raised an eyebrow when she saw my ring. "Is that
what I think it is?"

"Yes." I smiled hopefully. "It's an engagement ring."

She inhaled sharply and sat down. "Jesus."

"How about congratulations."

Ebony just smiled and started looking at the printouts of the airline schedules.

"I was wondering," I continued, "if you'd be my maid of honor."

"I—"

"Before you answer, you know I don't have many friends, and your friendship is precious to me. I really want you to be there on my special day."

A look of sadness shadowed Ebony's usually bright and cheerful eyes. She dropped her head, telling me her response before she even voiced it.

"I'm sorry," she said. "I can't be a bridesmaid in your wedding."

"Why not?" I asked angrily, my hands balled into fists.

"I just don't support your decision. I can't, in good conscience, stand up with you when I think you're making a horrible mistake."

The involuntary tears that had become a regular occurrence clouded my vision. I stood up from the desk and ran from First Lady's office. I was devastated that I didn't have Ebony's or First Lady's blessing. Why did this have to be so complicated? Why couldn't everyone just be happy for me?

CHAPTER
Seventeen

Past

"You two will be my only bridesmaids. Lynette, I'd like you to be the matron of honor." I let it slip out casually when Dayna, Lynette, and I were having a meeting at my home.

Dayna responded immediately. "You mean, *I'm* the matron of honor?"

Lynette's eyes widened. She knew that an ugly argument was brewing, but I was determined not to go there.

"Dayna," I continued, "Lynette is my best friend."

"But you were *my* maid of honor," Dayna whined.

"Well, that's because you didn't have many friends," I said before I could stop myself.

Dayna looked at me as if I'd just stabbed her in the chest. I hadn't meant to come across so bluntly, since it wasn't the complete truth. Dayna didn't have *any* friends.

In an attempt to keep the peace, Lynette said, "Well, it

doesn't make any difference at all to me. She can be the matron of honor."

"Oh, so now you're just *letting* me be the matron of honor!" Dayna spat. "I don't want it if it's going to be about all that."

"Do you want to be in the wedding or not, Dayna?" I asked wearily.

Dayna started to cry. She was so predictable. I'd had a countdown going on in my mind as to when the water-works would begin. She beat me by about two seconds.

"Yes," she sobbed, "of course I want to be in the wedding. I can't believe my own sister would treat me this way."

Lynette rolled her eyes. She'd seen countless similar exchanges between me and my sister. Dayna usually fussed, cussed, and cried and typically won out in the end. But I wasn't going to let Dayna destroy the one day that I would be the center of attention.

I replied, "If you want to be a part of this, you'll co-operate."

When Dayna was still not appeased, Lynette suggested, "Why don't you just have two matrons of honor. I've seen it done before."

"All right then," I decided. "We'll have two matrons of honor. Are you happy now, Dayna?"

Dayna's tears vanished as quickly as they had been produced. "Yes."

Even though I'd made the final decision, Dayna had yet again gotten the best of me.

In the midst of our hasty wedding plans, Travis and I had set aside time to have premarital counseling with Pastor

Jenkins. As we sat in front of his desk waiting for the session to begin, I was nervous that something would be revealed that would ruin my plans for a wonderful married life. If Travis was worried about the outcome of the session, I couldn't tell.

Pastor Jenkins started, "This is one of the facets of my job that I truly enjoy. Guiding young people who are in love is very rewarding."

"Thank you for fitting us in, Pastor," Travis said.

"Charmayne is like a daughter to me. Of course I'd make time for this, but I'm wondering why you all didn't choose to go with Travis's pastor. You will be attending his church, right?" Pastor asked me.

Travis replied, "Well, with my traveling to commence soon, I thought that it would be better for us to just come to Bread of Life. You are an anointed man of God, Pastor Jenkins, and I'd love to serve on your staff."

Pastor Jenkins patted Travis on the back. "And we'd love to have you. I'll talk to your pastor after you join officially."

Travis didn't respond, and I thought for a fleeting moment that I saw uneasiness in his eyes. I hoped and prayed there wasn't anything else that Travis was keeping from me.

Pastor Jenkins asked, "So how did you two meet?"

"We met in her office," Travis replied. "I came in and fixed one of her office chairs."

Pastor nodded. "Yes. Yes. I remember seeing you two together at Sister Lynette's wedding."

I smiled at Travis. "That was our first date, Pastor."

It was almost impossible to believe that just a few months after that first slow dance at Lynette and

Jonathan's wedding, we were sitting here in front of Pastor Jenkins, being counseled for our own nuptials.

"Wow!" Pastor Jenkins exclaimed. "That was a swift courtship. Is there any reason why you all decided not to give it more time?"

"I know that God has sent Travis to me, Pastor. I feel it deep in my spirit. I've prayed and prayed on the matter, and I know that I have peace." I gave my little speech with confidence. I hoped to convince myself.

"Well, typically I don't recommend that couples move so quickly, but I know that Charmayne is a prayer warrior. I know she hears from the Lord."

"We *both* heard from God on this one," Travis interjected. "That's what I call confirmation."

Travis took my hand in his, passively defying Pastor Jenkins's doubts. I felt him squeeze my hand determinedly, and I felt my own confidence swell. We both smiled at Pastor, presenting a united front.

Pastor said, "Let's first talk about the biblical structure for a marriage. Both of you turn in your Bibles to Ephesians chapter five. We'll read verses twenty-two through twenty-five, then skip down to twenty-eight through thirty-one. Travis, why don't you read that for us."

I listened while Travis read a passage I could recite by heart.

> *Wives, submit yourselves unto your own husbands, as unto the Lord.*

> *For the husband is the head of the wife, even as Christ is the head of the church: and he is the saviour of the body.*

Therefore as the church is subject unto Christ, so let the wives be to their own husbands in every thing.

Husbands, love your wives, even as Christ also loved the church, and gave himself for it; So ought men to love their wives as their own bodies. He that loveth his wife loveth himself. . . .

For no man ever yet hated his own flesh; but nourisheth and cherisheth it, even as the Lord the church:

For we are members of his body, of his flesh, and of his bones.

For this cause shall a man leave his father and mother, and shall be joined unto his wife, and they two shall be one flesh.

Pastor Jenkins asked, "Brother Travis, what is your interpretation of these verses?"

"Basically, that I should love Charmayne unconditionally as Christ loves the church, and that Charmayne should submit her will to me as she would unto Jesus."

Pastor nodded, "That's pretty accurate, son. As a matter of fact the *only* way that this model of marriage is successful is if both of you choose to fulfill your call as a husband and a wife. Travis, you can't expect her to submit her will to you if you don't show her that unconditional love, and Charmayne, you can't expect Travis to be able to display the love of Christ if you rebel against his leadership at every turn."

I commented, "Pastor, of course I agree with this passage, but I've been independent a long time and I've accomplished a lot in my life. Am I supposed to just follow Travis even if I believe he's making a mistake?"

Travis looked shocked at my response. I wanted it to be known up front that while I would be a submitted wife, I would have a voice. I didn't want to be treated like a child.

Pastor Jenkins replied, "I don't think Travis would've asked for your hand in marriage if he wanted a mindless drone. Since both of you are believers, this subjection is more about allowing him to be the priest of your home. Allow Travis to seek the Lord for the vision of your household. He has a very difficult and important task. Pray for him to make wise decisions based on the will of God."

"Yes, Pastor Jenkins. I can definitely do that."

Pastor Jenkins said, "Charmayne, I want you to answer this question. What do you think is the number one reason for divorce?"

I thought long and hard about what would cause me to want a divorce. I replied, "Infidelity."

"That's a good guess, but actually it's money issues that drive more couples to seek divorces."

"I don't find that hard to believe," Travis said.

Pastor continued, "Have you all discussed how you will handle finances?"

"What is there to discuss?" asked Travis. "As the head of the household, I will have final say on all financial decisions."

"Charmayne, what do you think of that?" asked Pastor Jenkins.

Obviously, Travis did think that I was going to be a

mindless drone, contrary to what Pastor Jenkins had just implied. What I thought was that Travis was out of his natural mind if he thought I was just going to turn the management of my carefully acquired wealth over to him.

"While I have no problem accepting the leadership of my husband, I plan to have a very active role in all financial matters."

Travis looked concerned. "I didn't know you felt that way."

The financial issue was a deal breaker for me. I had been independent too long and gained too much to give up total control immediately.

"Eventually, I'd like to turn over that responsibility to you completely," I said calmly and with a steady voice. "But it's going to take some time."

"Charmayne is very wise in the area of finance," Pastor Jenkins interjected. "I'm sure there are some things you can learn from her."

Travis nodded in agreement, but his brooding expression disturbed me. It simply became another warning in my spirit that I put aside.

Pastor asked, "What about children?"

Travis spoke again, "I want two, maybe three children."

"I, too, would like a small family."

Pastor said, "Since you both agree on having children, you all should discuss how you want to raise them and what forms of discipline you both find acceptable."

Travis laughed. "We're going to raise our kids exactly the way my mama and grandmama raised me. I'm going to light up the behind of any child of mine that gets out of line."

I inhaled sharply. It was my belief that there were very few occasions when a child needed to be "lit up." It sounded like Travis was a huge fan of butt whippings. I decided to cross that bridge when we came to it.

"Speaking of mamas and grandmamas, how do the two of you get along with each other's families?"

"I haven't really met any of Travis's family, but I do know that his mother is in a nursing home."

"My mother is it," Travis said. "I don't have any siblings, and Grandmama died when I was sixteen."

"And what about Charmayne's family?" Pastor asked. "Travis, what do you think of them?"

"Her mom and sister are nice. As long as they know not to meddle in our business, we'll be fine."

That was one thing Travis needn't worry about. I had been keeping Mama and Dayna out of my business for years. I wasn't about to start voluntarily giving the two of them any information to add to their arsenals.

Pastor Jenkins said, "There is no way that we are going to be able to cover every topic you both need to address. We'll get four more sessions in over the next two weeks to hit on the major areas of trust, sexuality, and prayer in marriage."

I replied, "Pastor, you've already given us a lot to think about."

Travis agreed. "Yes, Pastor Jenkins. This has been an enlightening meeting."

Travis's reply almost made me want to laugh. I didn't see where he'd been enlightened at all. He came into the meeting with his own views, and he was leaving with them intact. If anything, I had been enlightened on what issues I might have to address in the future.

I couldn't say that I was leaving the counseling session with a good feeling. I had no idea how I would submit myself to Travis's rigid take on the wifely role. What I did know was that I was getting married in less than a month.

It seemed that I'd waited my whole life to be validated and loved by a man other than my daddy. I wanted to prove that I was worthy of receiving the passion and affection that I'd watched others receive my entire life. All the weekends and holidays that I spent alone, yearning for companionship, would be erased as soon as I walked down the aisle with Travis. I wasn't going to allow a few doubts to hinder anything. I knew, in my heart of hearts, that whatever obstacles Travis and I faced, we'd be able to conquer them with the help of the Lord. That was all the confirmation I needed.

CHAPTER
Eighteen

Past

On the Saturday morning two weeks before my wedding to Travis, I was awakened by knocking at my door. I looked over at the clock and frowned. It was only seven o'clock. Lynette and I had been up late the night before trying to put the finishing touches on the wedding planning.

I pulled the covers over my head and willed the knocking to go away. When it didn't, I groaned and reluctantly got out of my warm bed. I looked in the mirror and frowned at the puffy dark circles under my eyes. I seriously needed to put on some foundation, too, because my summer tan had faded, leaving me looking pale and washed out. I heard the knock again and rushed to pull my wild mane of hair up into a ponytail. Whoever it was would have to be satisfied with my morning face. I put on my bathrobe as I headed for the door.

"I'm coming!" I fussed as the knocking continued.

I looked out of the peephole and discovered that my early-morning visitor was none other than Travis. I smiled despite my irritation. Of course I didn't mind him outside my door at the crack of dawn, but he could've called.

"Hey, baby," he said as I opened the door.

He embraced me as he walked through the door. I placed a hand over my mouth. I hoped he didn't want a kiss, because I had not made a pit stop at the bathroom sink to brush any teeth.

"Good morning," I said with questions in my eyes. I hoped I wouldn't have to ask for an explanation.

"How quickly can you be dressed?"

"In less than an hour, I think."

"Good. There's someone I want you to meet."

"Okay . . ."

I waited a moment for more, but I guessed that Travis intended on surprising me. He sat down and turned on my television and I headed for the shower. Since I didn't have a clue who I was meeting, I put on my dressiest blue jean skirt and a tan cashmere sweater. My hair was absolutely hopeless, so I pulled it into a neater ponytail on the top of my head. I put on a light layer of makeup, and when I was as satisfied as I was going to get, I emerged from my bedroom.

Travis smiled at me. "You look great. Let's go."

We pulled into the parking lot of a nursing home called Morningside Manor. It was a comfortable-looking rest home that looked as if it had been transformed from one of the many old mansions in the area. I wondered if I was going to meet one of Travis's relatives.

As I got out of the car, I asked, "Is this where your mother lives?"

"Yes. You didn't think I'd marry you without letting you meet my mama, did you?"

We walked into the nursing home, and a friendly orderly greeted us.

"What's going on, Travis?" he asked as he gave Travis a high five.

"I can't call it, man."

The orderly motioned to me and asked, "Who's the lovely lady?"

"This is my fiancée, Charmayne. Charmayne, meet Bobby, my mother's favorite person in this place."

Bobby extended his hand for me to shake. "Well, I don't know about all that, but I do have a way with the ladies."

It seemed odd to me that Bobby was the only staff member I could see. I didn't see any nurses or any other orderlies. It was only eight thirty in the morning; I supposed that everyone else came in later.

Travis quickly ushered me down a hall to a room at the end. He opened the door slowly and quietly as if he didn't want to disturb the other residents. I wondered why we didn't just come later in the day.

"Good morning, Mama," said Travis as he tiptoed over to the bed.

Travis's mother's tiny frame seemed engulfed in the queen-size bed. Someone was obviously taking good care of her, because her long silver hair was braided into two big plaits that had yellow ribbons on the ends. She was either blind or close to it, because although she turned her head toward Travis's voice, she didn't make eye contact with him.

"William, is that you?" she asked.

I raised an eyebrow at Travis. He smiled and mouthed the word *Alzheimer's*. I nodded with understanding.

"No, Mama. It's me, Travis. I want you to meet my fiancée. Her name is Charmayne."

Mama folded her arms and frowned. "I don't know any Travis," she said matter-of-factly, poking out her bottom lip.

Travis looked a little hurt, but continued. "Mama, we're getting married in two weeks. Charmayne, come over and say hello to Mama."

I said softly, "Good morning, Mrs. Moon."

"My name is Bertha Washington, honey, and I don't know anybody by the name of Travis."

I smiled and patted her hand. The chart at the end of her bed said MOON, as clear as day. I wondered how long she had been suffering from Alzheimer's disease. I silently thanked God that my mother was still in her right mind, no matter how much she got on my nerves.

Travis tucked an extra pillow behind his mother's head and kissed her cheek. I almost burst out laughing when she wiped his kiss off her face. It seemed almost childish, but her face was quite serious. In fact, she looked furious.

Travis came over and whispered, "This is not a good day, Charmayne. She's usually better in the mornings; that's why we're here so early."

"Maybe we should go."

Travis looked back at Mama and sighed. "I think you're right. We'll try again in a few days."

Travis and I both said good-bye to Mama Moon, even though she didn't respond. On our way out, a nurse was sitting at the station. She looked up at us strangely. Travis started walking briskly, pulling me along with him.

When we got outside, I asked, "Why did we speed past the nurse like that? Is there something wrong?"

Travis responded, "Visiting hours don't start until nine, but Bobby always sneaks me in early to see Mama. She's usually lucid as soon as she wakes up. Today she didn't know me at all."

I stroked Travis's arm. "How long has she been sick?"

Travis opened my car door. "Too long. It's going on six years, and she's only gotten worse."

"Do you have any other family? Any cousins, aunts, uncles?"

"I do have some great-aunts and one great-uncle, but I don't know any of them. They all live out of town."

"Oh," I said sadly. I was sure that it was hard for him to witness his mother in that state. I was relieved to see the tension ease from his face as quickly as it had come.

"What a way to start a Saturday, right?" Travis asked with a smile.

"Well, I'm with you, so something about it was right."

His smile widened. "So what are your plans for the rest of the day?"

"Lynette and I are going shopping for my dress."

"Mind if I tag along?"

"Yes! You cannot see my dress until the wedding day."

Travis laughed. "Don't tell me you're superstitious!"

"Not at all. I just want you to be surprised, that's all."

"Well, I know whatever you pick will be beautiful."

Lynette, Dayna, and I had visited five area bridal shops, but had not yet found the perfect gown. I was starting to believe that the perfect gown did not exist, and if it did, they did not make it in a size twenty. We were both weary and ready to go home, but Lynette was sure that we would find a dress. Plus we only had two weeks. It was crunch time.

I'd had no problem finding bridesmaids' dresses for Lynette and Dayna. They had figures that could fit into anything, but I chose modest two-piece silver dresses that came all the way to the floor. Dayna wasn't satisfied with my selection. She wanted something with more color, but I wanted them to have an understated look. It was bad enough that the two of them outshined me on a daily basis—they were not going to do it on my wedding day.

The bridal-wear consultant brought over several dresses for me to try on, and I groaned. I hated that part of the process. I was glad to have Lynette with me, because it was usually an emotional obstacle course for me when I had to try on clothes in public.

I was hoping to be down to a size eighteen by the time of my wedding, but at the time I was still squeezing into a twenty. The consultant kept looking at her watch, as if she didn't want to help me. I saw her looking longingly after another bubbly bridal party that would probably have been a lot more fun to assist. I couldn't blame her. Who would want to spend half their day catering to a bride on the verge of tears and an overly critical sister and best friend?

I tried on the first gown, a formfitting lace number. I looked into the mirror and immediately frowned. There was no way I was letting anyone see me in all that lace.

Dayna fussed, "Come on out so we can see it!"

Reluctantly, I stepped out of the fitting room. I could

tell by Lynette's frown and the shaking of Dayna's head that they agreed with my assessment.

Lynette said, "Let's try another one."

"We're going to be here all day," said Dayna as she took a seat and started to file her already manicured nails.

I trudged back into the fitting room, this time to try on a silk gown that was cinched directly beneath the bodice. My curves made me look like a buxom milkmaid in the dress. It certainly wasn't holy enough for me to wear in the sanctuary at church.

This time I didn't walk out of the fitting room, I simply opened the door. Lynette bit her lip and frowned, while Dayna puffed her cheeks with frustration.

"Let's try something with less cleavage," Lynette offered, trying to sound encouraging.

Gown number three solved the cleavage issue. It was designed to look similar to the Victorian-style dresses I'd seen in movies. It had a high neck, and there was a bustle attached. There was an opening in the shape of a triangle directly above the corset showing a small area of my back.

"Well, what about this one?"

Dayna said bluntly, "That's not it."

"Charmayne, you need something with more coverage," Lynette elaborated as she poked Dayna for her insensitivity. "Your back doesn't need to be out. I mean, you're getting married in the wintertime."

"I don't know what to pick, Lynette! None of these dresses was designed with my particular body type in mind." I was frustrated and tired.

The nonchalant bridal consultant suddenly looked as if she was having a stroke of genius. She rushed across the store and came back with a beautiful satin gown with long sleeves and a high neck. Around the sleeves and neck was white fur. The bottom had a hoop; fur lined the hem. It looked like something a Russian princess would wear for a trek across Siberia. She handed it to me gingerly, and Lynette and Dayna both clapped their hands with approval.

When I put the dress on I felt transformed. I looked into the mirror and imagined myself gliding down the aisle into the arms of my prince. I knew that I'd found the dress, and it fit perfectly. I felt tears welling up, because as I stood there gazing at myself, I realized that it was the first time I'd ever looked at myself in a mirror and thought I was beautiful.

"Well, come out, girl, and let me see you!" urged Lynette from the other side of the curtain.

"Okay . . . Here I come . . ."

I walked out of the curtain, and Lynette squealed, "Oh, my God! That's it, Charmayne! That is it."

"It's perfect," added Dayna.

The consultant was grinning and had her arms folded like she'd just saved the world from disaster. Well, she'd saved my world, or at least my wedding. I would be eternally grateful to her.

"So," asked the consultant, "you'll take it?"

"Yes! You can start ringing me up right now. I just want to look at it a little more."

Lynette walked over close to me and said, "Now we have the dress, but what about the groom?"

"What do you mean?" I asked uncertainly.

"You haven't said much about Mr. Travis lately. All is well, right?"

I raised a hand toward the heavens. "All is truly well, bless God! I met his mother today. Poor thing has Alzheimer's."

"I'm sorry to hear that," Lynette said, shaking her head sadly.

I mimicked her movements. "Yeah. She didn't even know who he was."

"That's a shame. Girl, what if you have to take care of her? Are you ready for that?"

"Travis and I talked about it," I responded confidently. "He believes that the nursing home is the best thing for her. They can give her the round-the-clock care that she needs."

Dayna butted into the conversation. "He better not think he's going to put our mother in anybody's nursing home."

I shook my head in an irritated manner. "What in the world are you talking about? We weren't even talking about Mama."

"I'm just saying," Dayna replied with her lips puckered into a grimace.

It seemed that all of a sudden, everyone was so full of advice. I didn't want another piece of wisdom about my decision to marry Travis from anyone.

I replied with a sarcastic tone, "Thank you for the advice."

"What's wrong with you?" Lynette asked defensively, immediately discerning the irritation in my voice.

"It just seems like every time I turn around someone is trying to give me a reason why I *shouldn't* marry Travis," I ranted. "If it ain't somebody wondering if he's got a job, they're hearing from heaven that he's the wrong man. I wish everyone would just let it go and be happy for us."

Dayna rolled her eyes. "Honey, don't nobody want you to get married more than I do."

"Now, wait a minute," said Lynette. "I'm your biggest supporter. Ebony is the one hearing from God about y'all. I'm probably the only one who believes that you two are actually going to make it down the aisle."

"What right does *anyone* have to wonder whether or not we're going to get married? I'm so sick of this. I can't wait to get it over with so that everyone can get on with their lives."

"I think people care about you, Charmayne. No one wants to see you get hurt."

"Well, guess what. I'm not a baby or a china doll. I'm a grown woman. I don't break that easily."

"All right then, I'm done with it. Whatever you like, I love."

I regretted taking out my frustration on Lynette, because she had supported me every step of the way. I knew that she was just stating the facts. But the fact that was most important to me was that Travis brought me a measure of joy that I'd never known, and there wasn't a naysayer in the world who would convince me otherwise.

CHAPTER
Nineteen

~⚬~

Past

I was walking quietly, stealthily across an immense field. I didn't know why I was being so covert, but it felt necessary. Off in the distance was Travis, and he was talking to someone. As I drew closer, I realized that it was his friend Les. They didn't seem to notice me as I approached, but they started walking. I followed them. For some reason, I couldn't quite make out what they were saying. They weren't whispering, but their words weren't making any sense. I trudged on behind them, but I was getting tired. Travis and Les started walking faster and faster until they were far in the distance. Suddenly I was filled with an indescribable panic. I started to run, faster than I'd ever run. The grass in the field started to grow around my feet until it was above my head. Even though I was unable to see, I continued to press forward, knocking stems of grass to the side. I started to hear Travis's voice again and focused on it. Following the sound took me out of the field of tall grass and into a clearing. I started running again and without warning, the ground beneath my feet disappeared. I was falling, and I could hear Travis's voice in the distance. I cried out, "Help me!" but no one listened . . .

I woke from the dream terrified and drenched with sweat. It was early morning, the day of my wedding, and I'd just had a nightmare that included my husband-to-be. I was a nervous wreck about my marriage to Travis, but I refused to admit it to anyone. I did take the dream as a sign that I should get on my face and pray. Something in me needed to restore my peace before I walked down the aisle.

I lay in the middle of my bedroom floor with tears streaming down my face. I prayed aloud, "I pray for peace, Lord. Peace in my decision to marry Travis. Lord, I ask that you bless our decision and make us to have a prosperous union. Lord, I am afraid! Show me that I am doing the right thing marrying this man!"

Even after praying so fervently I couldn't shake the feeling of absolute terror at the thought of exchanging vows with Travis. As the dawn drew near I thought the feelings would subside, but they only intensified. As the sun rose, I found myself praying again.

By the time Lynette and Dayna showed up at my house to help me get ready, I was nothing but a ball of nerves.

After trying for the fourth time to polish the fingernails on my trembling hands, Lynette snapped, "Look, girl! You are going to be fine. The Lord is not going to let you make a bad decision."

"Maybe the Lord has been telling me this whole time that this is a wrong choice for me."

Dayna said, "You know it's not too late to call the whole thing off."

I glared at my younger sister. She *would* be quick to encourage me to call off my wedding. My marriage to Travis carried the potential of overshadowing her little family, especially in Mama's eyes.

"Yeah, you'd love to see me look like a fool," I spat angrily.

Dayna replied, "No, I just don't want to see you make the biggest mistake of your life. You're the one doubting this whole thing. Don't start snapping at me."

Lynette intervened, "Charmayne, you're just nervous. Everyone is nervous on their wedding day. It's natural. But once you make it through, you'll be Mrs. Travis Moon. Just think of that."

Mrs. Travis Moon. I let the name roll off my lips. I'd never thought that I'd be Mrs. anything. I inhaled and exhaled slowly, forcing myself to let go of the worry. After a few moments I had successfully moved all my fears to the back of my mind, where they wouldn't ruin my dream wedding.

When we got to the church, Travis was already there along with Les, his best man, and Anna. Another brother from Travis's church was to serve as the other groomsman, but he had not yet arrived. Dayna went ahead of me and Lynette to make sure that Travis didn't see us when we walked into the church. I wasn't wearing my gown yet, but I didn't want him to see anything.

It took the full two hours of preparation time to get me into my dress and made up. Lynette worked skillfully on me and Dayna, and then we put the finishing touches on her makeup. Anna watched quietly from the sofa in the women's lounge.

Dayna asked Anna, "Aren't you going to go out into the sanctuary and make sure none of these hungry sisters is ogling your husband?"

She laughed. "Hungry sisters are the last thing I'm worried about."

"See, Dayna, some women actually trust their husbands," responded Lynette.

I refused to get in the conversation—I had other things to hold my attention. So many thoughts were going through my mind. I wondered what the people at Travis's church would think of me. I wondered if I'd meet Travis's expectations.

The time came to start the ceremony, and I only panicked a little. I'd managed to numb most of my emotions into silence. Still, Lynette came over and took both my hands in hers.

I said, "It seems like it was just last week I was doing this same thing for you."

Lynette laughed. "It almost *was* last week, why you playin'?"

Then we both laughed. I needed the release in tension, and was feeling almost normal when the usher came back to let us know that the ceremony was starting. Lynette and Dayna hugged me and took their places in line.

Lynette had chosen red roses to be used in the bouquets with little sprigs of baby's breath. The splash of color was perfect against the silver bridesmaid's dresses and my white gown. The entire effect was festive—which was exactly the opposite of how I was feeling.

Dayna walked out first. She deliberately took her time sashaying down the long center aisle of the church. She even stopped occasionally to smile and pose for pictures. When she got to the front of the church she leaned over and kissed Mama, who was seated in the front aisle. Mama had decided to wear an elegant winter-white suit. To accessorize she'd chosen a matching hat with a fur trim similar to my dress.

Next was Lynette. I was barely able to let her hand go as she walked down the aisle. She tossed her new hair weave left and right and strutted as if she were on a Parisian catwalk. Jonathan made sure to stand up and nod at his wife—a symbol to all the gawking men that she was taken.

My nieces, Erin and Koree, were dressed in miniature copies of my gown and pranced down the aisle with my nephew in the middle. Ronald Jr. looked so uncomfortable in his tiny tuxedo, but his sisters loved all the attention.

I was so nervous when it was my turn to walk down the aisle. I couldn't stop my hand from trembling even when my uncle Charles took it in his own. As I glided down the aisle to meet my prince, I received a standing ovation from my church family. I saw looks of joy and hope in the crowd. Joy from the ones who were glad I'd finally found a husband, and hope from the sisters like me who were patiently waiting on God to send them someone.

Ebony sat among the guests and smiled at me as I walked down the aisle. I appreciated the fact that she'd shown up even though she thought that I would soon regret my decision. She dropped her head as I passed, and I knew that she was praying for me.

Travis looked so beautiful to me as he reached out to take my hands in his. Coming to meet him in front of the altar was the most exhilarating moment of my life. Every other milestone and event that I could think of paled in comparison with Travis accepting me as his bride.

Pastor and First Lady Jenkins sat on the front row, nodding their approval. Pastor Jenkins had not had the pleasure of meeting Travis's pastor before, but he gave his silent endorsement of the ceremony. I must admit that I was so excited, I had to struggle very hard to listen to what Pastor Smith was saying.

I took in his admonition for our marriage to be a threefold cord with Christ at its center. He urged Travis to love me unconditionally, so that my respect would come automatically. Pastor Smith then told me to respect Travis's headship in all areas, and that if I did this I'd never have to worry about having his love. Travis held my hand tightly, visibly moved by the words. When I saw tears in his eyes, I couldn't help but shed a few of my own.

After the ceremony, we went to take pictures in the Cleveland Botanical Gardens. Everything had a coating of ice or frost, so we hoped that our pictures would have a fairy-tale feel to them. By this time, I was starting to feel the effects of my corset, girdle, and control-top panty hose. Beauty did not come comfortably for a big girl.

We got to the reception, and although the food looked

delicious, I was too wound up to eat—literally and figuratively. Instead Travis and I went around to all the tables thanking our guests for coming.

I endured what could've been an awkward moment with Marvin Baker and his "date." He had apparently convinced that new sister at our church that he was worth her time. On any other day, I probably would've felt a twinge of jealousy or even resentment, but since I was there marrying a man who was one thousand times finer than Marvin, I couldn't do anything but be happy for him.

Ebony took me off to the side, away from everyone else. I was curious to hear what she had to say, but I knew I'd be angry if she said anything to ruin my joy on my wedding day.

She handed me a package. "This is my gift to you. Open it."

I opened the package and smiled. It was Stormie Omartian's *Power of a Praying Wife.* Ebony and I embraced.

"Thank you."

Ebony replied, "I may not agree with your choices, but know that I'm always praying for you. There is nothing that will happen in any of our lives that prayer can't get us through."

After about two hours at the reception, Travis whispered to me that it was time for us to leave. I knew that we were on our way to the honeymoon suite at the downtown Ritz-Carlton, and I was terrified. It was the one part of the whole wedding process that was making me feel unsure.

Even though I was a virgin, I felt odd going to my mother for advice on how to please my husband on my wedding night. I thought that I was too old not to know, and that my mother was too old to give me anything of value. I sure wasn't going to ask my baby sister, though no doubt she could've schooled me well—after she got finished laughing for ten minutes.

I had to rely solely on Lynette's wisdom in that area. I had refused to allow her to throw me a bridal shower. I would've died of embarrassment opening up little packages of lingerie. Instead Lynette took me to a plus-size women's store that carried all the frilly little see-through unmentionables that they made for thin women.

I couldn't bring myself to buy anything too outlandish, although Lynette tried to make me pick up a peekaboo this or an edible that. I was already scared enough; I didn't need to wear anything that might make Travis laugh at me.

After a great deal of encouragement from Lynette, I had packed my white full-length silk gown and robe with some alluring-smelling lotions and soaps. Lynette had also promised to turn the honeymoon suite into something out of a romance novel, so I didn't have to worry about ambiance.

It would seem that after all this planning for one evening, I would feel ready, but I was frightened beyond words. When I saw some of the men slapping Travis on the back on our way out and making little suggestive jokes, my fear heightened. What if I didn't measure up to Travis's expectations?

I was silent all the way to the hotel. I kept wringing my hands and couldn't stop my knees from shaking. Travis was humming happily to himself in the back of the limo. He kissed me on my ear and I froze.

"What's wrong?" he asked.

"I don't know. I guess I'm just nervous."

Travis pulled me to him in a reassuring hug. "Don't be. Just relax and enjoy yourself. It's supposed to be fun."

Lynette had truly outdone herself with preparing the honeymoon suite. All we could do was gasp when we opened the door. There were rose petals scattered all over the bed and on the plush carpet. At least fifty candles were lit, providing soft romantic lighting and a pleasing scent. Completing the scene was a basket of chocolate-covered strawberries next to the bed.

Travis said he would use the bathroom first so that I could take my time. I perched on the edge of the bed, waiting for my husband to finish and not quite knowing what to do with myself. It didn't seem proper for me to turn on the television, so I sat there with my mind wandering.

After about ten minutes, Travis emerged from the bathroom surrounded by a cloud of steam. He had not bothered to put on a bathrobe, but had a towel wrapped around his waist. Staring at his chiseled body made me feel suddenly conscious of just how *unchiseled* I was.

I stood slowly and walked toward the bathroom. Travis told me that I could take my time, and I was going to do exactly that. On my way in he planted a warm kiss on my lips. I hoped that he didn't feel me trembling.

Sensing my fear, he said, "I don't want you worrying about anything. Remember that I chose you, and everything about you is beautiful to me."

I looked into Travis's eyes, trying to make sure that his words were sincere. All I could see in them was love and desire. I was overwhelmed but encouraged, and all I wanted to do was make Travis happy that he married me.

I squeezed his hand and went into the bathroom, no longer afraid, but determined. When I stepped out of the bath, I refused to dissect my imperfections in the mirror. I became the breathtaking beauty that Travis said I was. When I walked out of the bathroom and into Travis's arms, I was intoxicated with joy and I thought that nothing would ever be able to change that feeling.

CHAPTER
Twenty

❧❧❧

Present

I stared blankly across my dining room table at Ebony. She was talking, and I was listening, but I couldn't believe what I was hearing. She was trying to get me to apply for a job that she'd heard about on one of her speaking engagements.

She explained, "It's a mentor position at a battered women's shelter. You would be helping the women get back on their feet by preparing them for the job market."

I bit my lip and thought about the opportunity. Was I ready to mentor anyone? I couldn't even find a job for myself, but I was supposed to help women prepare for the job market? Not to mention that I was still close to being an emotional wreck. I'd just had a session with Dr. King earlier that day, and she seemed to think that I was doing better, even though I'd almost lost it that day in the grocery store. She called that a minor setback and told me not to dwell on it.

"Is it full time?" I asked.

"Yes, and it's pretty good pay, too."

"What do you mean by *pretty good pay*?" I questioned suspiciously.

"It's starting at thirty thousand a year," declared Ebony with enthusiasm.

I laughed out loud. That wasn't even a quarter of what I had been making at Grace Savings and Loan. But at the time I had no paycheck coming in at all. I thought about Travis and balled my hands into fists. How had I been stupid enough to let that man ruin everything I'd worked for?

Ebony discerned my change in mood and continued cautiously. "So should I tell my friend that you're interested?"

I searched my mind for a reason to say no. When I could think of none, I tried to think of an affirmation. *You are a gifted woman, and you are not defined by your paycheck.* It was true, and I didn't really need the money. Perhaps the Lord wanted to use me to touch someone's life. Perhaps he wanted one of the women to touch *my* life.

"Yes," I replied. "Tell her that I'm more than interested."

Ebony clapped her hands jubilantly. She seemed happier about all this than I was. The timer on the oven went off, and I went into the kitchen to put our baked herb-crusted chicken and rice pilaf on plates.

Ebony said as I handed her the place settings, "I'm so proud of you with this diet, girl. I've never seen you this dedicated. How much have you lost now? Fifty pounds?"

I smiled. "Actually, I've lost about seventy."

"Well, congratulations. I think you're going to really do it this time."

I sat down at the table across from Ebony. "I think so, too. Isn't it strange how it took a failed marriage to get me serious about weight loss?"

Ebony looked uncomfortable at the mention of my marriage. It still bothered her to talk about the subject. She felt an unnecessary amount of guilt for not trying harder to stop me from marrying Travis.

"You know it's okay to talk about marriage," I said lightheartedly. "I'm not angry with the whole institution of marriage. Only Travis."

Ebony slammed an open palm on the table furiously. "I just don't think it's fair what he did to you, Charmayne!"

"I used to get mad every time I thought about it myself, but Dr. King is helping me with that. Now I only get mad half the time."

"Well, he's going to pay. God's going to get him."

"Yes, I know."

Of course, I knew that the Lord was not going to reward Travis for what he'd done to me. For some reason, though, that knowledge was not enough. Something in me wanted to see that man suffer a terrible demise in plain sight of all of the people he'd wronged.

Ebony apparently knew me better than I thought she did, because the mentor position at the women's shelter was perfect for me. I knew it was from the Lord, even during the interview process. When they hired me on the spot, I felt like screaming *The famine is over* at the top of my lungs!

The shelter was called Dove's Haven. It was actually for battered women with children. A woman with some vision who had been victimized by an abusive man had started the facility. It was a renovated apartment building with eight two-bedroom suites. My job was to assess the eight occupants' backgrounds, education, and challenges and eventually get them all placed in career-oriented jobs.

Each of the women at Dove's Haven was set up in a rent-free apartment with her children. All of their physical needs were provided by the shelter. Whatever financial assistance they were receiving was placed in a savings account for them when they were ready to leave and reclaim their lives.

What attracted me to the program was the fact that the staff at Dove's Haven didn't just address the physical needs of the women. They had one-on-one counseling sessions, group therapy, and an evangelist who came in once a week for Bible study and prayer. Most of the women who entered the program were in and out the doors in less than six months. Those were the success stories.

Then there were women like Celeste. She was my first case. She'd been at Dove's Haven for two years. She was actually from Atlanta, but was in Cleveland hiding from her drug-dealing boyfriend. Her two boys were absolutely beautiful. She had been pregnant with the younger when she'd gotten to Dove's Haven.

She was sitting at my desk for our second meeting. We'd talked about some of her challenges in the first meeting. From what I could tell, her biggest challenge was lack of a steady employment history. I'd given her some homework assignments that she'd taken with very little enthusiasm.

"Celeste, did you finish the personality profile that I gave you on Monday?"

"Yes, Ms. Ellis, but I don't agree with what it said."

"You don't agree with the conclusion?"

Celeste nodded. "It says I should be some kind of health care professional. I don't want to do that. I want to work in an office, filing papers or something."

I had given Celeste a personality profile that was supposed to match her up with the field that would utilize her strengths and downplay her weaknesses. As generic as they seemed, I found the tests to be rather accurate.

"Let me see the test."

Celeste's responses showed her to be a nurturing individual who enjoyed working with a variety of people. Her weak areas were paying attention to detail and organization skills. She was a person who derived satisfaction from bringing joy to others.

"Well," I said, "your profile seems to be right on target for a health professional. You're a nurturer."

"I do enough nurturing of my sons. I want to work in an office."

"Okay, well, do you have any office experience? Have you ever done any filing or answering phones?"

"I don't have any experience doing anything. I been with Jerome since I was fifteen. He took care of me," replied Celeste flatly. I wondered if she was being difficult on purpose.

"Well, I guess we'll just have to start from square one."

Suddenly Celeste appeared distracted. "This is probably pointless. Why don't we talk about you?"

I was surprised that she was interested in my life. "What do you want to know about me?"

"Why you're always walking around with bags under your eyes. Do you sleep at all?"

"Well, yes. But not so well." I'd thought that my makeup covered the dark circles under my eyes, but apparently not.

"Does your husband beat you?" she asked boldly.

Despite her rudeness, I felt compelled to answer her questions. "I'm not married."

"Divorced?"

"You are quite nosy, Celeste."

Her lips curled into a smile. "You know all my business. It's only fair. So tell me. Are you divorced?"

"Not yet, but the process has begun."

Celeste sat on the edge of her seat, intrigued. "So it's fresh! That's why you're not sleeping well. Did he cheat on you?"

"Celeste!"

"Did the man cheat on you?" she asked again, ignoring my unspoken request for privacy.

"In a manner of speaking. Now enough about me. We need to talk about finding you some gainful employment."

"Are you serious?"

"Yes."

Celeste gestured to her emaciated body and disheveled hair. "Will you look at me? Who is going to hire me? I look like a zombie from *Night of the Living Dead* or something."

"You don't have to. I could help you with that."

It was Celeste's turn to laugh. "There is very little you can do for me. Besides, I'd rather talk about you. Why didn't you forgive your husband? Most of you church ladies forgive your husbands."

"I didn't forgive him because he's a liar," I responded immediately.

"Aren't they all?"

"I hope not."

"Well, I'm sorry. I don't share your optimism."

I bit the tip of my finger, reflecting again on how thoroughly Travis had ravaged my life. "My husband took a lot from me. He took everything, actually."

Celeste nodded, and her facial expression became an ugly grimace. "Your husband is a taker. My baby's daddy is a giver."

"For some reason, I don't think you mean that in a good way."

Celeste sat back in her chair. "You're lucky."

"What? Lucky? I don't think so."

"You're luckier than me. You'll live."

"What do you mean?" I asked, not knowing for sure if I wanted to hear the answer.

"My boyfriend gave me HIV. How's that for a parting gift?"

I was at a loss for words. No one had prepared me to counsel AIDS victims. I was just supposed to be helping people find jobs. My story sounded trivial compared with hers.

I asked Celeste seriously, "Even though you're sick, do you still want a job?"

"I don't think anyone will hire me, but of course I want a job. I want to leave my boys a will instead of a bill."

"There may be something I can do."

Celeste raised a skeptical eyebrow in my direction. "I've heard that before."

"But you haven't heard it from me. Give me a week or so, and I'll get back to you on this."

I smiled to myself. It was good to have some favors that I could call in, even if I couldn't use them myself when I needed a job. Celeste, still looking unsure, left my office possibly with hopes of a not-so-bleak future for her sons.

Celeste's story had given me some perspective. Travis had not destroyed me—not completely. He had taken a lot from me, but the most vital parts of me were still intact. Listening to Celeste had done more than cause me to remember an old business contact. She had inspired me to go and get my life back.

CHAPTER
Twenty-one

❧

Past

The first weekend after our honeymoon, I sat on the bed watching Travis pack for his four-day workweek, and I realized that I didn't want him to go. It was silly of me, because I knew probably better than he did what type of time-consuming effort was going to go into making his business a success. And I did want him to be a success— more than anything. I wanted to know that I had married more than a pretty face.

Travis gingerly placed his much worn black suit in a garment bag. I frowned when I noticed frayed edges on the pant hem and a rip in the lining of the jacket. Who was going to take him seriously if he was dressed that way?

"Travis, what time do you have to leave today?" I asked.

"Well, I want to get on the road as soon as possible. Why?"

"I think we need to go shopping. I'm sick of seeing you in that black suit. You can buy some suits and have them tailored when you get to Detroit."

His face lit up. "I was wondering when you were going to share the wealth."

I smiled, but I didn't know what he meant by that statement. Hadn't I been sharing the wealth already? Weren't we living in my home, and wasn't he driving my car? I knew that eventually I had to start thinking of things as "ours," but that was going to take some time.

Since I had absolutely no idea where to shop for a man's clothing, I let Travis lead the way. We went to a downtown men's boutique that specialized in top-of-the-line designer apparel. The owner of the shop was already acquainted with Travis; he gave him a big bear hug when we walked in the door.

"T! It's been ages. Where have you been hiding?"

Travis laughed. "I've been off falling in love, man. This is my lovely wife, Charmayne."

"It's nice to meet you." I beamed at Travis's compliment.

Travis continued, "Charmayne, this is Mr. Shane. He dresses the successful men in this city. I've been window-shopping here for years."

Mr. Shane took Travis to the back of the store to show him some new arrivals while I browsed around on my own. My eyes widened and my jaw dropped when I saw the price tags on the suits. Even the cheap-looking ones were priced eight hundred dollars and up.

Travis came out of the fitting room wearing a four-button gray single-breasted suit. There were very faint pinstripes that were only visible up close. Mr. Shane had accessorized the suit with a black dress shirt and a black, gray, and red tie. Travis posed in front of the mirror, and I had to admit that he looked like a model.

Travis exclaimed, "This is perfect! A couple more hookups like this and I think I'll be set. I'm going to need some shoes, too."

"Gators?" asked Mr. Shane.

"What else?" replied Travis as if the question were ludicrous.

By the time Travis was finished shopping, he'd racked up a bill of over five thousand dollars. I reluctantly pulled out one of my gold cards to pay for the purchases. I hadn't spent five thousand dollars on clothes in ten years.

Mr. Shane congratulated Travis as I handed him the credit card. "I see you done came up this time, man."

Travis grinned sheepishly. Somehow I felt like there was an inside joke that was being told at my expense. I looked at my husband for an explanation, and he put his hand around my waist and pulled me close to him.

"He's just jealous that he doesn't have a successful black woman at his side," Travis explained.

On the way home, Travis was in a great mood— humming along with the radio and clapping his hands. I, on the other hand, felt uneasy. I had the irrational feeling that I was getting him all dressed up for another woman. I didn't know how or when the feeling had emerged, but it was real nonetheless.

"So," I asked when Travis stopped at a red light, "what will you do in Detroit when you're not working?"

Travis laughed. "I'll be working the whole time, but if I have a free moment, I'll try to catch up with my boy

Les. Anna will probably cook a nice dinner for me. You don't have any problems with that, do you?"

"With Anna cooking you a meal? No. Of course not."

Travis teased, "What? You don't mind another woman feeding your man?"

I replied lightly, "Honey, you're a grown man. I hope that you can feed yourself. I ain't your mama."

A grinning Travis answered, "You my sugar mama."

I felt my face turn into a scowl. What in the world had he meant by *sugar mama*? Women got with sugar daddies just to make sure that their bills were paid. It had nothing to do with love or even lust—merely commas in a bank account. For Travis to say that after I'd spent five thousand dollars on him was tasteless and hurtful. Did he feel that way about me? *Was* I his sugar mama?

Travis noticed my turn of moods and said quickly, "You know I'm only playing, right?"

I nodded but didn't say anything else. I turned to look out of my window, still stunned by his choice of words.

When we got home, Travis packed his purchases into the back of his work van along with his other luggage. I watched him in silence, feeling insecure. I walked back into the house, and he followed me in to say his good-byes for the long weekend.

He pulled me into an embrace. "I'm going to miss you, sweetheart. Promise to call me every day."

"Of course I will." I smiled up at him, feeling helpless to make any further objections.

He picked up his briefcase and my laptop and headed for the door. He had asked to use my computer on the road, and I didn't see any problem with it, even though it was owned by the bank. He was only going to use it to check his e-mail, and it was just sitting on my desk gathering dust.

As if something had just jogged his memory, Travis said, "By the way, when I get back home, we have some very important things to discuss."

"Like what?"

"Like how we need to set up our finances."

"What's wrong with the setup that we have now?"

"There wouldn't be anything wrong with it if we were roommates. We're one flesh, but our money is separate."

I didn't like where Travis was taking the conversation. I had worked hard for every penny I'd earned, and I wasn't in a big hurry to put his name on everything, especially not after he'd just called me a sugar mama. Besides, he seemed *way* too eager for me to do so. I knew that as a Christian woman, I should submit to my husband and let him take the lead, but I could see that it was going to be a gradual process.

I kissed him on the cheek. "Well, let's talk about it when you get back home."

"I'm serious, Charmayne. I don't like feeling like you're keeping secrets from me. I didn't know that you had a gold American Express card."

I laughed. "Do you want to see my portfolio or something?"

"Yes," Travis replied. His face did not reveal one hint of humor.

"All right, Travis. When you get home, we'll meet with my financial planner."

This seemed to appease him. "It's not that I'm trying to take anything from you. I know you're successful. It's just that you know everything I have."

I thought, *Of course I know everything you have! You ain't got nothing!* But I didn't vocalize my thoughts; just nodded and hugged him again as he walked out the door. We would meet with my financial planner when he got home, but only after I'd talked to her first. I was going to protect some of my assets, and make sure that they stayed mine. Travis was my husband, but my mama didn't raise no fool.

CHAPTER
Twenty-two

～❧～

Past

While Travis was away on his first business trip of many, I got into the Christmas spirit. Since I had spent the entire month of November planning my wedding, I hadn't gotten a chance to do any shopping for anyone, including my new husband. Lynette was the queen of last-minute shopping, so we got together for a mall-dashing spree.

Lynette picked through a pile of discounted sweaters, frowning at the limited selection. She asked, "What did you get your mama?"

"Oh, she was easy. She's been hinting all year that she wants to go on a vacation. She told me last month that she wants to get on an airplane before she dies."

Lynette laughed. "So where are you sending her?"

"To an all-inclusive resort in Cancún with one of her bingo buddies."

"You're such a good daughter. I bet Dayna is going to be jealous."

"You're probably right, but Dayna always finds something to get in a huff about. I can't worry about her."

Lynette held up a cream-colored sweater with a huge tiger in the middle of it. It seemed a bit too much for Jonathan. I shook my head in disapproval, and Lynette threw the sweater back down.

"This is too hard! I have no idea what to buy him."

I nodded. "I know what you mean. I'm getting Travis some cuff links."

"That's a good idea, but I want to get Jonathan some clothes. He needs a new wardrobe."

"Have you ever been to Mr. Shane's downtown?"

Lynette laughed. "Are you serious? Girl, his prices are outrageous." She raised an eyebrow and asked, "Is that where Travis shops?"

"He got a few items from there before he went on the road."

Lynette sucked her teeth and said, "Umph."

"What?"

"I bet he couldn't afford that store before he hooked up with you."

I rolled my eyes. "Don't start."

Lynette decided to keep the rest of her thoughts to herself, until we got to the jewelry store to pick up Travis's cuff links. Each was in the shape of a cross, diamond-encrusted. They were expensive—a little under two thousand dollars—but Christmas came only once a year, and they would look good with his new suits. I also hoped that by my generosity, I would convince Travis that I want to share everything with him—including my money.

Buying the gifts also helped me to convince myself that I wanted to share with Travis. I was trying to get in the habit of viewing the money as ours. I knew Travis would have had no problem purchasing the cuff links for himself, so I shouldn't have, either.

Lynette commented, "Dang, girl! You already got the man. You ain't got to buy him now."

"Giving my husband a gift is not *buying* him. This little purchase is not hurting me, and you know it."

"Yeah, I know. But what is he getting you for the holiday? He could only afford to get you something like this if you gave him the money."

I replied without much enthusiasm, "Everything I have is his."

Lynette burst into laughter. "Girl, you need to practice that line a little bit more. You are not believable at all."

I took the little box with the cuff links from the salesperson and we walked out of the store. Lynette was still laughing, and I was getting a little bit irritated.

"What is so funny?"

Lynette mimicked me. "Everything I have is his. Come on! *Everything?*"

"Why don't you think I mean it?"

"Because that isn't like you! That man probably has no idea how much money you really have."

I stepped into the passenger's side of Lynette's car. "Okay, you're right. He doesn't. He asked me about it before he left, but I stalled him."

"You're going to have to tell him eventually."

"Why? Why can't he just know that I have his back financially, and that he doesn't have to worry about anything? Why does he have to know exactly what I have?"

"That's a man. He's not going to want you to have any secrets. Why don't you want to tell him?"

How could I explain my reservations when I didn't even understand them? It wasn't something tangible; it was just an ominous feeling. Usually when I felt that way, I realized that God was trying to warn me about something. I didn't want to admit I was feeling that way about the man I'd so hastily married.

I responded, "I don't know. But I guess I will when he comes home."

"All right then, moneybags. Let's go over to Marshall's, though. Some of us ain't got it like you. We still have to shop bargain basement."

I laughed. "Marshall's it is! I can get Dayna's present there."

Travis called me on Christmas Eve, when he was supposed to be on his way home. I was baking pies for the party at my mother's apartment on Christmas Day. It was a tradition that we all crammed into Mama's little family room and gorged ourselves on rich, fattening foods while we exchanged gifts. I was looking forward to finally having a husband to bring.

"What do you mean you can't make it home?" I asked furiously. I couldn't believe what I was hearing.

"The furnace in the retirement home decided to conk out today. I ordered a part, but because of the holiday, I can't get it in until the day after Christmas. I've literally got the furnace held together with a hanger and some duct tape."

"But it sounds like there's nothing you can do until you get that part. You might as well come home for the holiday and then drive back. It's only a three-hour drive."

Travis explained, "But what if the furnace quits and they can't get it going again? The pipes will freeze, and these elderly people will be without heat."

I was glad he couldn't see the big tears falling down my cheeks. "But this is our first Christmas. I wanted it to be special."

"We'll celebrate when I get home."

"Okay. But what about your mother's gift? Should I take that to her on Christmas, along with a plate of food?"

"My mother? You got her something?" Strangely enough, he sounded alarmed.

"Yes, I bought her a warm robe and some new slippers. I noticed that she was shivering when we went to visit her."

"That was sweet of you, but don't go up to the rest home without me. It would probably just upset her, especially on the holiday."

Travis's lack of concern for his mother was beginning to bother me. He claimed that he visited her three times a week, but I hadn't heard about him going to the nursing home since he'd taken me two weeks before our wedding. He hadn't even brought his mother to the ceremony. He'd claimed that when he and Les tried to pick her up, she'd refused to leave her room. If it had been me, I would've sedated my mama to get her to my wedding.

"Well, okay. I guess I'll see you when you get home."

Travis blew a kiss through the phone. "Love you."

I was still livid about Travis's absence on Christmas morning when I packed my two sweet potato pies into the car and headed for my mother's house. The only thing that lifted my spirits a little was the thought of the look on Dayna's face when she saw the gift I'd bought Mama.

When I walked into Mama's apartment, Dayna and her family were already there. The children were drooling and hovering over the stack of presents, but they rushed over to me when I walked in the door. They covered me with the *I-know-Auntie-bought-me-a-gift* hugs and kisses that I received from them each Christmas.

There was a huge box sitting in the middle of Mama's already cramped living room floor. From the looks of the immaculate wrapping, it was probably Dayna's gift to Mama. I figured it was that big-screen television that they couldn't afford to purchase the year before. I walked over to Mama and kissed her lightly on the cheek.

"Where's your husband?" she asked.

"Merry Christmas, Mama," I said, trying to avoid the question.

She persisted. "Is Travis parking the car?"

"No, Mama. He can't make it. He's out of town on business."

Dayna poked her head out from the kitchen. "What? Doesn't he have his own business? He didn't give himself the holiday off?"

I bit my lower lip and tried to hide my irritation. "Merry Christmas, Dayna."

"Well?" Dayna insisted on an answer to her question.

"His client had an emergency. The two of us will just have to celebrate later."

Dayna shook her head with pseudo-sadness. "Awww. That's too bad."

I ignored her and handed out gifts to my nieces and nephew. I'd gotten Erin and Koree dolls and three outfits apiece from The Gap. I bought Ronald Jr. a remote-controlled car and some expensive tennis shoes. I handed

Ronald Sr. my yearly gift to the children of a $250 savings bonds for each of them. It was my contribution to their college funds.

Ronald said, "Thank you, Charmayne. You spoil these kids."

"She can afford it," said Dayna as she emerged from the kitchen. "What did you get me?"

My sister and I exchanged gifts, and I also handed Ronald a small package. Dayna looked disappointed when she opened her gift—a sweater. Ronald got the usual silk tie. She was so ungrateful! I couldn't believe she had the audacity to frown on my gift when she'd bought me a pair of gloves and a scarf.

"All right," said Mama, "when do I get to open my gifts?"

Dayna grinned. "Right now, Mama!"

Dayna presented the gift from her family, which was a forty-eight-inch flat-screen television. The thing was so huge that it was going to practically swallow up Mama's living room. One thing was for sure: Mama would no longer have a problem seeing or hearing her favorite soap operas.

Mama gushed, "Ooh, Dayna! Y'all shouldn't have spent all this money on me."

Ronald mumbled something under his breath, and Dayna nudged him in the ribs. They probably *couldn't* afford the gift, but money was absolutely no object to Dayna—even if she didn't have it.

She looked over at me with a superior smirk on her lips. "Your turn."

I got up and handed Mama the envelope. Dayna hovered over Mama so that she could be the first to approve or disapprove of my gift. She realized what the gift was before Mama did, and her mouth dropped open at the sight of the plane tickets.

"Cancún? Who in the world will Mama go to Cancún with?" asked Dayna sharply.

Mama giggled, "I have friends! Thank you, Charmayne, baby. I'm gone finally get to ride in an airplane. I'm calling Ruby right now to tell her the good news."

Dayna rolled her eyes at me and went into the kitchen. I followed her so that I could help with the dinner—and try to contain the nasty conversation that was sure to follow. I knew it was going to be ugly when Dayna started slamming silverware and dishes.

"What is your problem?" I asked, wanting to get the whole thing over with.

She pointed at me with a huge serving fork. "You. You are my problem."

I shook my head angrily. "I haven't done anything to you, Dayna."

"You do the same thing every year. You find a way to upstage me with your money."

"Mama told me that she wanted a trip. Don't get mad at me because you couldn't afford to give it to her."

Dayna's eyes bulged furiously. "Do you have any idea how much overtime Ronald had to work to get that television? And then here you come, waving your magic credit card wand."

"The gifts that I choose for Mama don't have anything to do with you."

"Oh, yes, they do. Just like that man you married."

She caught me completely off guard with her reference to Travis. "What do you mean?"

"You had to find the prettiest Negro in the city, didn't you? It's all part of what you do to make Mama love you more."

She thought Mama loved me more? I wanted to ask her what world she was living in. I had heard our mother sing Dayna's praises since the day she was born, but *she* felt unloved?

Just then Mama came into the kitchen. Dayna and I both had tense expressions on our faces that we tried to soften as Mama approached. As angry as we were, neither one of us wanted her to know that we were arguing at all, much less about her Christmas gifts.

Mama asked, "Is everything all right in here?"

Dayna replied, "Yes, Mama. Go on back in there and enjoy your grandbabies. Me and Charmayne can take care of the dinner."

"Okay then." Mama eyed me and Dayna suspiciously, but decided to let the matter drop and went back to fiddle with her new television.

When Mama was out of earshot, I whispered, "The choices that I make in my life have nothing to do with you. Not what I buy Mama, and not who I marry."

I knew that the conversation was over when Dayna started humming. That was something that she'd picked up from our mother. Whenever Mama wanted to end an argument with our father, she would get in her last word and start humming a gospel tune. It's very hard to argue with someone who is humming "I Love You Lord" or "Amazing Grace." The person still trying to argue comes across as a devil. Dayna's tune of choice was "I Can't Complain."

I started boiling water for the macaroni and cheese

while Dayna prepared the corn bread dressing. With our backs to each other we did what Mama expected us to do. I didn't know how to recover from Dayna's verbal assault. She had cut me deep with her accusations, no matter how ridiculous they were in actuality.

I wanted to turn to Dayna and tell her how much I admired her family and her relationship with Mama. I wanted to tell her how beautiful I thought she was. But I didn't—couldn't. All I could do was stare into a pot of water and wish that I was a hundred miles away.

CHAPTER
Twenty-three

❧

Past

Travis returned home two days after Christmas, and as promised we celebrated on the night of his return. His gifts to me were a set of gold hair combs and a sweater that was two sizes too small. I was thrilled, even though the presents weren't perfect. He could've given me a blender and some hiking boots and I would've been pleased. His biggest gift to me had been marrying me—and I was still thanking God for that.

It seemed as if Travis had been gone forever, and I was excited to have him back home. I didn't know if I was keen on his business anymore, not if it meant that he was going to be away days at a time. It didn't really seem to be worth it.

I fed Travis the turkey dinner that I'd prepared, with all of the traditional fixings. I was tired of turkey myself, seeing that I'd just gorged myself on it at my mother's house two days before, but this was our first Christmas and I wanted to do everything right.

I wanted to top off our Christmas celebration with something extra special, so at bedtime I took a long bath and emerged into the bedroom wearing pretty lace lingerie. Travis seemed uninterested and barely glanced away from the television. I didn't know how to take his reaction. I'd never heard of a man willingly turning down sex with his brand-new wife.

"Travis," I asked, "is there something wrong?"

He smiled up at me, as if he'd just then noticed what I was wearing. "No, honey. I'm exhausted. It's been a long week."

"Well, why don't you let me help you relax," I offered.

Travis patted his hand on the bed, motioning for me to sit. "Come lie next to me. I don't have the energy for all that tonight, but I wouldn't mind some cuddling."

I obediently took my place on my side of the bed. I was confused and hurt, but I wasn't going to let Travis see that. He was blasting every stereotype that I'd ever known about men and about marriage. Men were supposed to be insatiable, and women were supposed to oblige them with their wifely due. No one ever mentioned anything about him being too tired for me.

I was so disturbed about Travis turning me away that I could think of nothing else when Lynette and I went out for lunch the following day. She was rattling on and on about the tennis bracelet that Jonathan had bought her for Christmas, and how he had spoiled her sons with gifts. I smiled and nodded at all the appropriate places, but she still noticed my detachment.

"Girl, what is wrong with you?" she asked.

"Nothing. Why do you ask?"

"Because you are a million miles away from here."

"Tell me," I ventured cautiously. "What would you think if Jonathan turned you down in the bedroom?"

Immediately she replied, "I'd think he was getting it somewhere else."

I believe it was the look of sheer horror on my face that told Lynette I was really asking about myself and Travis. Though the damage had already been done, she softened her answer and said, "Well, it doesn't have to mean that, but it would probably be the first thing that comes to mind."

Surprisingly, the thought that Travis was fulfilling his needs elsewhere had not even crossed my mind. I had just assumed that he didn't find me attractive or that I looked silly in the lace camisole. It was unfathomable that my brand-new husband would be cheating on me when we hadn't even been married a month.

"Well, I don't think that Travis is cheating. Forget I asked."

"Just don't let it happen more than once without asking questions."

I nodded quietly, wishing that I hadn't even started the conversation. Lynette had a worried look on her face that mirrored what I was feeling on the inside.

Since Travis was missing in action for the Christmas church services, I was relieved that he was going to be at my side for the New Year's Eve service. Not that I had anything to prove, but I wanted people to see us together. It seemed like most of my friends and acquaintances were waiting for us to fail.

We walked into the church, arm in arm—me wearing my new hair combs and Travis sporting his very expensive cuff links on one of his new suits. Lynette smiled reassuringly when she saw us, no doubt recalling our earlier conversation. But neither she nor I needed to worry, because the very night that I'd expressed my concerns to Lynette, Travis reaffirmed his desire and his attraction for me.

Our New Year's Eve services were festive occasions. There was always a lot of singing, a lot of dancing, and a lot of testifying. When I thought about what the Lord had done for me all year long, I started jumping and shouting, although my praise was usually low-key.

"You betta praise him, Sis," I heard someone say.

When I finally calmed down Pastor Jenkins said, "Sister Charmayne, do you have a testimony that you want to share?"

I noticed that Travis had disappeared from my side, but I testified anyway. "Yes, Pastor. I have been truly, truly blessed this year. I've been blessed in my finances, blessed with good health, and the Lord has seen fit to send me the husband of my dreams. But more than anything, I've felt my walk with God get stronger, and I know He's going to continue to do great things in my life. Hallelujah! Hallelujah! *Hallelujah!*"

The fervor of my testimony struck a fire in the congregation. Two sisters started shouting, and then Lynette joined in. Not missing a beat, the musicians started in with the shouting music, banging on the drums and organ like there was no tomorrow. I thought about the praise report I'd just given and I hugged myself.

When the intense shouting died down for a moment, I

made my way to the water fountain. My throat was parched, and I could feel the beads of sweat collected on my forehead and neck. As I walked up the aisle, someone patted me on my back and said, "It's all right, baby."

I took a long, thirst-quenching gulp of water and stood in the vestibule fanning myself. I looked through the stained-glass windows of our main entrance. It was a beautiful and still night. We'd had some warm weather that had melted all of the November and December snow, and the streets were as dry as in the middle of June.

I glanced up and down the street at the nightlife going on outside our worship center. I gasped when I saw my husband leaning into a car across the street. I squinted to make out the shadowy figure behind the wheel, but I just wasn't close enough to see who it was. I couldn't even tell if it was a man or a woman.

Travis started back toward the church and I panicked. I didn't want him to know that I'd seen him until I figured out what I was going to do and say. I dashed back into the sanctuary and slid into our pew just as Travis walked back through the double doors.

I shuddered as he placed his arm around me. I wanted to knock his hand away and slap the smile off his face. I needed an explanation and I needed it sooner rather than later.

I whispered to Travis, "Can I talk to you outside for a minute?"

"Now? It's the middle of service."

"Yes, now. It's important." I wanted to smack him up-side his head.

Travis and I got up and walked out into the vestibule. No one even noticed that we were up walking again, because the choir had started singing and had taken the praising and shouting up an extra notch.

Travis asked impatiently, "What is it that couldn't wait until we got home?"

I couldn't believe that he had the audacity to sound irritated. "Who were you just talking to outside?"

He shook his head in disbelief. "You spying on me now?"

"No, Travis. I happened to see something that I obviously wasn't supposed to see." I could hear my voice rising, although the church vestibule was no place to stage a scene with my husband.

Travis grabbed me by the arm and led me outside. Although the night looked calm, it was bitter cold. I wished that I'd put on my coat. I yanked my arm away from him when his big hands started to hurt me.

Travis spoke in an angry hiss. "Woman, why don't you trust me?"

I answered with a question of my own. "Why are you always surprising me?"

It had just dawned on me that Travis was *always* shocking me in one way or another. His initial interest in me was shocking, and every aspect of our relationship had seemed to just come out of the clear blue sky. Travis quitting his job, revealing his felonies, proposing to me, introducing me to his ailing mother . . . all of these things had blindsided me. I had come to expect the unexpected from Travis.

Travis scratched his head nervously. "That was my parole officer, Charmayne."

A sarcastic chuckle escaped from my lips. "Your parole officer? Surprise!"

I shook my head and started to walk back toward the sanctuary. In my mind, I was making the conscious choice to ignore the surprises that wouldn't destroy me.

Travis took my hand. "I wanted to tell you, but when I first told you about my felonies, you left me. I didn't want to lose you again."

"So you lie to me?"

"I never lied to you about this."

"Omission *is* lying."

"I didn't omit the fact that I just got out of prison. You could have assumed that I was still on parole."

I felt foolish. It was almost like I wanted it to be a woman in that car. Him having a parole officer wasn't a bad thing, but I didn't know how to get out of the conversation without making myself look like the insecure and jealous wife I had quickly become.

Marriage was not what I'd expected. I thought that it would be about sharing my hopes and dreams with my soul mate, and that we'd always lean and depend on each other. The union between myself and Travis was none of these things. He accused me of not trusting him, but he didn't trust me with even the most basic information.

We stood in silence for what seemed like too long. Travis was clearly hurt, and I was at a loss for words.

He broke the silence. "Why don't you trust me?"

"I do."

"No. You don't. You're constantly looking over your shoulder, waiting for me to drop some kind of bomb on you. It's not going to happen, Charmayne."

Travis opened his arms and embraced me. I felt the tears start to pour down my cheeks. Why couldn't I allow myself to be happy and why was there still no peace in my spirit?

"Travis," I sobbed, "I'm really sorry."

"It's all right. I know you didn't mean it."

But I *had* meant it. So I stood there in Travis's arms praying and wondering. Praying that my marriage would last, and wondering how in the world I'd ended up apologizing when Travis was the one keeping secrets.

CHAPTER
Twenty-four

～∽◦ᡣᡣ◦∽～

Present

"First Lady will see you now," said Sister Piper Willis,
First Lady Jenkins's new armor bearer.

With me sitting down from my post and Ebony accepting more and more speaking engagements, First
Lady needed a replacement. Piper and I had different
takes on what it meant to be an armor bearer. I thought it
meant being a prayer warrior, friend, protector, and con-
fidante. Piper, on the other hand, preferred to be some
ridiculous hybrid of secretary, security guard, and maid-
servant. She was even posted outside First Lady's office
door like a sentry. I could imagine her holding up one of
First Lady's hatboxes to ward off some imagined threat.
I was sure that she was driving Ebony up the wall.

First Lady was standing at the coffeepot making a
fresh cup. "Would you like some coffee, Charmayne?"

"No, thank you."

First Lady gingerly carried her hot cup back to the desk. "How is it working out with Evangelist King?"

"Wonderfully. She's a gifted counselor."

"She's an anointed woman of God," remarked First Lady Jenkins.

I was getting a little nervous, because First Lady had called the meeting in the first place, but I had no idea why. We hadn't talked much since I'd married Travis and resigned from being an armor bearer. The last conversation we'd had was when she'd recommended Dr. King.

"Are you wondering why I called you in here?" asked First Lady.

I exhaled with relief. "Yes."

"Well, I want to know when you're coming back to your post."

"You mean as armor bearer?"

"Yes. You can come back anytime you want."

I lowered my head sadly. "I'd like that, but I don't think it's for me anymore."

First Lady came and sat next to me. I could tell she was getting into prayer mode. "What do you mean you don't think it's for you?"

"How can I be a good armor bearer if I'm failing in my own walk?"

"You think that just because you've made some wrong turns, you're failing?"

"I knew that the Lord was telling me not to marry Travis. I never felt any peace with that decision, but I pushed His voice out of my spirit. Now look at me!"

"Charmayne, I *am* looking at you. The Lord has forgiven you of your sin of disobedience, and you've already paid a hefty price. But I also see a survivor in you. Tell me how long it took the Israelites to get into the Promised Land."

"Forty years."

"Right. They walked much farther than God would've had them to, because of their stiff-necked behavior."

"So you're saying I just took a detour?"

"You went down a dead-end road, honey, but now you're back on the right path."

"How do I know that I'm back?"

"Do you feel peace in your spirit, honey?"

"Yes. It's been awhile since I felt it, but my peace has returned."

First Lady beamed. "Well, you need to get on back, because that Piper is driving me crazy."

I laughed with First Lady. Everything was starting to feel normal again. I knew that I was back on the Lord's path for my life. I could feel the presence of the Holy Spirit like I had before I'd decided to take matters into my own hands. I was glad, too, because I didn't want to be like the Israelites. I didn't have forty years to get this thing right.

Later that day I had a session with Dr. King. She'd been hinting that our time together was almost finished, but I had come to depend on her for her wisdom. I hoped that we would continue to be friends once the sessions were through.

I told her about my conversation with First Lady. "She said that my marriage to Travis was like my wilderness experience."

Dr. King nodded. "I like that! Tell her I'm going to have to take that and use it."

I laughed. "I sure will."

"I'm going to have to agree with First Lady Jenkins. You had a momentary lapse of judgment when it came to marrying Travis. From your descriptions of the man, it's not hard to imagine many other women making the same choices."

"That's what really burns me! I know that Travis is going to use his charms and woo one of my sisters in Christ, and there's nothing that I can do about it."

Dr. King replied, "There is something you can do about it."

"Pray that the Lord smites him?"

She laughed. "Charmayne, I'm so glad to see that your humor has returned. No, you cannot pray for his demise, but you can pray for his deliverance. Jesus can work on his heart and repair his character."

"And make him the perfect husband for someone else, right?"

"Perhaps. I don't know that he will make a good husband for anyone."

"He sure wasn't a good one for me."

Dr. King asked, "Thinking back, were there any warning signs that your marriage was in trouble?"

I nodded slowly. "Dr. King . . . it was troubled from the very beginning."

CHAPTER
Twenty-Five

~~❧~~

Past

It was the Thursday morning of our meeting with my financial planner, and I was nervous. I'd taken the day off work so that I'd have enough time to devote to the meeting. Travis had gotten up early and made breakfast for the both of us, but I just wasn't hungry at all. I followed the smells of bacon and vanilla-flavored pancakes into the kitchen with a lackluster attitude.

Travis was standing in the kitchen cooking in his underwear. He liked to go around the house wearing no shirt, allowing his muscular form to get all the exposure that it needed. His chest and back were glistening with scented body oil. I'd never met a man more concerned with his appearance.

Even though he was half naked, I felt underdressed in my robe and slippers. He'd suggested to me that I try going around naked. He said I would feel liberated. I told him that in order for me to walk around the house naked, we'd have to paint all the mirrors black.

I sat down at the kitchen counter. "Good morning, Travis."

"Morning!" he said cheerily.

"Breakfast smells good. What are we having?"

"You are having a stack of my gourmet vanilla pancakes and warm crispy bacon. I am having a protein shake."

"What are you doing? Trying to fatten me up?"

"No. You're fine, and I'm about to start training, so I need protein."

"Training? For what?"

"Training, so that I can retain this physique that I've been blessed with. I'm also joining a gym. There's a new twenty-four-hour gym on South Woodland."

"Great! I'll join with you. I need to get in shape anyway, and that's something we can do together."

Travis furrowed his brow and shook his head. "I don't have any objections to you joining a gym, but not my gym."

"You don't want to work out with me?"

"I wouldn't be working out with you anyway. You need strictly low-impact cardio, and I'm doing mostly weight training."

"Well, we can still be in the same building."

"I'd rather not. I use my time at the gym to clear my mind and meditate. I don't need you there."

I was angered beyond words. "Is *clear my mind and meditate* another term for messing around on me with another woman?"

"Here we go again with the trust issue."

I shot right back, "No, here we go again with your surprises."

Travis placed the heaping plate of food in front of me. He then took his protein shake and marched right on out of the kitchen. I guessed that the conversation was over and the decision had been made. Travis would be joining a gym, and I would be sitting home getting even fatter off his cooking.

We were still not conversing with one another when we left for the meeting with my financial planner, Victoria Summers. I'd informed her ahead of time that I wouldn't be revealing all my assets to Travis. Vicki didn't think it was a good idea to keep anything a secret. She'd asked me what I would do if I needed to tell him somewhere down the road. She thought that it was the kind of secret that could destroy a marriage. I'd taken her admonishments to heart, but I was willing to risk it. I wasn't planning on being anyone's sugar mama.

Vicki greeted us at the door, as I was one of her most lucrative clients. She'd even ordered a catered lunch for our meeting. Travis was impressed, but I knew Vicki, and this was the typical red-carpet treatment she gave her best clients. I felt it was deserved, with the amount of money I paid for her services.

Travis handed Vicki his small stack of bank account receipts. She bit her lower lip as she read the information. I knew exactly what was going on in her mind. His $22,000 in assets paled in comparison with the $210,000 that I had stockpiled in mutual funds, bonds, annuities, and liquid cash. Vicki usually didn't even take on clients who had less than $150,000 in assets. It began to dawn on her why I only wanted to give Travis a limited picture of my net worth.

Vicki asked, "Mr. Moon, is it all right if I call you Travis?"

"Of course." Travis smiled broadly. He was finally getting the respect he felt he deserved.

"I've been with Charmayne for years, but I didn't want to take any liberties. You may call me Vicki."

"All right, Vicki," said Travis, "let's get down to business. What has my beautiful wife not been telling me?"

Vicki glanced in my direction and I smiled. I hoped that she was going to honor my request.

She responded, "Well, Charmayne has one of the best credit scores I've ever seen. She's above seven hundred, which is perfect. She has one hundred ten thousand dollars in a highly diversified portfolio that includes mutual funds, annuities, and bonds."

Travis looked from Vicki to me and then back to Vicki. "A hundred ten thousand? Is that all? How much of that is liquid?" His voice was ominously tense, and he was sitting at the edge of his seat.

Vicki chuckled nervously—she'd noticed Travis's demeanor. "It almost sounds like you're ready to cut and run, Mr. Moon."

"Of course not. I simply don't like being in the dark. What if something happens to Charmayne today? You could end up robbing me blind and I'd never know."

Vicki answered, "About forty thousand is relatively liquid, with ten thousand in a money market checking account that is totally accessible."

"So when are we putting my name on everything?"

That question was to me, and I looked to Vicki, hoping she'd stall for me.

"I can draw up the paperwork, and it will take about sixty days for everything to go into effect. I'll have the papers in Charmayne's office by next Wednesday."

Travis looked irritated. "Well, I guess that will do."

"I'm sorry it can't go any faster than that. But you know how banks are."

He shifted in his seat. "Yes. I understand. Is there a restroom in this office?"

"Yes." Vicki handed him the keys. "Go down this long hall and make a right, then it's the third door down on your left."

"Thank you."

When Travis was safely down the hall, Vicki closed her office door. She exhaled loudly and walked briskly back over to her desk.

She said, "He's a real piece of work. Where did you find him?"

"Don't ask. I didn't know he was so concerned with my assets until about a month ago. I paid for something with a gold credit card and he's been obsessed ever since."

"Well, don't worry. I'll handle it, and it will be painless for you."

"Thanks, girl."

Travis opened the door to the office noiselessly, as if he'd hoped to catch us in the act of doing or saying something. He kissed me on the forehead as he sat down. The kiss didn't feel genuine, and Travis seemed agitated.

Vicki finalized some forms and got Travis's signature on them. Signing the papers had a calming effect on him. I noticed the tension that was on his face melt away like hot butter.

"Well, I guess that does it. We're finally one flesh," Travis said joyously.

"We already were."

"In the spirit realm we were, but now we are on paper. Aren't you happy about it?"

"Of course I am."

I was glad that the Lord didn't strike me down right then and there for lying through my teeth. I didn't want Travis to be able to get his hands on even a fraction of my wealth.

We walked out of Vicki's office hand in hand. Travis's joyfulness was bothering me so much that I was happy he was leaving for the weekend. I was ready to go home and help him pack his bags.

While we were driving home he asked, "Is everything all right, Charmayne?"

"Yes, I'm fine. Just a little tired. I've had a long week. One more day and then the weekend."

"That's when my work begins," lamented Travis.

I wondered if he was already growing tired of running his own business. He sure didn't seem as excited about it as he was in the beginning.

"A little hard work never hurt anyone."

Travis answered quickly and sharply, "Yeah, well, I'm not going to be working like a dog my whole life."

Something about the way he looked at me when he made that statement sent a chill through my body. It was as if he blamed me for his hard work and was going to make me pay. His eyes turned dark and ominous as we drove on in silence. I felt troubled in my spirit; something malevolent was brewing in the atmosphere. I prayed silently as Travis drove, *Lord, I feel restless in my spirit. I pray that you keep me and protect me. Please give me light for my path. Touch Travis's heart and spirit* . . .

CHAPTER
Twenty-six

━━━◦ຄ◦━━━

Past

I felt a tremendous amount of guilt following our meeting with my financial adviser. How could I say that I loved Travis and not be completely honest with him about something so simply meaningless as money? I put myself in his shoes and found that I'd be willing to divorce him for a similar offense. I felt like the tormented murderer in Edgar Allan Poe's "The Tell-Tale Heart." It seemed that at any moment, my lies would be laid bare and I would lose my dream husband.

My guilt caused me to leave work early. I was going to go home and tell Travis all my deeds, then beg his forgiveness. I'd take him on a ridiculous shopping spree, maybe even a vacation.

On my way home I found myself stopped at a red light directly across from the nursing home where Travis's mother lived. I felt another pang of guilt. I hadn't visited my mother-in-law since that first meeting we'd had. I remembered Travis telling me not to stop by without him, but I didn't see what harm it would cause. Besides, it would be part of my penance for being such a conniving wife.

When I walked through the doors of the nursing home, it was abuzz with activity, quite unlike the day Travis and I visited. It took me a few moments to get the staff nurse's attention, because she seemed to be doing ten things at once.

Finally she looked up from a stack of papers and asked in an irritated tone, "Is there something I can help you with?"

"Yes. I'm here to see a patient. Her name is Mrs. Moon."

The nurse frowned. "We do not have a Mrs. Moon here."

"Oh, you must be mistaken. She's my mother-in-law, and I just recently visited her with my husband."

The nurse, still shaking her head, asked, "Do you know which room she was in?"

I led the nurse down the hallway to the last room on the right. We went into the room, and Mrs. Moon was lying in bed, sleeping peacefully.

I pointed to the woman and said, "This is Mrs. Moon, my mother-in-law. I'd just like to sit with her for a while."

The nurse replied, "I'm sorry, ma'am, but this woman's name is Bertha Washington."

"But doesn't she have a son named Travis?" I asked, feeling confused.

"Mrs. Washington doesn't have a son, but she does have three daughters who visit her daily. She has a grand-son named William, I think, but he's just a teenager."

I gasped upon hearing these facts, and ran out of the nursing home with tears streaming down my face. What kind of man was I dealing with who would lie about the identity of his own mother? I was afraid to think about what else Travis could be lying about.

I went home ready to confront Travis, but when I pulled into our driveway, his van was gone. I'd missed him—he was already on his way to Detroit for the week-end. I felt consumed with anger, wondering what he was *really* doing in Detroit.

Desperately I dialed his cell phone number, and the voice mail came on immediately. A frustrated roar came from my lips. It didn't even sound like me. I was at my wit's end and there was nothing I could do but wait.

I picked up the phone again, wondering who I could call for support. I dialed Ebony's home number, tears still streaming down my face. She answered on the first ring.

"Charmayne?"

"Yes . . . Ebony, I need you to pray with me. Right now."

Sensing the desperation in my voice, Ebony prayed, "Father, in the name of Jesus, I come to you right now. We're asking that you restore and renew, Lord. Send your angels in to bring peace, Lord. Right now, O God."

"Yes, Lord . . . ," I agreed as my leg shook uncon-trollably.

"We ask that you be a fence around Charmayne, dear Lord," Ebony continued. "Give her strength for this day and the days to follow. Protect her mind, Jesus, protect her heart. Lord, lead her and guide her. You will be a light to her path, O God. I speak peace into the atmosphere, in the name of Jesus . . . Amen."

We sat on the telephone, me not saying anything, and Ebony whispering "Jesus" over and over. Her voice calmed me somewhat, even as I felt myself unraveling. I thought back on all the warnings I'd received and ignored. And now the one who had warned me the most was praying for me.

"Do you want to talk about it?" Ebony asked.

"No, no, no," I sobbed. "I can't, Ebony. Just keep praying for me."

I couldn't speak Travis's betrayal out loud, because part of me wanted to believe that it wasn't happening. I wanted to wake up and realize I'd been dreaming. Then I could continue my fantasy of Travis being the loving husband and me being his respectful wife.

I spent the entire weekend waiting. Travis was set to be home on Sunday afternoon, when I would normally be praising the Lord at Bread of Life. But that Sunday, I had other plans. I wanted to confront Travis without giving him the luxury of preparing himself or finding out what I'd discovered.

I woke up early Sunday morning and drove down the street. I parked my car in the garage of a home for sale, then walked back home. My neighbor Clara watched my actions curiously out of her window. I supposed I looked demented, but I couldn't stand nosy people.

Back at home, I went into my bedroom and waited. At a little after noon, I heard Travis's van pull into the driveway. I braced myself for battle. Travis wouldn't know what hit him.

I sat tensely on the edge of my bed waiting for him to come upstairs, but instead I heard him talking. He was on the telephone. Cautiously, I walked to the bedroom door, so that I could hear him more clearly.

"Look, I don't want to have this conversation right now. I'm back home." He had an annoyed tone in his voice. "No. I cannot come back to Detroit! Not until next week . . . Of course I'll miss you."

My hands balled into fists and I felt my temperature rise. I wanted to scream. Not another woman! I thought I could handle anything but that. It was going to be more of a battle than I thought.

"Leslie . . . don't be like this . . ."

So the heifer's name was Leslie! My worst fears had been confirmed. I knew that there was another woman. My instincts had been correct. Hot tears splashed my clothing and the floor in front of me.

"I love you . . . no . . . say it back . . . I'm not hanging up until you do."

I was ready to explode. I had never been a part of something so surreal. It was as if I were watching my life unfold on the big screen.

Travis finally said good-bye and ended that torturous call. I stood frozen in place, unable to move but unable to dismiss what I'd heard. Travis was coming up the stairs, but I was still in a state of shock.

Travis saw me standing in the doorway, and his face paled. He hadn't expected me to be there, and I hadn't expected his affair to be revealed. We were both full of surprises that day.

"What are you doing home?" he asked.

"I live here."

"But your car—"

"Is down the street."

"Why?"

"I'm done answering questions. It's your turn. Who is Leslie?"

Travis sighed and dropped his head.

I repeated, "Who is she? Is she your mistress? Have you been seeing her all along?"

For a brief instant Travis looked puzzled. "Oh, you think Leslie is—"

I cut him off. "I think? I heard you on the phone, Travis! You told her you loved her! You said that you'd miss her. Do you think I'm an idiot?"

Travis shook his head. "No, Charmayne. But you're wrong about Leslie."

"What? Are you going to tell me she's your long-lost sister? Maybe your daughter? Another surprise for me, Travis?" I was furious, my questions coming back-to-back. I didn't even take a breath between words.

"Leslie is not my sister or my daughter. Les is my lover."

I must have heard wrong. "Les? As in the best man at our wedding?"

"Yes. We've been together for fourteen years . . . since college." Travis spoke slowly and deliberately.

My mind reeled. Travis had hit me with the mother of all surprises. It was something that only transpired on talk shows, but it was happening to me, in my house.

"If you're gay, why did you marry me?" The tone of my voice was sharp and piercing. "Was it the money?"

Travis sighed again and scratched his head.

"So it *was* the money! I can't believe this." I was

dizzy. I closed my eyes and held my head to keep the room from spinning.

I was frozen in time. I couldn't move. I couldn't speak another word. So Travis did all the talking.

"Charmayne, this has nothing to do with us. It's a side of me that I never thought you'd find out about. It doesn't diminish my love for you."

I stood there wondering if Travis was a lunatic. How could he think that I would accept his revelation and go on as if everything was fine and dandy? Travis obviously had no intention of letting all my liquid assets get away. Suddenly I remembered why I had wanted to confront him originally. "Why did you lie about your mother?"

Travis chuckled. "I'm just caught, huh? Like a rat in a trap. See, this is what happens when you don't trust people. I hope you found what you were looking for."

I ignored his ridiculous rhetoric. "You didn't answer my question."

"I lied about my mother because if I introduced you to my real family, they would've told you about Les. I couldn't bring myself to say that my mother was dead. I thought that was bad luck."

"Lying is bad luck," I replied angrily, pronouncing every syllable as if they were daggers.

"So it is."

We stared at each other blankly, neither one of us willing to take another step. For me the conversation was going to lead to the inevitable. The demise of my marriage.

Travis ventured into dangerous waters. "Charmayne, I've been bisexual ever since I can remember. I can't be satisfied by just one sex. I've tried, but it doesn't work."

"That's probably the first truthful thing you've said to me since we met," I said, shaking my head at the irony of it all.

The most devastating lie of all wasn't that his best friend was also his lover. Nor was it that Mama didn't really suffer from Alzheimer's. The most heart-wrenching lie was Travis telling me that he loved me. Those three little untrue words spoke more about his character than anything else. Travis was a cruel monster, and I had been his prey.

After a deep, mind-clearing breath, I declared, "You disgust me."

"So what are we going to do?"

"You are going to get out of my house."

His eyes flooded with tears. "Can I at least pack my things?"

"What things? You ain't got nothing here! Everything in this house I bought. It's all mine."

Travis stood up straight, perhaps to be menacing, but I was not afraid. "You gone keep my clothes, Charmayne?"

"Uh, no. I'm gone keep *my* clothes."

Travis tried at first to go around me into the bedroom. When he saw that I was serious about not moving out of his way, he backed down.

He said, "I'm going to give you some time to cool off. Then we can talk about this."

Travis walked away from me and down the hall. He looked back once, and after taking in the rage on my face he continued downstairs.

"Leave that cell phone on the table. I got that account. It belongs to me," I called down the stairs.

"You know I need this phone for work."

"I know you use it to contact your lover. I'm not going to be a part of your sin. Leave my cell phone on the table."

Travis looked back once more, his eyes pleading for understanding. I gave him nothing. Not even a hint of sadness that he was leaving. I just wanted him gone.

I watched from the window for a sign of remorse or of the love I believed that he'd felt for me. The only expression Travis wore was one of silent resignation, as if he'd just done something as simple as losing a basketball game. I stood at my window with tears streaming down my face, the gravity of Travis's offenses weighing on me heavily. Violated, I fell to my knees, sobbing. Finally I found a voice that croaked out two words. *Why Lord?*

Going to work the following Monday was torture. It had crossed my mind to call in sick, but I was afraid that I'd spend the entire day crying over Travis. It was bad enough that my eyes were bloodshot and swollen from crying all weekend. I'd avoided everyone, and I'd even missed church.

My assistant, Donna, noticed that I was out of sorts, and I could tell that she was looking for clues as to the reason. I didn't share the details of my personal life at work, however, so I had no intention of telling her anything.

On my way into my office I said, "Let me know if tech support calls. I just dropped off my laptop to be upgraded."

Donna replied, "I sure will."

"Thank you."

Donna asked tentatively, "Is everything okay? You look tired, or ill."

I responded blandly, "I'm fine. Hold my calls this morning, okay? I've got a lot of work to catch up on."

I sat down at my desk and attempted to weed through the mass of papers that I called an in-box, but I spent most of my energy trying to keep from crying. Listening to my voice mail was what finally caused me to break down. Hearing Travis's voice saying that he loved me was too much.

I had barely had a chance to pull myself together when Donna burst into my office and frantically proclaimed, "Charmayne, the board of directors has called an emergency meeting. They said that the meeting is today at one o'clock and that your attendance is mandatory."

"Wait a minute, Donna. Slow down. Who said there's a meeting?"

"Bishop Gordon just called."

"That's funny. I usually get an e-mail from the board."

Donna shrugged and walked out of the office. I tried to go into my e-mail account, but for some reason the password wasn't working. It was strange, because I knew my password. I wasn't one of those clients who had to call technical support because they forgot a password over the weekend. I tried my password once more, making sure the CAPS LOCK key wasn't on and that I typed very slowly. I was still denied access. I called electronic mail support to fix the problem immediately because I was not in the mood for computer system issues.

"E-mail support. May I help you?"

"Yes. This is Charmayne Ellis, and I'm calling about my e-mail account. My password isn't working."

"Hmm . . . Charmayne, what error message are you getting when you put your password in?"

"Um . . . it says, USER ACCESS REVOKED."

"Really? Let me take a look at your account."

I heard a flurry of typing and then silence. After a few moments there was more typing, and then the support person put me on hold. I couldn't stand being put on hold, even if I was asked nicely. And this support person didn't even ask. Maybe he didn't know that I was the president of the bank.

"Charmayne? Thanks for holding."

"Yes. I'm still here."

"Well, it looks like Corporate Information Security has put a freeze on your e-mail account. There is a fraud alert on your account. As soon as that is lifted, I can unfreeze your password."

"Info Security? What is going on? Who do I need to talk to over there?"

"I'm not sure, but their extension is—"

"I know the number."

I could feel myself getting irritated and a little bit worried. First a surprise board meeting, and then a frozen e-mail account? It seemed too coincidental. And what did they mean by *fraud alert*? Instead of dialing Corporate Information Security, I dialed Bishop Gordon's office.

"Praise the Lord."

"Bishop Gordon. It's Charmayne Ellis. What's going on? Who called the board meeting?"

"Charmayne. You used your maiden name. Was that done on purpose?"

"No."

"I am not at liberty to discuss anything with you now, Charmayne. Just be sure to attend the board meeting."

When I walked into the boardroom, I wore my brightest smile. Not one of the board members smiled back. A few of them actually looked angered by my smile, as if I had no right to it. I tried to read Pastor Jenkins's expression, but even he was wearing a poker face.

Bishop Gordon said, "Charmayne. Please have a seat."

There were several chairs available, but I selected the one that gave me the best view of all of the board members. I supposed that no matter what seat I chose, it was obvious that I was in the hot seat.

I said, "I would really appreciate us dispensing with any formalities and getting right to the point today. I've been put off all morning."

Bishop Donaldson replied, "I'll be happy to get to the point. But first, let me ask you . . . when is the last time you used your company credit card?"

"It's been weeks . . . I don't use it on a regular basis."

"Well, do you know of the card's whereabouts?"

"Yes. I keep it in a safe at home."

Bishop Donaldson cleared his throat. "Well, somehow it has made its way out of your safe and into the hands of your husband."

"What!"

"Flags are raised when there are more than two cash advances on the card in a five-day time span. The card was used at several different ATMs, and a grand total of five thousand dollars was withdrawn."

I scoffed, "Surely you don't think that I authorized or had anything to do with those transactions."

"Maybe not, but we pulled camera tape from each of

the locations where the card was used. It is clearly your husband. He seemed to know the PIN number by heart. That is what concerns the board."

I couldn't think of anything to say in my defense as I stared into ten pairs of unsympathetic eyes. I thought about the little piece of paper with the PIN number written on it that I had taped to the front of the card. I had no reason to believe that anyone was going to go into my safe and conduct unauthorized business.

Bishop Gordon asked, "Sister Moon, do you have anything to say in response?"

"What can I say, Bishop? Obviously Travis obtained the number from me. My question is, What are we going to do about it? I can write a check right now to cover any improper withdrawals. Let's dispense with this matter quickly so that I can get back to work."

"Before you take out your checkbook, let me give you all of the offenses," continued Bishop Gordon. "Travis has also used your company phone to rack up fifty thousand dollars in calls to pornographic nine-hundred numbers."

I shook my head in disbelief. "I don't understand—"

"And lastly, it has been brought to our attention that you approved Travis's twenty-thousand-dollar small-business loan. Don't you think that approving the loan for a fiancé is a conflict of interest?"

"All the documentation was there. The loan officer just needed a second opinion. What can I do to make this all go away?"

Bishop Donaldson said, "I'm afraid that it's not that easy, Charmayne. By allowing your husband to gain access to sensitive information, you have opened the bank up to a security breach and the possibility of losing thousands of dollars."

I asked in desperation, "Can we not just apprehend Travis and press charges? I won't object."

"If this was merely a financial matter, then perhaps. However, there have been more disturbing findings."

"Bishop Donaldson, what are you talking about?"

"Charmayne, when tech support upgraded your laptop, they performed a scan on your hard drive, including all the cookies and registry entries. There is an alarming amount of pornography downloaded onto your hard drive. Additionally, there are cookies for porn Web sites that correspond with charges placed on the company credit card account."

I could not open my mouth to respond; my face was frozen in shock. I couldn't even blink back the tears that were forming in the corners of my eyes. In the whole group of men, there was not one sympathetic face. Not even Pastor Jenkins, my own father in the gospel, seemed understanding. Some of the board members even looked disgusted . . . but they couldn't have been more disgusted than I was. It was my mate they were talking about.

Pastor Jenkins asked, "Daughter, were you aware that any of this was going on?" There was loving concern in his voice.

"Of course I wasn't, Pastor."

Bishop Donaldson said, "Well, whether you knew or not, you are still responsible for everything that has transpired. You must make this right by paying Grace Savings and Loan one hundred seventy-five thousand dollars."

"One hundred seventy-five thousand dollars! What if I don't pay?"

"Then we'll be forced to prosecute Travis. At the very least you would have to testify against him in court, but you may also be viewed as an accomplice."

"You would prosecute me?" I asked with tears burning my face. The thought of testifying in court terrified me. Everyone would know what Travis had done to me; there would be no hiding from it. I had no choice but to pay the bank almost everything I'd saved.

Pastor Jenkins said, "We wouldn't want to, Charmayne. But surely we can expect to receive your resignation immediately."

I was shocked beyond words. "My resignation? You want me to resign?"

"You must know that the president of the bank must be above reproach. We could've fired you. But since we know that you didn't conduct any fraudulent activity personally, we will allow you to resign with dignity. I need your resignation on my desk by the end of the day."

"But what about my projects? Will you even give me time to prepare my replacement?"

"There's no need for that," said Bishop Gordon. "Your biggest endeavor, the Teach a Man to Fish program, will be terminated. It posed too high of a financial risk to the bank anyway."

I got to my feet angrily. "This is not fair! I've given you and this bank my heart and soul! I've worked too hard to build this place up from nothing! And this is how you treat me?" I crumbled back into my seat lifelessly.

Pastor Jenkins said, "Charmayne, you know that if you need a letter of recommendation . . ."

"Thank you, Pastor."

Everyone started hastily packing their briefcases. I believed that my tears made them uncomfortable. They all left one by one, including my own pastor, so I assumed that the meeting was over. We had been in the conference room for less than half an hour. My career had been completely eradicated in under thirty minutes. It hardly seemed long enough to destroy hopes and dreams. You couldn't bake a cake in half an hour. You couldn't even watch a good movie in half an hour. Thirty minutes was just long enough for a television family to solve some trivial problem with lots of hugs, kisses, and *I love yous*. But to take everything I'd worked for all my life and make it disappear like a puff of smoke? Thirty minutes just didn't seem long enough for that.

CHAPTER
Twenty-seven

~⁊⁊~

Present

I awoke from yet another nightmare in a cold sweat. My silk nightgown clung to my body like a wet piece of tissue paper. I placed a hand on my chest and tried to regulate my breathing, which was shallow and fast.

Dr. King had warned me that I might remember my breakdown suddenly, and she had tried to prepare me for it. For some reason my conscious mind had blocked out the tragedy that had left scars all over my arms and hands; the memory was intact, though, and waiting to surprise me in the middle of the night.

When I realized that I was shivering, I vigorously rubbed both my arms. I wanted to call Lynette, but it was three o'clock in the morning. She had been there at the hospital when I was hurting. That much I had remembered. Lynette had done much more than I required from her as a friend.

I sat up in the bed and wiped the tears away from my face. Next, I inhaled and exhaled until my breathing was normal. Then I bowed my head and prayed to the Lord for peace, direction, and guidance. Finally I started from the beginning in my mind, and reconstructed the events that had landed me in the hospital.

Past

I woke up in a hospital emergency room. Confused and disoriented, the first thing I tried to do was sit up in the bed. I was shocked and afraid when I realized that I was strapped to the bed with two very short restraints. A nurse was attempting to take my blood pressure. For the moment I ignored the bandages that covered both my arms and hands. I couldn't remember why I needed them, and I wasn't sure that I wanted to.

"Are these arm restraints really necessary?" I asked the nurse. "I feel like a criminal."

"I'm sorry, Mrs. Moon. The doctor said that they need to stay on until the medication takes effect."

"First of all, do not call me Mrs. Moon. That is not my name. My name is Charmayne Ellis. Second . . . what medication?"

"I'm sorry. Your identification said Charmayne Moon. And the doctor has given you a mild sedative and some Valium to calm your nerves."

"Well, my identification is wrong. But you wouldn't know that. And I don't want any medication. I feel fine."

"Well, Ms. Ellis, according to your chart you had some sort of episode."

"What happened? I don't remember. Wait. I remember

baking a cake. But I don't remember taking it out of the oven."

"Don't worry about it. Everything has been taken care of."

"Really? How do you know? And why are my feet wrapped in bandages? They hurt."

"You've got twenty-two stitches in your right foot and thirty-seven in your left. You cut them up with the glass."

"What glass?"

"You really don't remember?"

I shook my head, annoyed at her questions. "When can I go home?"

"Not for a while. They have to make sure that you're not a danger to yourself or anyone else."

"You can't be serious! Of course I'm not a danger."

I said that, but I didn't know who I was trying to convince—the nurse or myself. The truth was, I had no idea what I'd done. All I knew was that it had something to do with glass. My feet, arms, and legs felt like they were on fire, so I assumed that I'd cut them doing something. What that something was, I couldn't quite place a finger on.

"Ma'am, I'm sure you're fine. And as soon as the doctor tells me, I'll get rid of those nasty restraints."

I was practically old enough to be the nurse's mama, and she was talking to me like I was a child or an imbecile. I was ravenous, but I was afraid to ask for anything to eat. I thought it might delay my getting home, and all I wanted to do was feel my head hit the pillow.

The nurse finally left to attend to a patient across the hall from me. She'd put my television on a channel that was showing old sitcoms. For some reason I didn't remember *The Jeffersons* being so hilarious. George had on a little suit with a kick pleat in the back, and it reminded me of Willie Brown, that guy Lynette had fixed me up with. I probably should have married him. I would've been cleaning hair dye out of the pillowcases, but I wouldn't have been sitting up in the hospital room looking like a fool.

The nurse popped her head into my curtain and said, "Your sister is here to see you. Should I send her in?"

Without thinking I replied, "Absolutely not! I don't want any visitors."

I heard Dayna arguing with the nurse in the hallway. "What do you mean she doesn't want to see me? I'm her sister!"

No way was I going to let Dayna see me tied to the bed like a lunatic. I did have some pride left. All I needed was for her to carry the information to Mama. By the time she finished embellishing the story, I'd be in a straitjacket and locked in a room with rubber walls. And all over a man. She'd probably think that would clinch her number one spot in Mama's heart. There was no way our mother would prefer the crazy one. I didn't need her faked concern to add to my frustration, especially when I was trying to convince the doctors that I wasn't a danger to anyone.

As a matter of fact, I didn't want anyone to see me like this, not even Lynette. I just wanted to close my eyes and wish the past hours away. Whatever had happened during this episode was going to have to be between me, the doctors, and the Lord.

After practically an eternity, a white-coated female walked into my room. I hoped she was a doctor, so that we could get the matter resolved. I was ready to go home and start my life over.

"Mrs. Moon. How are you feeling?"

"Please call me Ms. Ellis. And I'm feeling one hundred percent better. Can we take these arm restraints off?" I pleaded, hoping that I didn't sound too desperate.

"Yes. I don't see why not. There's nothing in here that you can break."

The petite, chocolate-colored doctor took off the restraints one by one. For some reason I was relieved by the fact that she was a black woman. Maybe she would understand what I was going through. From what I could tell, all I'd done was broken a few glasses. I could've had a real episode and taken a knife to Travis. But clearly I was not insane.

After I came out of the bathroom, the doctor was sitting in the orange armchair next to my bed. Instead of getting back in the bed, I had a seat in the yellow chair. I was ready to have a talk with the doctor, but there was no way I was getting back in that bed—not with those restraints still attached to the rails.

"Ms. Ellis, you may call me Dr. Taylor, or Barbara if you wish."

"I prefer Barbara, and you can call me Charmayne. You just saw me tied to a bed, so we can pretty much dispense with the niceties."

Barbara smiled, "Charmayne, it's good that you haven't lost your sense of humor. That's a very good sign."

"A sign that I'm not a total head case?"

"A sign that you're going to make it through whatever is troubling you."

Well, I didn't think that I'd ever doubted my ability to make it through this whole thing with Travis. I was just admitting to myself that something had snapped, but I didn't feel broken. I hoped it wasn't the medication making me feel at ease. If I was losing my mind, I wanted to be the first one to know about it. I didn't want a false sense of wellness.

"Barbara, what do you call what happened to me?"

"What do I call it? Well, some doctors would give a general diagnosis of a nervous breakdown."

"I didn't ask about some doctors—"

"I know. I would say that you're experiencing post-traumatic stress disorder. Do you know what that is?"

"I thought that was something war veterans went through."

"It's not just war veterans. It can happen to anyone who has gone through a traumatic experience. Tell me about yours."

"You sure like to get straight to the point, don't you?"

"You do want to go home as soon as possible, right?"

"Yes."

"So let's talk about it."

When I still hesitated, Barbara continued, "Look, Charmayne. Talking to me does not label you as a nutcase. Think of it as medical treatment. Your responses were generated by a reaction to stress in your central nervous system. This is a real medical issue that can respond to proper treatment and medication. Would you be hesitating if you'd had congestive heart failure?"

"Of course not."

"This is the same thing. Charmayne, you need to let yourself heal. So let's talk."

"I don't even know where to start."

"Try the beginning."

So I sat there and told Barbara everything. Starting from the first day that I met Travis in my office. When he fixed my chair. I told her how he swept me off my feet, and how I allowed myself to be caught up with all the pretty-girl treatment. I was fairly cool up until I started telling Barbara about how he ruined my career. I didn't notice that I was banging my fist on the side of the chair until one of my bandages ripped loose and blood started to trickle down my arm.

Barbara said, "Okay, Charmayne. Let's stop here for a moment."

"Okay." My voice was trembling. Barbara pretended not to notice the blood, either, so I just wiped it on the side of my hospital gown.

Barbara wrote something down in her notebook, and then looked up at me and smiled. She continued, "Now, Charmayne, I am positive that you can get past Travis fooling you into marriage. But I am concerned about the anger you've displayed at having your career destroyed."

"Do I not have the right to be angry about that?"

"You sure do. But we have to find some constructive ways to deal with that energy."

I knew I wouldn't be waiting long for the psychiatrist mumbo jumbo to start. *Constructive ways to deal with that energy?* What I wanted to do was break my foot off in Travis's behind. How constructive was that?

"I don't know what you want me to do, Barbara."

"Well . . . I don't want you to keep breaking glass."

"Okay . . . so I broke a few dishes . . . what's the big deal?"

"Is that all you remember?"

"Actually, I don't really remember too much of anything. I do recall breaking some glasses—which is obvious, from the cuts."

"Charmayne . . . you did more than break some dishes. You broke every single window in your home, and then you went outside barefoot and broke every window in your car. You were on your way to your neighbor's home swinging a bat when she called nine-one-one."

My God. I didn't know. I must've scared Clara half to death. I was going to have to apologize to her. No wonder they had me tied to the bed. Travis had turned me into a menace. Maybe I did need some medication.

"I don't know what to do," I responded in a very small, timid voice.

"Let me ask you, Charmayne, do you have a church home?"

"Yes. I do. But I can't go back there."

"You might need to do that. I've found that with a lot of people, medication doesn't help as much as going back to your roots. Religion is a place of rescue, where we can find peace."

"Peace." I repeated the word as if it were another language.

"Here's what I'm going to suggest. I think we'll keep you here for a couple more days, lightly medicated with Xanax, and then you can sign yourself out. I don't think you need a prescription. How do you feel about that?"

I nodded, even though I wasn't sure I agreed. I didn't want to stay one night in that place, but I was afraid to see what I'd done to my home.

Barbara asked, "Is there a friend you can call to bring

some of your things from home? It might make you feel
a little better."

As ashamed as I was of all this, Barbara was right yet
again. The first thing I did when I got settled into that
sterile little room was pick up the phone and call Ebony.
I needed my prayer partner and friend more than anyone
else.

"Hello."

"Hi, Ebony. This is Charmayne, I'm at Mount Sinai
General." I tried to make my voice sound normal.

"Is everything okay? Is it Travis?" she asked.

"No. I need you to do something for me. Go to my
house and get me two changes of clothing."

"Okay. Anything else?"

"Yes. Bring my Bible."

CHAPTER
Twenty-eight

❧❧❧

Past

I woke up in that hospital feeling utterly lost, not wanting even to open my eyes. But the good thing about being in that environment was that they wouldn't let me lie around and mope all day. I had to attend group sessions with folks who had a lot more problems than I had. There was a poor girl who was strung out on crack cocaine. Her name was Letha and she kind of attached herself to me. I think they put her in my room on purpose.

My first roommate was having electroshock therapy. I'd thought that was some archaic treatment no longer in use, but the poor woman must've had serious issues. Her husband and children were constantly by her side. It was sweet and all, but I needed some privacy.

The next morning I woke up to Letha standing over my bed. She actually scared me. Her hair was standing straight up in the air, and her lips were white like she'd been eating a whole box of powdered doughnuts.

"What's your name?" she said.

"Charmayne. Who are you?"

"I'm your new roommate. They moved Gracie on out of here."

"Well, what's your name?" I asked, trying not to turn my nose up. The girl's breath smelled as if she'd been munching on garbage.

"Letha. My friends call me Lee-lee."

"Well, Letha. It's nice to meet you."

"What? You don't wanna be my friend?"

"I didn't say that . . . but we're not friends yet. We just met."

"What yo' friends call you for short?"

"Char."

"I like that. It sounds like a rich girl's nickname. When I get me some money, I'm gone have to think of a new nickname. Lee-lee sounds kinda ghetto, I think."

Just when I thought I was going to pass out from holding my breath, the food service person came in with our breakfast. Letha had grits and bacon, and I had the works. Eggs, grits, bacon, and two slices of French toast. Letha smacked on her grits, which she added an unholy amount of sugar to, and looked over at my tray.

"Dag. You must be hungry."

I smiled. "I'm a growing girl."

Letha laughed out loud. "Yeah . . . you got that right."

I ignored her insult. From where I was sitting, I looked a sight better than she did. Fat and all.

"You could probably use a few more things on your plate, honey."

Letha looked down at her tray, "Maybe. I don't eat much, though. I just get high."

I thought, *At least she's honest.* That was the first step to getting some help. At the time, I was still in denial.

Letha licked her finger, "So what you in here for?"

"I don't think that's any of your business."

"They gone make you say it in the group sessions anyway. So you might as well get it out."

"Who is they?"

"The doctors. If you don't tell everybody your business in group, they make you stay longer."

I was skeptical, but Letha looked like she'd done the whole thing before. She probably knew the ropes.

"I broke some glass."

"Went and had yourself a nervous breakdown, huh?"

"So you're a doctor now?"

"My last roommate had one. Except she didn't break any glass. She cut off all her hair and all her kids' hair. She had four little girls and shaved them completely bald."

Letha stood up and walked over to the window. There was no way I'd be breaking that glass. It was so thick that even if I'd attempted to break it, I'd break my hand first. She breathed on the window and scribbled her name, like a little girl. Her legs were so skinny that from the back she looked no older than thirteen. Her little nightgown was open in the back and her underpants, which probably used to be white, were a dingy shade of gray.

"Okay, now it's my turn to ask a question. If you've been here before, why are you back?"

Letha replied, "'Cause I like gettin' high. They think I'm crazy 'cause I don't want to stop, even though I know it's gone kill me one day."

"Well, why don't you want to stop? Do you want to die?"

"Everybody dies. Sometimes I don't think it would be so bad."

I was thinking that this child must not have grown up in the church. Even backslidden folks didn't want to die and end up in hell. But when your life was hell on earth, it was probably hard to imagine anything worse.

I supposed that Letha didn't want to talk anymore, because she got into the bed and turned her back to me. I thought she was asleep, until I noticed that she was shaking. I walked across the hall to the nurses' station.

"Can somebody help Letha? She's lying in there shaking. Maybe she's got a chill or something."

The nurse didn't even look up from her paperwork. "Letha? She's just going through withdrawal. She's used to it. It'll pass."

Well, maybe she was used to it, but I wasn't. I went back into the room and did the only thing I knew to do. I laid hands on her and prayed. After a little while the shaking stopped. I looked down, and she was finally sleeping.

While she rested, I called Ebony and asked her to do some shopping. How could the child want to live when she probably only had one pair of panties to her name? And who would want to walk around all day in hospital clothes? No wonder she was starting to feel like a permanent resident.

Hours later, when she woke up, Letha was like a child on Christmas. She ripped through the neatly packed bags with a huge smile on her face. I'd even included some personal toiletries on my list.

"Why did you do all this?" she asked suspiciously.

"Because I wanted to."

She thought for a moment and squinted. "You ain't gay or nothing, are you? 'Cause I don't get down like that. Not even for no rocks."

I laughed out loud. "No, girl. Hasn't anyone ever just done anything nice for you?"

"No."

I didn't even know how to respond to that. Letha couldn't have been more than twenty years old, but to go that long and not remember anyone doing anything loving or caring was tragic. I used to always wonder how a person could ever start taking drugs. Letha showed me that day.

Letha asked timidly, "What was that thing you was doing when I was feenin'?"

"You mean when you were shaking? I was just praying for you."

"Like to God? Ain't nobody ever prayed for me, neither."

"Well, somebody just did."

She grabbed up a few of her new things and went into the bathroom. She looked back at me out of the corner of her eye. I supposed she was still trying to figure out my angle. I'd never truly met anyone who needed Jesus more than Letha. I wondered if that was why I'd gone through all the mess with Travis . . . just to get to the one space in time where Letha would be . . . so that she could get saved. It never occurred to me that she would be a tool in my own deliverance.

On my second and last day of being hospitalized, Lynette and Ebony brought First Lady Jenkins to see me. I was speechless, embarrassed, and furious at Lynette for bringing anyone else to witness my pitiful state. I looked a mess and felt even worse, and there First Lady was looking at me and feeling sorry for me.

I scowled at my friends as I said, "You brought First Lady."

"She made us bring her," replied Lynette apologetically.

"Well, I'm standing right here," said First Lady Jenkins, "and I can hear you talking about me."

"I'm sorry, First Lady. I didn't want anyone to see me like this, that's all. I *thought* Lynette knew that."

First Lady responded, "I'm here to pray for you. Your pride need not be an issue."

"We're all here to pray for you," Ebony added.

Sufficiently rebuked, I bowed my head as First Lady came and laid her hands on me while Ebony lifted her voice in prayer. Her touch was healing, as were the words of her prayer. Even Lynette was in agreement and whispering "Hallelujah" and "Thank you, Jesus."

When they were finished I said, "Thank you."

First Lady nodded and replied, "You're welcome."

Lynette started packing up my things, which didn't amount to much. I had a little bag of clothing and some books along with my Bible. I was waiting for an official discharge, but I didn't want to stay in that gray room a moment more than I had to.

"Dayna and I cleaned up your house," said Lynette casually, as if she weren't dropping another bomb on me.

"Dayna helped you?"

"Yes. She was so upset that you wouldn't see her when she came to visit. She wanted to do something. I couldn't stop her."

So Dayna knew about my breakdown, and Lynette had probably told her about Travis, too. She and Mama were no doubt having a field day wagging their tongues about my misfortunes.

Lynette attempted to explain her motives. "She's your sister. She cares about you. I didn't think it was right to keep her in the dark."

I didn't want to have the conversation in front of First Lady Jenkins, so I just nodded and sat on the edge of the bed. I would tell Lynette off later, but I kept civilized in front of First Lady.

First Lady asked, "So where is your husband? Why isn't he here with you? He's the cause of all of this, right?"

Obviously, she'd heard about the demise of my career. I answered, "Travis is gone."

She didn't ask for any more details, so I didn't volunteer any. Besides, I hadn't told anyone about Travis's affair with Les. It was bad enough that everyone knew about Grace Savings and Loan; they didn't need to add *all* of my shame to the gossip circuit. Ebony sat down on the bed next to me and put her arm around me. Her silent showings of support were as effective as her prayers.

First Lady pulled a business card out of her purse and handed it to me. She said, "Evangelist King is a Christian therapist. She has helped quite a few people get back on track. Me included."

I couldn't imagine First Lady Jenkins ever needing to see a therapist. She was so together, and such an example of perfection. I just couldn't see her falling apart and doing anything as extreme as I had.

I placed the card in my wallet, not sure if I'd use it. I

actually felt better after my two days of solitude. I'd spent time reading my Bible and letting the words minister to my broken spirit. I thought that if I could just get through the following days, I'd be okay—without anybody's medications or anybody's counseling.

Finally I was discharged and ready to go home. First Lady Jenkins had driven her own car, and Ebony had ridden with her. We said our good-byes in the parking lot. Lynette didn't look too thrilled about getting in the car alone with me. She knew me well.

As soon as we were on our way I said, "Lynette, first of all, thank you for everything you've done over these past couple of days."

"You didn't even have to thank me. That is what best friends are for."

I took a deep breath and continued. "But I didn't ask you to include my sister—or First Lady Jenkins, for that matter. I would've appreciated it if you'd asked me first how I felt about other people knowing. It wasn't like I went to the hospital with pneumonia."

"Now, wait a minute. As far as Dayna was concerned, I didn't tell her anything she didn't already know. The hospital contacted her, and your mama, too. I brought First Lady Jenkins because you needed someone to pray for you, and that's not my forte." Lynette's voice sounded hurt when she responded.

Immediately I was apologetic. Who was I to ream Lynette out when she was trying to help me in my time of need? She wasn't trying to put my business out in the streets; she just wanted me to get better.

"I'm sorry, Lynette. I guess it's just my pride talking."

"It's all right."

When we pulled up to my home, any remaining anger at Lynette completely disappeared. If anyone had put my business out in the street, it was me. Anybody who drove past the house would've realized that some type of disaster had happened. There were boards up on all the windows, and it looked abandoned. Realizing that I was the cause of the destruction was too much to bear. I broke down and sobbed. Lynette didn't say anything, but she cried, too.

Eventually I was able to stop crying long enough to go into my house. The boards didn't allow any sun to come in, so it was dark and dreary. Lynette went around turning on all the lights while I stood in the middle of my living room in awe.

She said, "I was going to order you some new windows, but they weren't going to be able to install them before you got home."

"It's okay. I needed to see this."

The message light on my answering machine was blinking. I was surprised that I'd had any phone calls while I was away. I pressed the button to hear the first message and cringed when I heard Travis's voice.

His message said, "Charmayne, we need to talk. I want to explain everything."

I felt my entire body shiver as I hastily erased the message. The next two messages were from him as well, all asking that I reconsider my decision. He even declared his undying love in the last message.

Lynette asked, "Are you sure things are over between the two of you? Maybe you could work it out."

I looked at Lynette and shook my head. She only knew part of the story, so of course she would think that there was something salvageable to my marriage. But I knew the truth, and so did Travis, which is why I found it hard to believe that he would have the audacity to pick up the phone and call me.

After I assured Lynette that I was not going to fall apart again, she left me alone to contemplate my next steps. The first thing I did was locate a window retailer that would come and replace all of my windows the next day. Next, I called Evangelist King and made an appointment to see her. After seeing my home, it was obvious to me that I needed help. I hoped Dr. King was as good as First Lady thought she was.

CHAPTER
Twenty-nine

❦

Past

Dayna and Mama sat slack-jawed as I recounted an edited version of what had happened with me and Travis. I would've preferred not to tell them anything, but I couldn't let them just think I was crazy. Besides, I felt some sense of gratitude to my sister for helping Lynette clean my home. She didn't have to do that for me. I hoped it meant that this crisis I was having would supersede any animosity still between us.

In response to my story Dayna said, "I knew that brother was too good to be true."

Before I could respond Mama added her two cents. "That's what happens when you hook up with them pretty men. They ain't no good. Next time, stay in your own league and you might stay married."

I could feel salty tears stinging my eyes, but I refused

to let them fall in their presence. I didn't know why I'd expected them to be sympathetic to my situation. By their responses, it was obvious that they'd formed their opinion even before hearing anything I had to say.

I answered Mama. "You are right, Mama. I will stay in my own league in the future. I could've done much better than Travis. I played myself short."

Dayna let out a giggle that she only barely tried to stifle by covering her mouth with her hand. I wanted to slap her and give myself something to laugh about. Instead, I took the high road and said, "Thanks for helping clean up my place."

"Well, what else was I supposed to do? You wouldn't let me in your hospital room. I was hoping that Travis would be home, and maybe he could give me some answers."

I felt my irritation escalate into full-fledged anger. She'd only helped Lynette to assuage her curiosity. It had nothing to do with caring about me or about being a good sister. I didn't know why I'd expected her to be any different than I knew her character to be.

"About that," said Mama, "why you want to go around tearing up all the stuff you paid for with your own money? If that man did you wrong and you wanted to get back at him why didn't you tear up some of his stuff?"

"Mama, please . . ." I was tired of trying to explain myself to her.

"I mean, seriously, Charmayne. That doesn't make any sense," Dayna chimed in.

I bit my lower lip in an attempt to maintain my composure and stood up. I wasn't going to take any more of their abuse. I walked out of Mama's apartment without even saying good-bye.

When I got to the car, I glanced up at Mama's window and saw the two of them glaring out at me. I twisted my own face into a scowl and swung open my car door. After I drove off, I immediately felt a sense of relief. I turned my palms over on the steering wheel and noticed little red indentations from where I'd had my fists balled up.

I took a deep breath and started to cry. It wasn't fair that I couldn't go to my own mama for sympathy and support. She was supposed to tell me that everything was going to be all right. And wasn't my sister supposed to have my back at all times? I violently wiped away the tears. I was angry at myself for caring about what Mama and Dayna thought, and angry that I'd allowed them to get to me. I planned to do much better in the future, even if that meant not telling them anything about my life.

It was with much trepidation that I entered Dr. King's office. Truthfully, I didn't want to be there, but I'd spent my first weekend home crying and praying. In my desperation I'd even contemplated calling Travis, just to hear him out. Although I didn't want to admit needing a therapist, I truly did.

There was no receptionist—nor any receptionist's desk, for that matter. It looked like I'd walked into someone's apartment. I was checking the outside of the door to make sure I had the right office when Dr. King emerged from a room in the rear.

"You must be Charmayne. Welcome to my sanctuary. Have a seat."

I looked around the office and tried to figure out where I, the patient, was supposed to sit. It wasn't obvious from the office's setup. I chose a deep purple chaise that looked comfortable. Dr. King smiled. I wondered if she was able to tell something about me from my seat selection.

"Would you like something cool to drink? I have water and herbal iced tea."

"Yes. Iced tea would be fine." I was glad she asked, my throat was parched.

Dr. King talked while she poured two large glasses. "So how is First Lady Jenkins? I haven't seen her in a while."

"She's doing well."

"That is good to hear. I'll have to give my friend a call."

She handed me the tea and then sat down across from me on a love seat. My eyes widened when she kicked off her cloth slippers and put her feet up. I had never met a therapist like her before.

Dr. King asked, "So where would you like to start?"

"I don't know."

"Something brought you here."

I replied, "A two-day hospital stay brought me here."

"Well, let's talk about that."

"I broke out all the windows in my house, and they took me to the hospital."

Dr. King sat up. "What were you thinking about when you broke the windows?"

"I don't know. I don't remember doing it," I replied honestly.

Dr. King took a long sip from her tea. She looked as if she was in deep thought. I didn't think I'd given her enough information to form any conclusions, but she was thinking nonetheless.

"We'll work our way up to that, then. For now, why don't you just tell me a little bit about yourself."

"I'm thirty-six years old, currently unemployed and single. My dad died when I was eighteen, so now it's just me, my mom, and my younger sister, Dayna."

Dr. King cracked a little smile. "Charmayne, you just told me about some situations. I want to know about you. What do you like to do? What are your hobbies? What makes you stand up and take notice?"

It took me a moment to respond. It had been a long time since anyone had genuinely wanted to know about me.

"I like to roller-skate in the park and cook. I'm a really good cook. I enjoy being active at my church and reading historical fiction. An educated black man makes me stand up and take notice."

Dr. King grinned, and the entire room seemed to brighten. "All right. Now we're getting somewhere. I enjoy singing, although my voice is only fit to be heard in my shower, and I do needlepoint projects in my spare time. I love reading, and a wonderful fragrance will make me stand up and take notice."

"A wonderful fragrance?"

"Yes. Like a pie baking in the oven or a field of lavender. I am guided by my sense of smell. I'm one of those people who associate events with smells. I've been doing that since I was a child."

I felt totally at ease with Dr. King. By the end of that first session, it was as if I'd known her for years. I decided to save my story of Travis for later and talked about Mama, Dayna, and my relationship with Lynette. Dr. King didn't judge or scold, she just listened like an old friend would've listened. When I was done talking, Dr.

King held both my hands and prayed with me. I felt connected to her in the Spirit. Her soothing words gave me reason to hope for the first time since Travis had walked out of my life.

Still feeling encouraged by my first meeting with Dr. King, I walked into the health club determined to join. It was time for me to do something serious about my weight, without having a man as my motivation. To me, getting control of my eating addiction was one of the first steps in regaining control of my world.

I took one look around the spacious gymnasium and was daunted before I even got started. There were a large number of hard-bodied men and women—some of them appeared to be chiseled out of stone. My cellulite rolls seemed out of place in the same room with such physical perfection.

Just as I was about to leave and do my Tae-Bo tape at home, a bubbly young woman approached me. "Hi! I'm Sheila. May I help you with anything today?"

I took the plunge, and there was no turning back. "Uh, y-yes. I guess so."

"Are you interested in trying out some of the equipment?"

I nodded. She seemed pleased at my response. Maybe I was her first customer of the day.

The young woman described herself as a Personal Fitness Consultant. She said that it was her job to help me construct a plan that would allow me to reach all my fitness goals. She would work with a nutritionist to create a meal plan for me that would maximize my weight loss, and develop a workout regimen that I could truly stick with.

Sheila made everything sound good, but I was a bit concerned about working out. I'd never done anything athletic in my life. In school the closest I came to sports was playing table tennis in gym class—and that was mandatory.

I said, "I've never really exercised before so I'm totally out of shape. I don't want to hurt myself."

Sheila looked perplexed for a moment, as if I'd made her lose her thought. Then as if struck with an epic revelation, she replied, "I've got something perfect for you. Follow me to the aquatic center."

I burst into laughter. I guessed I hadn't stressed to Sheila how completely nonathletic I was. I didn't know how to swim, although classes had been offered at my high school. I had simply refused to put on a swimsuit.

I followed her into the aquatic center anyway and immediately was impressed with the size of the pool. The senior aquatic aerobics class had just ended. I saw men and women in their sixties and seventies emerge from the pool, completely unashamed at what time and age had done to their bodies. They looked as if they were having fun, and Sheila assured me that they had just endured a rigorous workout.

She said, "Some of the members of the senior class can swim up to ten laps in the pool."

"But I can't swim."

Again, I had seemed to perplex Sheila. She quickly rebounded. "In the water aerobics class, there's no actual swimming. That might help jump-start your fitness routine."

Just as I was about to raise another objection, a woman emerged from the dressing rooms and walked toward the pool. She was a big girl—even bigger than I was—yet she confidently strode across the pool deck as if she weighed 110. I would've definitely been wrapped in a towel and cover-up, but she wore only her modest one-piece bathing suit. I watched in awe as she perched at the edge of the pool, dove in, and swam a full length of the pool in under sixty seconds.

Inspired by the sheer bravery of the woman, I interrupted Sheila's spiel. "Do you all offer swimming classes?"

"Yes. On Mondays and Wednesdays at five thirty in the evening."

I grinned as the big girl completed her fourth length of the pool. "Sign me up."

CHAPTER
Thirty

~∞~

Present

I sat in Dr. King's office feeling as if I'd had yet another setback. After vividly remembering my breakdown, the feelings of anger that I'd had for Travis were greatly intensified. I wanted to hunt him down myself and exact my own personal brand of justice.

I vehemently expressed my frustration to Dr. King. She listened patiently while I ranted on and on about Travis deserving prison time. When I was done, I sat back on the couch and waited for Dr. King to agree with me.

Instead she asked, "What sparked this new anger, Charmayne? I thought we were making a lot of progress in the opposite direction."

"I remembered, Dr. King. I remembered breaking down, and how hopeless I felt when I was breaking that glass. It's not fair that Travis should get away with making me feel like that. The God I serve wouldn't allow such an injustice."

Dr. King nodded. "I see. You want Travis to pay, and you want to be there to see it. It would be even better if you could inflict his punishment, right?"

"Absolutely."

"And then what would you gain?"

A jaded-sounding cackle escaped my lips. "A wonderful sense of satisfaction."

"I don't think that will happen. As a matter of fact, I think it's time we started talking about forgiveness."

I retorted defensively, "I have forgiven him, but that doesn't mean he shouldn't reap what he's sown."

"Forgiveness is more than a word. I can tell you what you should be doing with reference to Travis, but I'm going to let God tell you. Open your Bible to Matthew five, verses forty-three through forty-five, and read them out loud."

I opened my Bible and read.

> *Ye have heard that it hath been said, Thou shalt love thy neighbour, and hate thine enemy.*
>
> *But I say unto you, Love your enemies, bless them that curse you, do good to them that hate you, and pray for them which despitefully use you, and persecute you;*
>
> *That ye may be the children of your Father which is in heaven: for he maketh his sun to rise on the evil and on the good, and sendeth rain on the just and on the unjust.*

I knew the verses well; in fact, I'd even used them when giving advice to one of my sisters in Christ. It was always easy for me to give counsel, but adhering to it myself was a whole other issue, especially when we were referring to a man who had ruined my life.

Dr. King said, "Look closely at verse forty-four. What are the verbs in the passage pertaining to you?"

I responded slowly, "Let's see . . . *love, bless, do good,* and *pray.*"

"What about the verbs for your enemy?"

"*Curse, hate, despitefully use,* and *persecute.*" I felt myself getting angry just reading that list.

Dr. King said, "So you see, Charmayne, God knows you been done wrong. He wants you to forgive anyway."

I said flatly, "I know that Jesus wants me to forgive that man."

"So what's the problem?"

"He doesn't deserve it. Anyway, how can I forgive him when my life is still a wreck?"

"You've lost over seventy pounds, you have a rewarding career, and you're financially independent. Where's the wreck?"

I reflected for a moment before answering. It was true that I didn't have exactly what I'd lost, but I couldn't look at my life and not see restoration. Jesus had restored my confidence through the shedding of pounds, and He had given me a job that I truly looked forward to going to every day. Even the feeling of loneliness that had led me to Travis in the first place had been replaced by a newfound purpose. Yet I still wasn't satiated. I still wanted vengeance.

"You're right, Dr. King."

"The last step in your healing process is forgiveness. And stop acting like you're doing him a favor. Do it for your own freedom. The Bible says that by forgiving you become a child of your Father in heaven. Don't you want to be a reflection of Him?"

There was only one answer to that question. Of course I wanted to reflect God's nature in my own imperfect life. But saying a thing and doing a thing were two different matters.

I replied, "Don't just tell me what I need to do, Dr. King, tell me how to do it."

It was Dr. King's turn to pause before replying. I hoped that I hadn't stumped her, because that was not my intention. I wanted to know where to look for forgiveness in a heart turned cold against Travis. I didn't want to be accountable to Jesus for not extending mercy to Travis. It was bad enough that he'd taken my material possessions; I didn't want him to be the cause of my spending an eternity alienated from God.

Dr. King finally answered my question. "You can start by forgiving yourself."

"What do you mean?" I felt myself an innocent victim; I didn't think that I needed forgiveness.

"You haven't truly excused yourself for choosing Travis in the first place. I guarantee that being at peace with your own choices will free you to forgive Travis."

I considered with interest Dr. King's theory. It was true that I was still kicking myself for getting duped by Travis. I was still telling myself that I had been stupid to believe he'd ever loved me. I still thought that there had been signs of his ill intentions, and that I'd purposely ignored them.

I'd had so many good friends warn me of my actions, especially Ebony. I remembered how sad she was when she refused to be a bridesmaid in my wedding. I knew that I should've listened to her and to the voice of the Lord. My disobedience had cost me so much. Forgiving myself had not entered into my mind, even though I'd asked God for forgiveness for my sin of disobedience.

Dr. King continued, "Are you still doing those affirmations?"

"I haven't done one in a while."

"Well, we're going to do one right now. Repeat after me. I am beautiful, gifted, and talented."

I stated confidently, "I am beautiful, gifted, and talented."

"I am God's woman, capable of great things."

I liked what she was saying, so the words were easy to repeat. "I am God's woman, capable of great things."

"I have made unwise choices, but I will recover."

"I have made unwise choices, but I will recover."

Dr. King finished the affirmation by saying, "I have sown in tears and will reap with songs of joy."

Tears welled up in my eyes as I stammered the words. "I-I have s-sown in tears and will r-reap with songs of joy."

I put my head in my hands and sobbed out loud. I had said the words, but I didn't know if I truly believed them. I felt that I'd never be whole again, and that singing songs of joy was a long way off.

I reflected on how God forgives us for sins. All we have to do is repent and we're washed clean with His precious blood, as if the sin never happened in the first place. I was filled with peace at the thought of His love. I wanted so much to see myself as Christ did. I prayed in my spirit. *Lord, help me to change my perception. Help me to see myself as your daughter.*

Dr. King smoothed the hair out of my face and handed me a tissue. She sat down beside me and took both my hands in hers. Her hands were incredibly steady and secure, while mine shook uncontrollably.

"Go ahead and cry. Remember the tears of Rizpah?" I thought back to Rizpah and her season of mourning. "These are not wasted tears. They have a purpose."

CHAPTER

Thirty-one

~∽~

Present

When the director of Dove's Haven told me that she wanted to have a very important meeting with me, I instantly became nervous. The last time I'd been called into a meeting with my superiors, I'd lost my job. I didn't know what I'd do if I was fired again. Dove's Haven had become more than a job for me. I had become totally invested in the women I'd helped, and that investment made for many success stories.

Besides Celeste, I'd used my contacts to place six women in jobs that would do more than give them a minimum-wage paycheck. Celeste was a research analyst for a lawyer friend of mine. All of the women were in career positions that would change their lives if they wanted it. And most of them seemed to really want it.

I walked into Rhonda's office wearing my confident

face. That was another thing I liked about Dove's Haven. Everyone was on a first-name basis with everyone else. There was a familial atmosphere that was important to some of the women who had never experienced family.

"Good afternoon, Charmayne. Have a seat." I relaxed a little. Rhonda sounded entirely too cheerful to be firing anyone.

"Good afternoon." I sat in front of Rhonda's desk as she finished typing something on her computer.

When she finished, she turned to me and smiled. "Charmayne, I have great news, and an offer."

"An offer?"

"Well, let me start by saying that Dove's Haven was awarded a two-hundred-thousand-dollar grant from the Parthenon Corporation!" Rhonda exclaimed.

"They're software distributors, right?"

"Yes. They're giving grants to faith-based organizations that are making a difference in the community."

"That is great news. That money will do these women a lot of good."

Rhonda continued, "Wait. There's more. I believe that we received that grant because I used Celeste's story as a case study in our grant proposal."

I nodded enthusiastically. "That was brilliant. She has a tremendous testimony."

"And she had a tremendous mentor. I was wondering if you'd like to expand your role. We want to launch a job readiness program for the entire community, and I'd like for you to direct it."

"I'd love to." It was a huge undertaking, but I felt ready.

"I'm happy to hear you say that! I thought you were going to say no."

My smile must've stretched from one side of my face to the other. The job offer was an answered prayer.

I replied confidently, "I just can't wait to get started. I'm going to compile all the ideas I have and present them to you next week."

Rhonda laughed. "I'm glad you know what to do, because I really didn't know where to start."

"Just leave it to me."

After hearing the good news at Dove's Haven, not even spending my lunch hour with Dayna was going to steal any of my joy. Actually, the lunch date was an olive branch from me to her. I didn't want our relationship to be as strained as it was. She was the only sister I had, and I knew that one day we'd need each other.

I had chosen an informal setting for our lunch—the food court in the mall. I saw that Dayna was already in line at the Taco Shack, so I headed for the Japanese grill. I ordered chicken teriyaki with no rice and found a table with a view overlooking the Cuyahoga River. When Dayna joined me I was watching an elderly couple stroll past the boats hand in hand. I wondered if I'd have someone to share my old age with.

"What in the world is that?" asked Dayna, referring to my food.

"Chicken teriyaki. I see you got your usual mystery-meat burritos."

She laughed. "Well, mystery meat or not, it tastes good."

"I'll remind you that you said that when the doctor is unclogging your arteries."

"Oh, I forgot. You're Miss Healthy now. How many pounds have you lost?"

"Seventy-three."

Dayna's eyes widened. "That's a lot of weight. Congratulations."

"Thank you."

It was comical to me that my sister and I were doing the small-talk thing. We both knew that we were here to talk about what had happened on Christmas. It had been almost six months and we still hadn't talked about the feelings Dayna had expressed on that day.

After a brief, uncomfortable silence, Dayna asked, "So how are you doing, Charmayne? Me and Mama are worried about you."

"I'm getting there. It's going to be awhile before I'm back to normal," I replied honestly.

"So the therapy is working out?"

"It's helping a great deal."

Dayna nodded. "I'm glad. I don't like to see you falling apart. You know you're the strong one."

It was true. I had always been the strong one in our family—the one everyone else leaned on. When our father died, Mama had fallen apart and Dayna had pretended that it was all a dream. At age eighteen I had made the funeral arrangements and taken care of insurance and outstanding debts. I had grieved behind closed doors when everyone had gone home.

When I didn't reply, Dayna continued, "You know it's time to start planning Mama's birthday party."

"It's only June, Dayna. Her birthday's not until September."

"Why leave it to the last minute?"

I shrugged. "Why do we have to have a party? Why can't we just do something as a family?"

Dayna said, "If it's about the money, I will pay for mostly everything."

She obviously thought I was broke. "It's not a money thing, Dayna. I just thought that me, you, and Mama could do a spa day or something."

"You'd actually want to spend an entire day with me and Mama?"

"Sure."

Dayna clasped her hands together and looked intently into my face. "Charmayne, I need to say something to you and I don't want you to interrupt. Just let me get it out."

"Okay—"

"You're interrupting already."

I placed one hand over my mouth to ensure silence for Dayna's speech.

She continued, "I'm sorry about Christmas. I don't ever want us to fight on the holiday again. It just seems like my jealousy gets the best of me sometimes."

"You're jealous of me? But why, Dayna? You have it all."

"I guess we can both look at each other's lives and find something to envy," she said reflectively. "But we're sisters, and I want us to be there for each other. Please forgive me."

"I forgive you," I responded simply. Before I'd begun therapy with Dr. King, I would've tried to find something that I'd done wrong in the situation and offer my own apology. But I hadn't done anything to apologize for, so I offered only my forgiveness.

"Was your relationship with Travis already in trouble when he didn't show up for Christmas?" Dayna asked. I was sure that she'd been dying to ask me that question. I wondered what had taken so long.

"No, it wasn't, not to my knowledge, but then again it was pretty much doomed from the beginning. There is much that you don't know about the situation with Travis."

"Are you going to tell me?"

"Maybe. When I'm ready." This response was also birthed directly out of my therapy. I didn't owe anyone an explanation for why my marriage had broken down.

"Well, even if you never tell me all that happened, I'm still praying for you."

I smiled warmly at my younger sibling. "That's what sisters are for."

CHAPTER
Thirty-two

~&~

Present

Lynette and I were having a celebratory spa day in honor of my completing therapy with Dr. King. I'd had my final session at the beginning of the week, and for the most part I felt healed and delivered. Of course, the healing and delivering had come from Jesus; Dr. King was just my guide along the way.

The spa day was Lynette's idea. She'd had to twist my arm to make me spend hundreds of dollars on pampering. No matter how much money I had in the bank, I would forever be frugal. She'd finally convinced me by reminding me how much money I'd spent buying clothes for Travis. She was right, too. If I could go on a shopping spree for a man who was robbing me blind, then I could surely afford a pedicure and a massage.

We sat in the lounge area in big fluffy robes, waiting

to be called back for our massage. I sat back on a comfortable chaise and closed my eyes. For the first time ever, I'd opted for the full-body massage. I'd never gotten one before, because I was embarrassed about my body. I didn't want anyone seeing all my rolls up close. But since I'd shed the pounds, I found myself doing a lot of things I wouldn't normally do.

"Girl, he is checking you out," commented Lynette.

I opened my eyes. "Who?"

"That fine dark chocolate brotha who just walked in."

The man Lynette was referring to was indeed fine, and he did appear to be looking in our direction.

"I think he's checking *you* out. Are you wearing your wedding band, you little fast-tailed heifer?" I was trying to keep from laughing out loud.

"Believe me, Charmayne, I know when a man is looking at me. Why don't you make eye contact with the man?"

I waved my hand in dismissal of Lynette and closed my eyes again. I was in no way ready to enter the romance and dating arena. I certainly wasn't about to try my hand at flirting. I'd heard that it was an art—an art that I had not mastered.

A few moments later I felt Lynette nudge me in the ribs. Ready to fuss at her for ruining my relaxation, I opened my eyes. Standing in front of me was the fine brotha who was formerly standing across the room.

"How are you beautiful ladies enjoying your spa day?"

I was speechless, so Lynette replied, "We are having a blast. What about yourself?"

"I'm just getting a manicure today. I've got a business meeting this afternoon, so I don't have time for my usual facial."

Lynette frowned. "Oh, that's too bad. My friend Charmayne was just going to invite you to join us for lunch."

My eyes widened in horror. Lynette would never change. It was her continuing mission to make sure I was happy. In her eyes, happiness meant having a man. I seriously could've wrung her neck.

I said, "Yes. It's too bad. Maybe next time."

Mr. Fine Chocolate-Brotha smiled widely, exposing his beautiful veneers. "Here's my business card. Call me later, maybe we can have dinner."

I reached for the card. "Perhaps."

He looked down at his watch and was suddenly in a hurry. "I've really got to run."

After the man was a safe distance away, I rolled my eyes at Lynette. She put on her innocent face.

"What?" she asked, knowing full well what she'd done.

"Don't do that mess, especially if you're going to hook me up with a loser."

"What makes you think he was a loser?" she asked, her voice full of curiosity at my newfound wisdom.

I shared my observations. "First of all, the brother's shoes were jacked up and ran over. Any man of substance wouldn't be wearing those raggedy shoes to a business meeting. And his so-called gold watch was fake. It had already started to tarnish."

"You saw all that in a two-minute conversation?"

I nodded and leaned back again, closing my eyes. Travis had caused me to be extra cautious when evaluating men. I was constantly on the lookout for any hucksters or con artists.

Lynette continued, "Maybe he was just trying to impress you."

"A brotha can impress me by being real."

"Don't be getting all jaded on me now. Every man is not Travis."

I knew that sincere, honest men were still present in the world, but I felt they were as scarce as a blooming flower in winter. I even thought that there was still hope for me, and that I might find love one day.

I replied, "I know, but I am not about to repeat my mistakes. The Lord only has to show me once."

"If you ask me, you're taking all the fun out of love."

I shook my head and marveled at Lynette's naïveté. She had been fortunate to find a good man who loved her and the Lord. But who could blame me if I treated love like serious business and not fun and games?

I answered, "I think you should leave my love life up to me and Jesus."

CHAPTER
Thirty-three

Present

"Are you ever going to talk to me again?"

I blinked rapidly and tried to stop myself from trembling. Headed out for work, I'd stepped into my driveway—and a shadowy figure came from behind the bushes. It took me a few moments to focus and realize that the figure was Travis and that he was talking to me. This man was not the charmer who had conned his way into my heart. He hadn't shaved in a few days, and he needed a haircut. There was nothing debonair about his faded jeans and worn-out T-shirt.

He asked another question. "Do you miss me, Charmayne?"

I responded with a question of my own. "Why are you here, Travis?"

"I wanted to know if it was really over between us.

I've broken things off with Les. I was hoping you'd give me another chance."

After the initial shock of seeing Travis standing before me, I became strangely serene. I stood tall and lifted my chin in defiance to his presence. There was nothing he could say or do to affect me. At one time I'd had many questions for him that I felt required an answer. But seeing him in the flesh was enough to sate my curiosity. He was the one who looked helpless and insecure, as if he was anticipating some heinous act of vengeance from me.

"I want nothing to do with you, Travis."

Travis smiled. "You can't say that you don't want me. I know you too well."

Annoyed, I responded, "You don't know me at all. I really need to be going. Is there anything else I can do for you?"

Ignoring my tone, he said, "You look good, Charmayne."

My former self—that low-self-esteem, desperate-for-love former self—would have shuddered in awe at the compliment. The new me was not impressed by Travis or his smooth-talking tongue. I placed a hand on my slimmed and toned hip and clicked my two-hundred-dollar shoes on the pavement.

"You don't," I replied bluntly. Indeed, Travis looked like he'd been through some trials and tribulations.

He gasped and placed his hand over his chest in a *clutch-the-pearls* motion. I didn't know if he was truly shocked or still trying to play mind games with me. I almost laughed out loud when I realized that I didn't even care.

I moved toward my car. I hoped that Travis would take

the hint and move on—out of my driveway and out of my life. He just stood there, slumped over, looking at me with a slight grin on his face. I couldn't believe I'd ever allowed him to gain so much power over me. But that was truly a thing of the past.

He took a step toward me, and I took a defensive stance. I didn't know what he was there to do, but he would not be harming me without a fight.

Travis laughed. "Girl, you ain't got to be all like that! I'm not here to hurt you."

"Then what are you here for?" I asked.

"I wanted to make sure you were okay. I'd heard that you'd lost it for a while. I never meant for that to happen. I thought you were stronger than that."

I felt heat begin to churn in my stomach. I reached for the door handle and got in my car. I needed to get Travis out of my sight before he said something that he would regret.

"I'm stronger than you'll ever know," I said through clenched teeth and a window that was only opened a crack.

I pulled out of my driveway so quickly that the tires squealed. I left Travis standing there looking after me. A peek in the rearview mirror told me that he hadn't finished; there was more he'd wanted to say.

One thing that he hadn't said was *I'm sorry.* In a perfect world he would've been on his knees begging my forgiveness, and graciously I would've given it to him. But there was nothing perfect about my world.

A part of me wanted to do a U-turn, go back home, and demand an apology. Truthfully, though, I didn't know what to do with an apology from Travis. A hollow *I'm sorry* from the man who had destroyed my world would not compensate. It would surely be too little, too late.

As I drove farther from my house, I felt the tension leave my body. I was surprised to feel the wetness on my face. I didn't know that I'd had any tears left to shed for Travis. I remembered Rizpah's tears and wondered if my own tears had anything to do with the man.

CHAPTER
Thirty-four

◈

Present

It had taken me awhile, after my ordeal with Travis, to get back to worshipping in the house of God. I was self-conscious, thinking that everyone knew my story and that they were sitting in judgment of me. It was nearly impossible for me to focus on Jesus when I was busy making sure no one was focusing on *me*.

When I finally got past my pride issues, my worship was elevated to another level. I was walking in the doors with praise on my lips; I was bringing the worship in with me from home. There were still folks who looked at me sideways, but I refused to let them hinder my praise.

On this one Sunday morning I was especially high in the Spirit. I was expecting an awesome move of

God, although I had no idea what it might be. The air seemed almost electrified with the presence of the Lord. I waved my arms, welcoming and ushering in His Spirit.

The choir began to sing "When the Saints Go to Worship," and I could feel the atmosphere intensify even further. I watched people start to go and lie before the altar before anyone started to lead a prayer or preach a word. A thin figure stumbled down to the altar wearing blue jeans and a hooded sweatshirt. I couldn't tell if the person was male or female, but obviously he or she needed prayer.

The altar call lasted over an hour, with people getting up at their leisure. Some were led back to their seats, and others downstairs to prepare for baptism. I heard the person in the hooded sweatshirt accept Christ as savior through loud, wounded sobs.

Pastor Jenkins situated himself behind the pulpit and began to speak. "I feel the Lord in this place today. Hallelujah! I don't even need to preach the word this morning. The word has already gone forth!"

Four people came up from downstairs dressed for the baptism pool. One of them looked familiar from a distance, but I was unsure. I'd have to get a closer look after service was over.

The baptisms were done one after another, with loud applause after each one. Our congregation was always excited when somebody went down in the water. A newly baptized person could expect plenty of hugs and congratulations after the service ended.

It was when they lined the new members up in front of

the church that I finally recognized the hooded figure. It was Letha from the hospital! Her short hair was wet from the baptism pool and slicked back. Her hands were stuffed in her pockets. She looked unsure but joyful nonetheless.

I was the first person to greet her after service concluded. She hugged me tightly—as if her life depended on it. "I'm so glad you're here! I thought this was the church name you gave me, but I wasn't sure."

"I'm glad that *you're* here. How are you doing?"

Letha looked down at her feet. "I ain't doing too good. I'm trying to get clean, but it's hard. The closest thing I've ever felt to peace was when you prayed for me that day. I want to feel that all the time."

I felt tears spring to my eyes. "God is going to do it, girl. He is so happy that you finally decided to come to Him. He's going to heal you, in the name of Jesus!"

"What about you? The Lord was with you but you were breaking glass?" asked Letha.

"Honey, you're right. The Lord was with me, but I was disobedient to His voice and to His word. That path took me farther than He ever meant me to go. But the Lord is faithful. He healed me of my pain and broken heart. He can do that for you, too."

"I believe it."

The prayer and deliverance team came to pray for Letha before she left the sanctuary. After they were done, I offered to drive her to the closest rehabilitation center in the area. After a moment of hesitation, she accepted my offer, and decided to do what she knew was necessary.

All the way to the center, I listened to Letha tell me her life story. The girl had been abused in more ways than anyone I'd ever heard—and by people she loved and trusted. She had been using the drugs as a way to forget. As long as she was high, she didn't feel any pain or inner turmoil.

I began to marvel about how good God is. Only He could take and use me for His purpose, even at my lowest point. At my most broken, He had used me to plant a seed in the heart and mind of a lost soul.

It was at that moment of revelation that I truly forgave myself. I forgave myself the impatience and lonely desperation. I forgave myself the foolish and impetuous choices. And lastly, I forgave myself for not waiting on God to send me the man he would have me marry.

Although I forgave myself—I would never forget. Remembering that pain was only going to make me stronger. Sharing my heartbreak with another lonely sister might ease her own suffering.

When I pulled up in front of the rehabilitation center, Letha looked at me and started crying. "I'm afraid. What if I can't do it?"

"You can't do it alone. But Jesus is with you." I opened up my Bible to Hebrews 13:5–6 and read the verses aloud.

For he hath said, I will never leave thee, nor forsake thee.

So that we may boldly say, The Lord is my helper, and I will not fear what man shall do unto me.

Letha nodded as I continued, "He will never leave you or forsake you. Do you believe that?"

"I believe it because you said it."

I pointed toward heaven and back to the Bible. "Believe it because *He* said it."

READING GUIDE

1. Charmayne is inclined to deny the relevance of her spiritual health to her psycho-emotional condition. In your experience, what is the connection between our spirit self (1 Corinthians 2:6–16) and our physical or mental health?

2. Does Charmayne strike you as being selective or picky, possessing high standards or being impossible to please? Why? How do you make decisions about an eligible dating or marriage partner?

3. How does meeting Charmayne's mother shed light on Charmayne's character, personality, and hang-ups about her body image—among other things? How do the voices of your childhood echo in your present sense of self? How does your faith help you respond to the negative messages?

4. Reread 2 Samuel 21 in a modern Bible translation. What do *you* think of Rizpah? In what ways can you identify with her? What do you think it was about her that drew a response from King David?

5. In your assessment, what's to like about Travis? What's to be concerned about? How you discern whether the voice in your head is God—or your own insecurities?

6. How would you react to an announcement like Travis's (that Charmayne was to be his wife)? What faith would you put in a man's conviction that God had "given" you to him? What would hold you back—fear, lack of faith, low self-esteem ... or common sense and the Holy Spirit?

7. What is your usual means for discerning God's will in your life? Does your method of discernment differ for decisions that are more important—such as career, marriage, children, relocation, and the like? Why or why not?

8. Read Genesis 29 for yourself. With whom do you more readily identify—Leah or Rachel? Why?

9. What qualities do you prioritize in a man? Which characteristics disqualify a brother from your consideration? What role does scripture or prayer have in your selection process?

10. How is Charmayne's recollection of her grandmother's bruised-peach pie comparable to a parable of Jesus? What spiritual or practical insight do you glean from the story?

11. "Just give me something to hold on to," Charmayne tells Travis. What do you hold on to in your life—especially in your relationships? How does your

hold on God affect your grasp on other people or things? (See Matthew 6:33; Philippians 2:4–8, and 3:9–14.)

12. As Christians, what responsibility do you think we have to take a chance on someone with a past—be it financially, relationally, or otherwise? If God is a God of second chances, if we are called to forgive and restore, how do we balance that calling with guarding against wolves in sheep's clothing? (See Psalm 86:5; Luke 6:37, and 17:3–4; 2 Corinthians 2:5–11.)

13. What's your philosophy on a long engagement, and why? What are the pros and cons? (See Proverbs 14:29b; 1 Corinthians 7:9.)

14. What is the value of premarital counseling? (See Proverbs 11:14, 12:15, 15:22, and 19:20.)

15. Scripture makes clear that God may speak through dreams (see Genesis 37; 1 Kings 3; Daniel 2; Joel 2:28). Have you ever perceived God speaking to you in such a way? How can you responsibly interpret a dream with spiritual meaning? (Again, look to Proverbs 11:14, 15:22, and 24:6.)

16. What experience have you had in the reciprocal benefits of ministry—gaining as much as you give, learning as much as you teach? (Consider Luke 6:38; 2 Corinthians 9:6.)

17. Did the pastor's revelation about finances being the prime cause of divorce surprise you? Why or why

not? How do (or will) you handle money in your marriage? Do you feel strongly about finding a sugar daddy—or being a sugar mama? Do you think the Bible dictates roles or responsibilities in family finances? If so, what scriptures guide you, and why?

18. "His biggest gift to me had been marrying me." What is your reaction to Charmayne's thought about Travis? Do you identify with that feeling? Why or why not? In what sense is such a perspective healthy—or unhealthy?

19. Consider the biblical story of the Israelites' forty-year wandering in the wilderness. When have you taken an unnecessary detour in your life—walking farther than God intended you to go? How did the Lord bring you back around—and what good did He redeem from it (Romans 8:28)?

20. Consider how Charmayne reacted to the shocking truth about Travis, their marriage, and her job situation. What do you do when the world seems to crumble around you? Where do you turn—and to whom? (Psalm 121 offers a good starting place!)

21. "For some reason I was relieved by the fact that she was a black woman." Why do we feel safer talking to someone who (even on the surface) seems most like us?

22. Tell someone in your group about yourself—not just the situational statistics (age, race, marital status, occupation, family) but the *real* you. Consider it

a glimpse of the future promised in 1 Corinthians 13:12!

23. Reread Matthew 5:43–45 and consider it in the context of a personal struggle with forgiving an enemy. What would it look like for you to put that verse into action? What keeps you from doing so?

24. Throughout this novel, Charmayne's self of sense is tied inextricably with issues of her weight. (Even in her healing process, she perceives that Jesus boosts her self-confidence by helping her lose weight.) Why do you think women are so hung up on appearances, biblical exhortations notwithstanding? Read again scriptures such as Proverbs 31 (which says nothing about physical appearance), 1 Samuel 16:7, and 1 Timothy 2:9–10 as *affirmations*.

Take a sneak peek at
Tiffany L. Warren's
new inspiring novel!

Please turn this page
for a preview of

In the Midst of It All

Available in February 2010

PROLOGUE

"Zee, are you going to get that?"

Zenovia blinked a few times, glanced at the clock and shook her head. "Three a.m. It's not good news."

She closed her eyes and buried her head under the covers; trying to escape the ringing telephone. Her husband reached over her and took matters into his own hands. Zenovia was grateful that he was home. This kind of news didn't need to be left on an answering machine.

Audrey lay in a pool of her own diluted blood, but the room was permeated with the scent of lavender. Pink bubbles floated on top of the pool. Scented by lavender; stained by blood.

Zenovia's husband talked for a few moments then pressed the 'end' button on the cordless telephone. He touched Zenovia on the shoulder. She jumped. She was expecting him to wake her; to be the town crier of her misery, but she was startled nonetheless.

"That was your stepfather. Your mother has passed away."

"How did she die?"

"He says in her sleep."

Zenovia rolled her eyes. "He's a liar."

"Did you see it?"

She nodded. "But not in enough time to stop her."

Zenovia turned away from her husband and buried her head into the pillow. A salty river trickled down her face, but Zenovia was not ready to share her tears with her mate. She wanted two minutes of private grief.

She heard him pressing buttons on the telephone.

"Who are you calling?" she asked.

"Bishop. You can't preach in the morning."

"I'm preaching."

"It's okay, Zee. He'll find someone else. You need to handle your mother's affairs."

"That can wait. I've got a word from the Lord that cannot."

PART

One

CHAPTER

One

❧

Zenovia heard knocks on the door.

They were not the soft knocks of the children in the apartment next door. There were two of them—a boy and a girl. Always dirty, with unwashed faces and mismatched socks if any. Their mama was on crack, like so many of the mothers in King Kennedy, one of Cleveland's most notorious housing projects.

The two chidren visited Zenovia and Audrey every morning looking for breakfast. But it was ten a.m. and they were probably plopped in front of their television, watching the Saturday morning cartoons.

Zenovia waited for the knock again. This time it came with a voice. "Hello? Is anyone home? We'd like to share the Gospel with you today."

Zenovia laughed. She had been thinking that the person behind the door was a drug boy running from the police or a crack head hustling some stolen property. But it was a lady, and she wanted to share the Gospel. No harm there.

Still, she didn't answer the door.

Audrey rushed from the bedroom of the one-bedroom apartment. She was wearing a ratty yet colorful housecoat. Wild red hair framed her face like a flame, complementing perfectly her freckles and green eyes.

"Why don't you get the door?" she asked.

She didn't wait for a response, but went to the door herself. She swung it open wide and smiled at the two ladies that stood before her.

"Good morning!" sang Audrey.

"Well good morning to you too!" said the lady who'd knocked.

Audrey asked, "Did I hear y'all say, y'all was talking about the Gospel this morning?"

"Yes you did. The Gospel of our Lord and Savior Jesus Christ."

"Well, come on in and keep talking! Zenovia, something told me we were going to have good news today."

Zenovia felt a smile tickle the sides of her lips. That *something* was a vision. Audrey had been having them since she was a little girl, and Zenovia had started having them when she'd turned twelve. They were haphazard messages, sometimes future, sometimes past. Usually there wasn't enough information contained in the visions to do anything useful. Most times, Zenovia was annoyed by the visions; treated them like unannounced visitors. Just like the two Bible ladies.

Both of the ladies stepped gingerly into the spotless apartment. Their eyes darted back and forth; inspecting. Their nostrils flared; inhaling the scent of the ocean breeze candles that Zenovia had lit. Zenovia watched their facial expressions change from cautious to pleasant surprise.

Zenovia narrowed her eyes. "You can sit down. Although I'm sure you saw roaches in the hallway, none of them have taken up residence here."

The ladies smiled nervously as they took a seat on the worn, but clean sofa. Audrey sat across from them in her leather recliner.

"My name is Charlotte Batiste," said the lady who'd knocked.

Audrey's smile beamed. "Charlotte. Like the little pig in that book."

"Actually, the pig's name was Wilbur," Zenovia corrected. "You're talking about the spider."

For a fleeting instant, Audrey looked irritated, but it quickly faded. "Well, that doesn't matter. My name is Audrey and the smarty pants is Zenovia."

Both ladies looked from Audrey to Zenovia with tight yet friendly smiles on their faces. The second lady, not Charlotte, actually wasn't a *lady* at all. She was a girl, no older than Zenovia, but she was dressed in a much older woman's apparel—a long corduroy skirt and sweater with a turtleneck. At their feet were little bags stuffed to the hilt with tracts and pamphlets.

"Well, it's nice to meet you both. This is my daughter Alyssa," declared Charlotte with yet another smile.

She never seemed to run out of smiles. Zenovia wondered if her face was sore.

Charlotte continued. "I am here this morning to share a wonderful thought from the Bible. Do you have a Bible?"

"Of course!" replied Audrey.

Audrey reached into a side compartment on her recliner and pulled out a huge, white, leather Bible. The kind grandmothers pass down to their grandchildren with the family tree on the inside cover and the picture of Jesus in the center. There was no family tree in the front of Audrey's Bible; only her name, in big block print.

"I'm going to read you some verses in the book of Revelation chapter 21. It's the last book of the Bible."

"Oh, I know where Revelations is," said Audrey.

Zenovia cringed. She wanted to say, *It's Revelation not Revelations,* but since she had already been labeled as a smarty pants, the critique went unspoken.

Charlotte read. "And I heard a great voice out of heaven saying, Behold, the tabernacle of God is with men, and he will dwell with them, and they shall be his people, and God himself shall be with them, and be their God. And God shall wipe away all tears from their eyes; and there shall be no more death, neither sorrow, nor crying, neither shall there be any more pain: for the fomer things are passed away."

Zenovia liked that scripture. No tears and no sorrow sounded like just what she needed. Apparently, Audrey liked it too, because there was a tear in the corner of her right eye.

"Well, I can't wait to go to heaven and see Jesus. He's going to take away all sadness and death. I believe that," stated Audrey with conviction.

"What if I told you that this scripture was talking about a paradise here on earth?" asked Charlotte.

Zenovia almost slipped from her usual academic self and said *What you talkin' about Charlotte?* like Arnold querying Willis on *Different Strokes*, but she held her tongue. She wanted to see Audrey's response.

Audrey asked, "This scripture ain't about heaven?"

Charlotte went on to explain how God was going to make the earth over into a big park and that believers were going to live there in a utopian nirvana. She said that children would have lions and bears for playmates and go unharmed. Zenovia was a little skeptical, but Charlotte flipped through her little orange Bible with such skill that she had to be telling the truth.

After she was done, Charlotte let out a loud sigh. "Now, Audrey, don't you think God wants you and your sister to live in paradise and not squalor?"

Audrey looked confused, but Zenovia laughed. It was not the first time that she and her mother had been mistaken for sisters. Audrey was a young-looking thirty-two Zenovia was a mature-looking seventeen.

"She is my mother, not my sister," said Zenovia.

"Oh," replied Charlotte, and then . . . with recognition, "*Oh!*"

Audrey dropped her head. "Had her when I was fifteen."

"Well, that's all right," said Charlotte cheerfully. "That doesn't matter once you give your life to God and get baptized."

"I've been baptized," replied Audrey defensively.

"Oh, but not like this. When you get baptized as one of the Brethren of the Sacrifice, your life will surely be changed."

Zenovia cleared her throat. "I've never heard of the Brethren of the Sacrifice. What denomination are you?"

"We're not a denomination at all. We are *true*

Christians, teaching *true* Christianity." She said this with such conviction that Zenovia wanted to pump her fist, yell *power to the people* and hand her an afro pic.

Charlotte turned her attention back to Audrey. "Would you like to come to one of our services?"

"I'd like that," responded Audrey eagerly.

Zenovia rarely saw her mother get excited about anything, so again she held her tongue. She wanted to object, and tell Charlotte that she and Audrey had a church home. First Gethsemane Baptist church, up the street, was where they had fellowshipped for the past two years.

But maybe it was time for a change. Audrey had gotten into a particularly embarrassing scuffle with one of the usher board members. The usher, Sister Brown, had told Audrey that she couldn't sit on the Mother's row. Audrey had responded by accusing Sister Brown of being jealous because Audrey was pretty and Sister Brown was "black and greasy."

After the altercation, Zenovia had done what she always did. She apologized to First Lady Benson and Sister Brown. She'd explained that Audrey had just been prescribed new medication for her schizophrenia and that it had not yet taken effect.

That all happened a month ago, and they hadn't been to church since. Zenovia liked to let things die down before they returned to worship. Admittedly, though, she missed the anointed singing of the choir and the spirited preaching.

Audrey looked over at her daughter. "What do you say, Zee? You want to join a new church?"

Zenovia shrugged and answered her mother's question with a question. "Why not?"

Debra.

- FA will lose my (unemploymt)

- TRADE SCHOOL

- WIA #

- WIA & FA